Kings
of the
Water

Also by Mark Behr

The Smell of Apples
Embrace

Kings
of the
Water

Mark Behr

ABACUS

First published in Great Britain as a paperback original in 2009 by Abacus

Copyright © Mark Behr 2009

The right of Mark Behr to be identified
as author of this work has been asserted by him in accordance
with the Copyright, Designs and Patents Act 1988.

Nothing Personal by James Baldwin with Richard Avedon,
used by permission of the Estate of James Baldwin.

Every effort has been made to contact all copyright holders. If notified, the publisher
will be pleased to rectify any errors or omissions at the earliest opportunity.

A CIP catalogue record for this book
is available from the British Library.

ISBN 978-0-349-11370-8

Typeset in Centaur by M Rules
Printed and bound in Great Britain by
Clays Ltd, St Ives plc

Papers used by Abacus are natural, renewable and
recyclable products sourced from well-managed forests and certified in
accordance with the rules of the Forest Stewardship Council.

Mixed Sources
Product group from well-managed
forests and other controlled sources
www.fsc.org Cert no. SGS-COC-004081
© 1996 Forest Stewardship Council
FSC

Abacus
An imprint of
Little, Brown Book Group
100 Victoria Embankment
London EC4Y 0DY

An Hachette UK Company
www.hachette.co.uk

www.littlebrown.co.uk

For my mother and father
who raised two of us

And love will have no choice but to go into battle with space and time and, furthermore, to win.

James Baldwin, *Nothing Personal*

I recognized, like a perfume remembered, my time-altered body, when, from the furthest future, you held the tall mirror to my long-entombed skeleton.

Dambudzo Marechera, 'The Waterman Cometh'

Clouds pass overhead like a fleet with sails billowing against the blue, their shadows rallying across the veld under the noon sun. A white bank masses beyond where the town sits in its hollow this side of the river. The route on horseback he remembers like lines on his own hand, like a story known without quite imagining all that could be found in its reading. Early spring rain, surely. When he sees the collapsed roof of Ounooi's old farm stall he gears down and fumbles for the indicator on the wrong side of the steering wheel. He turns on to the gravel as Leonard Cohen's voice on the radio sings, *ring the bells that still can ring, forget your perfect offering, there is a crack in everything, that's how the light gets in.*

He steps out, leaving the car to idle. The gate is unlocked, as Benjamin said it would be. The smell of recent rain on grass and soil fills his head. It is as if he has never been away. Sky and cloud reflect in the water beneath the cattle grid as he pushes the gate across it. Tire-tracks mark the sand and gravel, the roadside undisturbed except for shoe and foot prints. He sees purple and pink cosmos that have shot up out of season through fences above new green. *Paradys — Dawid & Beth Steyn.* Rust has nibbled away part of the white lettering. A stranger might take a moment to infer the P and s of the farm's name. But he is not a stranger.

The plane landed well ahead of schedule and he'd planned a detour along back-roads as his one indulgence before he leaves again tomorrow night: a few hours' drive, skimming beauty that could make him weep. After the paperwork at Avis and exchanging dollars for rands he found his way around the construction work at Johannesburg International. No longer Jan Smuts, as it still was when he left. Free of the slow morning traffic he sent a text to Kamil: *Got in early. Now in car. Sleep well, Love M.*

He'd called his brother on the farm. 'Welkom tuis, Michiel,' Benjamin said – welcome home – and asked about the flight and whether he'd slept. A few hours from Atlanta he'd tried to watch a movie. Unable to ditch the virulence of memory he took a pill. He slept for at least eight hours across the Atlantic and woke from a dream – a waking dream from which he'd almost reached sideways to feel for Kamil – of Ounooi bodysurfing, and faces and voices he could not distinguish from what was there before he thought he'd fallen asleep. He gazed at the dry landscape growing visible as if it were lifting towards him. Angola. He was sure he recognized the green Kunene as they passed over into Namibia. His head dropped low to the window to see eastward into the sun, searching for what might be the Caprivi corridor and the Kwando or Zambezi rivers.

'Your wife not with you?' From the woman beside him, her eyes on his ring finger as he filled out his passport number on the landing form.

'I came alone.' It's against the law for me to get married, Kamil would have said, giving his bittersweet smile, enjoying the consternation, the uncomfortable silence or hurried disavowal.

Ochre and brown thirty thousand feet down; space and land vaster than ever in memory, divided here and there by a straight white road. Into his drowsy mind came a convoy of Buffels on a track of fine white powder, a prehistoric centipede, each military vehicle a tiny rectangular vertebra. Occasionally he'd make out a homestead or a kraal, dry riverbeds . . . *here is my hand, take it, let's jump into the abyss, whatever happens; even if we fall to death, let us at least be hand in hand* . . . Ounooi or Karien had underlined the words in a copy of a Brink novel, kept with the other Bs on the highest shelves behind Ounooi's desk. Had the book once been banned?

'We've been taking our anti-malarials for the past month.' The passenger beside him invited conversation.

'You should be fine.' He smiled before twisting his back to see further out.

Had he dreamed of the doctor? Or Lieutenant Almeida on a quiet hot night with the glow and smell of cigarettes? On his flight out of here he'd sat at the back of the plane, in the smoking section. This morning, for the first time in years, he'd longed for a cigarette. Over Botswana the pilot announced the Makarikari Salt Pans and the Limpopo River; then marks of denser population, bigger towns, smoke rising from coal power plants, tarred roads tying everything into a net of scars. Land more deliberately mapped and fenced. Like crossing from Mexico into California. Waiting in line for the bathroom he set his watch nine hours ahead. In the cubicle's drone he hunched awkwardly to wash his face and clear his head, brush his teeth and take a pee.

'Watch for potholes once you reach the Free State. Keep to the right side of the road,' Benjamin had said on the phone.

'The left.'

'Left is right here, wise-guy. Don't forget. Alida can iron your church clothes while you take a shower, and she'll have a bite ready for you.'

'I thought I'd take a look at things on the way and stay at the hotel in town. I can have lunch at the Wimpy.'

'The Wimpy closed years ago, Michiel. They're opening a McDonald's. Are you sure you want to stay in town?'

'I think it's easiest.'

There was a long pause from the phone. 'Do that then. We'll meet you at church. My wife and children are looking forward to meeting you.'

A while later his phone rang. Benjamin again: 'Seeing as you're early, Oubaas suggests you fetch him from Paradys. Giselle and I'll go ahead to see to everything at church.'

'You think that's a good idea, Benjamin?'

'It was his suggestion, Michiel.' A pause after his name, long enough for the guttural *ch* of his brother's Afrikaans to register. 'He's reaching out. It's time you quit your crap. He and Alida will be waiting for you.'

'Oubaas and Alida both?' He tried to keep skepticism from his voice. It's a funeral, he reminded himself. Take the path of least resistance. Get it over with.

'Alida is like his shadow. She'll have him ready and dressed. Use the disabled parking space at the church.' Michiel heard the signal of an incoming text message.

'I'll go by the farm, if you think that's wise.'

'Alida has the remote for the homestead gate and she'll lock everything again after you drive out. This must be difficult for you, Michiel,' Benjamin added. 'But more so for Oubaas than for any of us.'

Beyond the cattle grid, towards the koppie, cattle browse in the unplowed field. He again inhales the smell. This, then, is where the reunion with the old man is to take place: with him in his Levis and Nike Airs made in Cambodia, on the prohibited soil with a name that reads *arady*. Not beneath the spire with its bell (which tolls in B flat, Karien said), within the tall white walls and oak paneling, attired in formals. Not quite as he has imagined over the past few days. Not with his father, anyway. Though with Benjamin it *will* be at the church after all. And with Karien, too, who will not, he knows, miss Ounooi's service. Mourning overshadows resolve, if only temporarily. *I figured things out on my own and took care of it. What I know today is that I have no need to hear from you or see you again.* In the early years – in England and Australia, when his thoughts still came mostly in Afrikaans, before San Francisco and Kamil's domestication of him – his mind played with encountering anyone from here. He had pictured the other's face and his own feigned indifference when, offhandedly, he would say *oh, that was a long time ago. I scarcely remember those days.* The one time he bumped into someone he knew — the woman on the jetty in the Solomons — he'd tried, only to see the deception register at once. Mostly he'd imagined seeing Karien. Had he come across her he would have fallen to his knees before her. He'd pictured De Niro in *The Mission*, climbing beside the Iguazu Falls to the Guaraní. With what he would have weighted himself in place of armor and weaponry, he did not know.

Oubaas suggested you come to Paradys. Transport him to the church. Difficult to reconcile with all he knows, remembers. Have age and the shakes indeed mellowed the old goat? Nothing Ounooi said during her visit gave any such thing away. Echo to her husband's Narcissus, her loyalty rarely allowed recognition that her sons' father was an impossible man. And what of Benjamin's *it's time you quit your crap?* The phrase's ordinariness suggested that culpability — the source of individual and shared grief in a decade and a half of silence — somehow belonged to Michiel. During Ounooi's visit, with the exception of the night on Market waiting for the trolley, both Michiel and his mother had circled around things of long ago. Without having planned it, they'd stuck to the simple but remarkable achievement of again being in each other's presence. She was the retired high-school English teacher visiting her son in the US, at his invitation. He (the apple had not fallen far from the tree), with an MA in English Literature from Berkeley, the director of International House, a transnational company that teaches English as a Second Language. He'd shown his mother the people and the spaces of his life. She had managed to be, or to seem, happy, though living above the everyday sadness of being human was her forte for as far back as he can remember. He has a picture of her in his mind of the morning after *A Streetcar Named Desire*. An unseasonably mild day for December in San Francisco. He is in the kitchen rinsing something they have picked up at Whole Foods for the lunch salad. He feels like shit for the way he spoke to her last night. He looks up and sees her on the balcony, in profile, on one of the Adirondack chairs.

5

What is she reading? He strains to recall, yearns almost. Something in paperback bought at Borders the evening before. He tries to picture the book's cover. Margaret Atwood? Was it Roth — *The Human Stain*? The Michael Cunningham? She has on dark glasses, her bare legs and feet are stretched out on the bench where red geraniums bloom in summer beside Kamil's concrete Buddha. In her right hand she holds a pencil to mark sections of text. Kamil has walked into the kitchen and follows Michiel's gaze.

'You have her nose,' Kamil says.

'Sundays on the farm were like this. My father warned us to be quiet when he and she went to "rest" after lunch. We three boys winked at each other. We'd have the crap beaten out of us if we disturbed the ritual. She'd come out after a while to read in the living room — we called it the sitting room — beneath her bookshelves. She read whenever she didn't have grading for school or bookkeeping for the farm.' She sits on the balcony with the Monterey pine's branches behind her, her hair swept up in a knot on top of her head, the way she often has it.

'You can see she was quite something. More so now for being slightly faded,' Kamil says. Ounooi looks up, peers over the top of her dark glasses. Smiling, she asks what they're whispering about. 'I was telling Michael how lovely you are, Beth.'

She throws back her head, her laughter filling the garden below. 'If I stopped coloring this lot every three weeks,' her fingers holding the pencil, smoothing back her hair, 'no one would be fooled.'

He'd always expected his father would be the first to die. So much older than Ounooi and with high cholesterol (inherited by Michiel), the old man would have a heart attack, fall from a horse or have his head knocked in by a disgruntled farm-worker. Marauders of the land. However he went, Oubaas's going would unclose a tiny window of possibility. When Ounooi brought news of the Parkinson's, Michiel had asked his and Kamil's physician about the prognosis; had spoken about it in therapy to Dr Glassman.

But then things happen differently: the phone rings at 2 a.m. and you know. Not who, but you know. So healthy! Michiel had taken her around tourist New York for two days, then back to the West Coast to meet Kamil. (*Your suburb isn't named for Fidel, surely, my child?* For José Castro, Ounooi, Commandante General of the Mexicans who fought the settlers a century and a half ago. Our place is on the boundary with the Lower-Haight. An old neighborhood that's being gentrified.) There had been their daily run through the park along John F. Kennedy Drive – she kept up with Michiel, urging him not to slow down. She insisted they walk in good weather rather than use public transit or cabs. Mornings after he went to work, she went for breakfast at Café Flore or across the road to the Bagdad. (*The waitress says the missing 'h' is deliberate!*) She helped America vacuum and wash the windows; carried the recycling – plastics, paper, glass, cardboard – down to the corner collection bins; went shopping on her own; found crickets at the pet store on Divisadero to feed to *La Creatura Felice,* America's name for Xanthippe. They attended the theatre; she read the *Chronicle* every morning; loved the red wine from Napa. *Amplexus* from Toad Hollow was all she wanted from the first time Kamil introduced her to it. She delighted at finding the tarot card Kamil placed blindly beneath each plate when friends came for dinner. Hers, *The Empress*. No sign of a hooded figure clutching a sickle. 'Like juxtaposition in books,' she'd said, clapping her hands. 'With the tarot your job is to figure symbols' meanings through their relationship to each other and to history.'

'Take the card home with you,' Kamil had said.

She and Michiel spoke about what had become of this one and that. Of Benjamin and his wife. She showed him pictures of the grandchildren. The new dogs. New horses. She still enjoyed riding. She spoke of laborers that had come and gone. Those who stayed: Pietie, now de facto running the farm, and Alida, invincible at seventy-five, smiling over her simmering resentments, taking care of

Oubaas whenever Ounooi was away. *It's not easy for him either. He's a proud man.* And Little-Alida, *Michiel, you won't believe it,* in charge of all of Anglo American Corporation's paper industries, with talk of her getting on to the board; *my little black princess from Paradys!* Grandparents now all passed on; aunts and uncles, cousins. The town. The changes: the township now has electricity and running water; there is renewal and a buzz of energy in the education system; the New South Africa where *things are positive, growth as far as the eye can see. The country looks like one enormous building site.* She'd just read and admired *Long Walk to Freedom*. Michiel and Kamil had shown her their life with fair integrity ('No oversharing required,' Kamil had said with his arms in an O above his head before Michiel's departure to the East Coast. I'm taking the plant downstairs to Paul and Paul. And you'd best leave Hanna, Iris and Vanessa out of the narrative till you've tested the water.) They shared with her their thoughts of adopting from China or Cambodia. Dirk and Karien — first mention of her name — Ounooi said, adopted two children from the townships; were taking them to the Kruger National Park for Christmas and then further on, for the eldest to see the site of Mapungubwe. Left unsaid was that the children's parents had died of AIDS-related illnesses and that the kids, too, might be living with the disease.

'She had no other children?' Michiel asked, contriving a mix of indifference and polite interest.

'Only the adopted two,' she offered in a way that let him understand she knew at least some of what he wanted confirmed. More she could not bring herself to say. No sentence in which his and Karien's names came together. No word on their issue. Did anyone but Ounooi know? Did *everyone?* And Peet's name had not been uttered; not by Ounooi, not even in response to his own outburst. It was as if there had always been only two sons.

Your mother needs to be grounded in the present, Kamil said in bed that night.

Denial, Michiel countered, same-old, same-old as always.

'Forgiveness,' Kamil fetched a phrase from early in their own relationship, 'is accepting the distance between how we would have wanted things to be and the way they are.'

'And how hard you made me work for yours.'

'I am not your mother, Michael. Parents don't redeem themselves. Rarely to their children, anyway. It is a relationship of blood, not choice.'

'Easy for you, with Malik and Rachel in your veins.'

'I've seen little evidence of Beth being as odd as you've made her out to be over the years. So she isn't speaking about the crap of the past. Malik and Rachel like going back after a few drinks. It doesn't mean they don't think about it constantly.'

After she left, neither Michiel nor Kamil could recall an observation or inquiry that acknowledged Michiel's lost years. Not a word linked to his leaving the farm and the country. No comment beyond *how long your hair was* at a picture of him and Kamil from the time he was returning each of her letters, unopened, to sender: almost a decade younger, tanned in bathing suits, their arms around each other on the dive boat in the Solomons with Michiel's hair in wet slithers down his shoulders. At the end of their new beginning, when he and Kamil took her to the airport – when he could have buckled under the weight of this goodbye read against their last – they kept up the tone of the previous two weeks. They helped her check her luggage. At the gate mother and son held on to each other for a moment longer than is usual; a moment that recognized how much was being left unsaid.

'I have loved you, child of my heart, through everything,' she whispered in Afrikaans. Through everything: a curtsy before their omissions, or a nod at the wound he'd inflicted on the rainy night when the young naval officer had arrived to await the trolley beside them? In a slow movement she loosened herself from his embrace. Her hands cupped his elbows and with her eyes looking into his she said: 'A mother understands. And I know you do too. Love takes a thousand and one shapes.'

And he answered: 'And I have loved you, Ounooi. A thousand ways and more.'

Kamil blew kisses that she returned, smiling, as she went through the departure gate. Since then they had received fortnightly letters, the last only a week ago. 'Some farms have internet and email, and it's all over town,' she wrote, 'but there's something about sending and receiving a letter with a stamp, wetted by the sender's tongue, that feels more like how I want to speak to you. Maybe I'll give in soon and go electronic. I hate to be thought old-fashioned.' He had written back once a month, his letters addressed only to her.

He stopped at a new toll booth on the N2 near Kroonstad. Paid with currency exchanged at the airport. Given that he wouldn't, after all, require money for a hotel and meals he'd swapped way too many dollars. Unless he was kicked off the farm again before day is done. His eye fell on his wallet and passport, the return ticket and Kamil's envelope on the passenger seat beside his phone. He remembered the message: *Midnight. Off to bed. Text me when its over. Think of u constantly. Love, K.* Back at speed, he picked up the envelope. ('Put it on her coffin, from me.') The card, with a silver dollar coin, had been stuck into the book he had brought for the plane but not read, choosing instead the mindless movie and then sleep. With his hands on the wheel he'd read: *Beth, and now you have brown clouds of roots overhead, a rank lily of salt on your temples a rosary of sand, and sails on the bottom of a boat in foamy mist, a mile away where there is a bend in the river — visible — invisible — like the light on a wave, you are truly no different — abandoned like us all, Kamil.* The poet he recognizes, much admired by Malik.

Standing at the gate with the car still idling, he takes in the farm road all the way to its curve around the koppie. Along here Ounooi ran, most mornings of her married life, accompanied by the farm dogs and, for a while, by him too. The shadow of a cloud passes over the dilapidated barbed-wire fence that separates the farm from that of their neighbor, the late Oom Oberholzer. It must be years since these fences were tightened. A job the three of them did during the Christmas holidays. From the morning after the Day of the Covenant to December 18th: two days on horseback, sleeping in the caves, every mile of fence firmed with pliers, mended where it had snapped or where the binding wire had rusted and come loose. He looks skyward. Will the burial proceed if it rains, he wonders. By now the lucern should be at ankle height. Though no trace of a hoe's markings can be seen on the fields near the gate, he hears Oubaas's voice: 'The saplings look good this year.' He gets back into the car and turns off the radio and air conditioning, opens all four windows. He sees the tips of khaki bush and redgrass through the cattle grid move in the breeze. Driving across, the vehicle shudders. Again he leaves the car on as he returns to shut the gate. He now sees them as boys, back then, at the concertina gates between the outlying stock camps: up and down from the bakkie while whoever is behind the wheel pretends to speed off; Peet expressionless behind his grin, playing on his own terms, striding at his own pace until the vehicle finally stops; Benjamin laughing while shaking his fist and spitting threats as he races barefoot after the truck; and Michiel's own, fat-lipped resentment that made him every driver's most cherished target. *How early the patterns are set*, he hears Glassman.

Stalks from another harvest stand waist-high, with leaves drooping over weeds on unplowed fields. Fallowing? Things falling apart? Paradys was never wealthy, not by the standards of some farms in the district or by the lifestyles of the town's doctors, dentists and lawyers. Nor weighed against enterprises that catered to the constant stream of business from across the Lesotho border or sold goods on hire purchase to people from the township. Certainly, the

Steyns had always been well off. *No question*, Michiel learned to quickly qualify overseas, *by the standard of almost every black South African we were rich.* The homestead's sandstone design was based on one by Sir Herbert Baker, architect of the Union Buildings in Pretoria. Family lore had it that the farm had fallen into English hands after the genocide of Boer women and children in the Aliwal North and Bloemfontein concentration camps. The Steyn side of the family hadn't had it hard since the first half of the previous century, as government grants to white Afrikaners enabled the purchase of the land with its impressive home built by the Englishman. Most other farms relied on state subsidies and the Land Bank's leniency to survive, but much of the Paradys land, nestled between the folds of koppies and low-lying mountains, offered protection against plagues and received rain like clockwork. During the time of economic sanctions in the eighties – before Michiel left for good – Oubaas toyed with entering into a partnership with city businessmen and weekend farmers to buy up struggling farms to create a more competitive conglomerate. This had happened elsewhere as fewer traditional farms were sustainable in the face of government subsidy cuts and the ailing Land Bank. Before things were signed and sealed, and in defiance of Benjamin's letters from Angola, Oubaas pulled out. The conglomerate went on to generate vast profits. With farms under irrigation along the Orange River, the venture found ways around the international prohibition on South African products. Boxes of cherries, peaches, apples, grapes and citrus fruits with logos and names like *Hartebeeskraal*, *Bitterput* and *Oumoedersdrift* were replaced by packaging that read *Product of Maluti Farms, from the Mountain Kingdom, Republic of Lesotho.* In an aisle of Sainsbury's, during the first winter he worked at the hotel on Leicester Square, Michiel came across sealed packages in the fresh produce sections bearing the Lesotho stamp. He stuck his fingers through the ventilation holes, the cherries cool against his finger-tips. He'd wondered at the depth of his father's regret, his brother's business-minded irritation, or if they had in fact joined after he left.

Cattle raise their heads to peer at his approach. He changes from second to first gear, slowing to allow a cow to cross. As she passes the hood her udder sways heavily. She turns, stares intently at the car. He continues slowly up the road. He crosses the spruit's low cement bridge. Yes, it has already rained this season. Above the steady stream red bishops fly from the reeds and zip skyward, then plunge like drops of blood. When he turns to round the koppie at the end of this field, the homestead will be in view. *Standing by the side of a kopje, very early on that September morning, it was a relief to see the majestic tops of the mountains of Basutoland, silhouetted against the rising sun, beyond the Caledon River that separates the 'Free' State from Basutoland.* He rotates his neck and again wishes for a cigarette. Verdant around the boulders and rocky outcrops, with the sugarbush aflame in early orange and yellow bloom, the koppie must have had a fire. Out of season and out of place in this region, the patch of proteas blooms. If the hill had burned in winter the flowers would be more lavish. From now till long after school started again in January, he and Peet were up there, breaking off the rough stems to display in the vases on the long dining-room table. Once a month, when it was Ounooi's turn to do the church arrangement, they carried arm-loads of sugarbush and calla lilies to the kitchen door. She did the flowers at home, as long as there was no wind. If her three sons were beyond her voice's reach she and Alida lifted the enormous triangular arrangement on to the flat bed of the open bakkie, maneuvering it so that its back was against the window, the huge vase resting on a thick piece of foam rubber. Then, with Little-Alida spreadeagled, her long legs on either side of the arrangement and her skinny fingers clasping the crystal vase, Ounooi carefully drove to town.

On the acres of harvest, through the valley, along the dust road and up the hill he sees cherry blossoms that look like patches of snow. With one sweeping gaze he takes in the sandstone house with its stoep all around, the red roof, the lawns, garden, Ounooi's orchard and the stables — all now enclosed by a tall fence. Then the sheep kraal and the dairy. The laborers' compound, a few hundred meters beyond Ounooi's orchard and the kraal, is fenced in too. Of the cement dam he can make out only the curved upper wall; the rest is hidden by reeds and fruit trees. A tractor pulling a trailer crawls around the orchard, past the cemetery's oaks, up the hill towards the compound. Who, he ponders, is to keep this going? Is the solemn Pietie really up to it? *I can't stand it*, he hears Ounooi, angrily reverting to English, *that Pietie is such a sourpuss.* And then, when she sees her three boys' smirk, *puss is a cat, you filthy-minded creatures!*

The jacarandas on either side of the gateposts have a few early blooms. Two bull terriers come bounding across the lawn. The dogs Ounooi brought photographs of. He finds the electronic gate open and drives through. He parks under the shade-cloth beside a new white Volvo. Before turning off the ignition he looks at the dogs, tails wagging, their small eyes seeming to smile up at him. The bull terriers were brought in once the Rottweilers had become too rheumatic to be kept alive in good conscience. Before the Rottweilers, the Rhodesian Ridgebacks from the last litter of Miemie — the dog Michiel had grown up with — had got tick-bite fever and died. And Miemie herself, Ounooi told him during her visit, was torn to pieces by baboons. 'We were in town and when we got back I had only to see Alida on the stoep to know something was wrong. She came across the lawn, you could see her pink overalls covered in blood. It was Saturday so there hadn't been any slaughter or butchering of livestock.'

When he alights the dogs do no more than sniff at his pants.

All around him is the *koer-koer, koer-koer* of turtledoves and from the other side of the house, up in the dam's poplars, the high-pitched cry of the piet-my-vrou. He hears something called out in seSotho from up at the workers' compound. The stoep, he notices, now has a shell of white metal bars. He opens the trunk and lifts out his luggage. With the dogs trotting at his side and his nose full of the vague scent of cherry blossoms, he walks across the lawn.

The seven steps still lead up between the terracotta-colored cement balustrade and boxes of strelitzia, with its dark foliage and spathes of robust blue, white and gold. For a moment he himself is sitting there, unshaven, nineteen years old with Miemie's head in his lap.

The stoep glimmers red, smelling of Cobra polish. The gate is locked but the front door beyond the enclosure is open. Less dusky than memory has had it, the hallway's floorboards shine where light falls from the bedrooms in skewed rectangles. Food is either being prepared or already in the warming oven. Leg of lamb, he imagines. Rice with raisins. Sweet potatoes in cinnamon and lemon. Sliced carrots in brown sugar sauce. Green beans.

He searches for a bell. There is none.

'Fuck.' He curses under his breath, looking across the yard. 'You knew I was coming.' The dogs sit, looking up at him. He could go to the kitchen or the side entrance. Resentment rises in him, a literal release of something in his stomach. Later he would recall with some surprise that he was thinking of Glassman in that instant: *note what you're feeling, in your body.* He sets his suitcase and bag down. He looks over the valley, finds the church steeple. The township — *the location*, they'd often still called it when he left — has grown further out as well as in. The once bare strip of veld, the train track running south and the tall screen of eucalyptus no longer keep things apart.

He cups his hands around his mouth and calls down the hallway: 'Pa!' He won't, he resolved way back, ever again speak the word *Oubaas*.

The dogs each let out a short bark.

'Alida!' He calls out.

He goes down the stairs and starts around the stoep. One dog follows while the other stays, sniffing at his suitcase. The side entrance, now cut off by gate and bars, is locked. Through new glass sliding doors, in the master bedroom he sees the tall oak headboard of his parents' bed. *Beside Oubaas. When he woke in the morning she was already cold.* Two suitcases, their contents spilling out, lie open against new built-in closets. The lawn has been mowed and watered to a green velvet sheen. Sprinklers chug in flowerbeds. The furrows around the rose gardens and footpaths are trimmed with geometric precision: Adam, in Michiel's mind's eye, with his foot on the spade, moving from bed to bed, snipping off grass shoots to maintain each border perfectly. Adam's neck and head thrust to one side as Oubaas smacks him with the flat of his hand. Had the rose shears been left out overnight?

At the kitchen entrance he again hears the piet-my-vrou's relentlessly repeating call. His nostrils flare with the scent of rose, honeysuckle, day lilies and camellia. The noonday heat is suffused with the sound of turtledoves in mulberry and poplar, and he recognizes the orchard's hum of bees and cicadas from up around the spring. Beyond the hedge of figs the orchard shimmers in a haze of white. *I want to do with you what spring does with the cherry trees.* His first Valentine card to Karien. Standard Six A. He'd found the Neruda on Ounooi's shelf, the poems in English on the left-hand page, Spanish on the right. He copied what his mother had underlined; he memorized the lines in Spanish and English to say to Karien. And in later years into the ears of strangers. In Seville a whisper had come back: You trill the 'r' perfectly, but it is not '*cerillos*', it is '*cerezos*'. *Quiero hacer contigo lo que la primavera hace con los cerezos.* Trusting the night's lover, he'd wondered how he'd misremembered or memorized incorrectly? Could it be that Ounooi's translation or the man in his arms were mistaken?

He tugs at the locked kitchen gate and calls Alida's name into the house and then in the direction of her kaya. He returns to the front gate with the one dog still at his side. The other now lies in the shade at the bottom of the stairs, its hindquarters stretched out, head neatly on the front paws. On the landing Michiel notices a shiny wet stain on the fabric of his suitcase.

'Poes,' he says, glaring down at the prostrate dog.

'The American arrives with an Afrikaans curse on his lips.'

He almost smiles as he turns. Behind the bars, in a wheel-chair, his father exists only in voice and cobalt-blue eyes. Old fingers control the contraption's wheels with visible tremors; his head nodding slightly, incessantly. Despite the sunken mouth and the nodding, the jaw is still locked. Neither the photographs Ounooi brought nor what she said or wrote has prepared Michiel for this.

'Dag, Pa.' Soft plosive of the p, odd to his ears.

''n Jammerte,' Oubaas says, talking with his eyes on his son's as he wheels the chair closer, 'Ounooi is nie hier om gevette kalf te slag vir haar verlore seun nie.' A pity Ounooi isn't here to slaugh-ter a fatted calf for her prodigal son.

From the landing Michiel towers over the old man in the striped cotton pajamas. So much, then, for mellowing. This is to be every bit as miserable as expected. Not time, disease nor the fresh face of death have made the old man relent. Why, in the name of all the gods, did he agree to come to the farm?

'Benjamin . . .' Michiel hesitates. 'Benjamin said you suggested that you and Alida come with me.' And then, 'To church. I have to get changed, Pa. I see you, too. Can Pa let me in?'

'Even your Afrikaans sounds American.' Oubaas relinquishes Michiel's gaze to take in his son's height. The head, at a permanent angle, creates the impression that he's looking at everything askance. 'I heard you call, I'm not deaf,' he says. 'My keys are miss-ing. Nothing's in its usual place with your brother and his family here. Real rough-and-tumble grandson I have. You'll have to go and find Alida. She has the master key.'

17

He descends the seven steps, almost tripping as he takes the last two in a single stride. One dog, the female, again follows. Behind the reed enclosure of what was Peet's rondavel he notices the movement of children and sees Alida on the footpath from her kaya. She wears heels and into the hem of the blue frock held up by one hand she places the curlers she removes from her hair. When the dog trots past Michiel Alida raises her head. She pauses mid-stride and brings the hand from her hair down to her chest. She crosses to meet him on the lawn. Smiling, he reaches out and hugs her to him. He is aware of one hand tentatively on his forearm, the other, still holding up her skirt, awkwardly between them.

'Alida, you've barely aged a day!' he says, without flattery. But for what must be a few extra pounds and some gray at her forehead, the tiny woman who as a girl helped raise Oubaas, then the three of them and her own daughter, seems miraculously close to the way he remembers her.

'Kleinbaas! It's like looking at Oubaas when he was a young man!'

He thinks of letting the address form go, but then, forcing a grin, says, 'Please call me Michiel, Alida.' She looks down, nods. 'I'm thirty-five, Alida,' he smiles, drawing attention from what she might have taken as a rebuke. 'Look,' he bends his neck, showing the balding beneath his short hair. 'A few minutes in this sun and my scalp will be red as boiled beetroot.'

'Ai, all the children are getting too big,' Alida says, shaking her head. There's a crack in her voice, and a sibilance that may come from dentures. He notices dark markings of sun on her cheeks, fine lines around her narrowed lips and eyes. Her skin is a lighter brown than he remembers. Yes, she has aged. She is indeed an old woman. She looks to the house and asks, 'Has the Kleinbaas seen the Oubaas?'

The old man has misplaced the keys, he says.

'He forgets like that,' she replies. 'It's been quite a morning here.' She is standing still again. 'People coming and going from early. We served tea and cake for friends and family before . . . because afterwards it will be too late.' She meets Michiel's eyes and says: 'He now suddenly won't let me bath him, Kleinbaas.' Then, almost conspiratorially, looking away, 'Since Ounooi . . .' She removes a curler and drops it into the fold of her skirt. 'I bath him and dress him when Ounooi isn't here.'

'It's good to see you looking so well after all this time.'

'I wanted to get Oubaas ready before I got dressed. I don't want to kneel at the bath in my church clothes. But he's obstreperous.' She looks closely at Michiel. 'Must I phone Benjamin and ask him to come back?'

'Perhaps it's his way of postponing the inevitable? Does he understand she's gone?'

'There isn't much wrong with that head, Kleinbaas. Mostly he knows everything. It's the body that can't do what the head wants.' She speaks softly now, clicks her tongue and lets her free hand shake, suggesting the disease's tremors. 'He speaks almost like normal. Hears and understands everything.' Then she smiles. 'But Jissis, Kleinbaas, he's just as hard-headed as always.'

Michiel is the last person to whom Oubaas will lend an ear, this much Alida must know. Had he gone to the hotel, or if the others had been here when he arrived, he would not be facing locked gates, dog piss on his luggage and a father as recalcitrant as in each of a million memories and thousands of dollars to Glassman. 'If he won't get dressed, Alida, we'll take him in his pajamas. Otherwise let him stay right here for all I care.'

'Now you're talking, Kleinbaas Michiel.'

From the rondavel comes a squeal of laughter.

Alida smiles. 'My Lerato's two. They're already this high.' She gestures to rib height. 'Lerato also came this morning.'

He is too embarrassed to inquire who she is referring to.

'You won't know her, Kleinbaas. She has a degree from university and her husband is a businessman from Nigeria. Big shot. They live in Jo'burg.'

19

Lerato. Little-Alida. Ounooi had stuck to their family's name for her.

'How considerate of her to come. And to bring her children.' He does not ask how his late brother's rondavel became a retreat for Alida's offspring.

'Ounooi had a thing for those two. And Benjamin's two, *Ounooi was erg oor hulle*.' She adored them.

'Alida,' he says as they approach the front of the house, 'how many bars are there around this stoep?'

The electric fence and burglar bars — also at her kaya and the rondavel, she says — came after the thing with Baas and Miesies Oberholzer of Diepfontein, the neighbors who, a while back, were murdered in their home. Through the bars the old man watches from his wheelchair. They have reached the front door without resolving what is to be done about getting him ready. Alida produces a set of keys and unlocks the gate. Michiel lifts his luggage and along with the dogs follows her on to the stoep.

'Look who I've brought, Oubaas,' she announces, her tone now whole-souled.

Michiel and his father study each other while she lowers the hem of her dress and lets the curlers roll on to a side table. She smoothes her skirt and, turning the wheelchair, solves the problem of whether Michiel will shake his father's hand. Or hug him. A kiss would have been unthinkable.

'The iron is still hot, Kleinbaas, if anything has to be pressed.' She speaks over her shoulder. 'And is Oubaas ready now for Oubaas's bath?' The absence of personal pronouns. Similar to the way Afrikaans kids never addressed their parents or other white adults without the honorific. Alida wheels the chair up the wooden ramp that connects the yellowwood hallway with the stoep. The wheelchair is surprisingly quiet on the floor. He hears sighs as the dogs make themselves comfortable on the red cement.

'Alida has prepared your bedroom,' Oubaas says. 'It's a full house.

The rondavel's got Little-Alida and her lot. We didn't know if you would be staying here.'

'For tonight, if that's okay by you, Pa.'

'Stay where you want, Michiel. For how long are you here?'

'I fly again tomorrow night, Pa. I'd have stayed longer but I have a trip next week. To China.'

He sets his luggage down at the door of his old bedroom. Alida signals for him to follow into the guest room where Oubaas and Ounooi have slept the past few years. 'You know, there are the two steps up into the master bedroom.' The difficulty of getting the wheelchair up and down necessitated the move. Over food aromas he now finds the smell of his mother. An intermingling of scents he never deciphered: freshly ironed white linen, and marjoram, and something sweeter, orange maybe. Or peach. She wore no perfume. The smell lingered for weeks on sheets, on towels and in her closet after she'd gone from San Francisco. Your guilty conscience, Kamil said. I can't smell a thing.

The small windows he remembers have been replaced by large sliding doors. The room is white, cream and beige. A breeze nudges at drawn lace curtains. Mohair drapes hang heavily on either side of the doors. The space has a contemporary look at odds with the conventional farmhouse exterior. Ounooi's taste. Here, in fact, is his parents' enormous bed with the tall oak headboard. An heirloom, from the first Oubaas Steyn. A pair of white men's underwear is folded neatly at the foot end. From a door handle, on a hanger, hangs a black suit and beside it a white shirt with a black tie draped over the shoulder. On the floor a pair of black shoes and socks. The yellowwood floors are without rugs: probably because of the wheelchair. The walls are bare save for a large oil painting of an Nguni cow's face in tan, chocolate brown and white. The glassy gaze above the moist black snout contains shadows of whom- or whatever she is looking at. The painting is reflected in its entirety in a full-length mirror on the opposite wall.

'Karien's,' Oubaas says, his eyes an accusation on Michiel. 'She became a child in this house after you left.'

Let it go, Michiel thinks. You will exhaust yourself responding to each recrimination.

On the white dressing table are Ounooi's cosmetics. Her hairbrush. Here she dropped her head between her knees and pulled the brush through her hair a hundred times before bed. Beside the brush is a vase of open yellowish roses, with fallen petals on the glass top of the dressing table. Did she cut them herself with the buds still shut? How many days for *Gloire de Dijon* to open and begin shedding petals? His eyes move to her side of the bed. Her bedside table holds a small stack of books. A dog barks and from outside comes the sound of children's exuberance. A woman's voice calls out. 'Over here, Mommy,' he hears a child's answer in English. But for the language, it could have been any of them, three decades ago. The white cloud of Ounooi's orchid shimmers through the lace curtains. Nothing to suggest that someone died in here.

'You're going bald,' Oubaas says.

'I've heard it's a gene from the mother's side, Pa. Grandpa Ford never had much hair.'

'Your mother's child, in bone and marrow.'

'And what about Benjamin, Pa? Does he still have a full head of hair?' He at once regrets the spark of sarcasm and stops himself before actually saying: *is your Chosen One not also of Ounooi's bone and marrow? Would not the late Peet have been bald by now?*

'You can go, Alida,' Oubaas says, taking his eyes from Michiel. 'You drive to church with Little-Alida and her piccanins. Remember your curlers on the stoep table.'

Alida glances at Michiel. She protests that the Oubaas has not bathed or dressed. She looks to Michiel to intervene. But Michiel has had no contact with this man for almost fifteen years and has no language for the moment.

'Let's forget the bath, Oubaas,' Alida says. 'Let's just dress and shave.'

'Go and get yourself ready, Alida,' the old man replies. 'Michiel is here. If we need you I'll call on the intercom.' Michiel notices an electronic box fitted to the wall on Oubaas's side of the bed, with its handset on the nightstand.

The old man swivels to face Michiel directly: 'Your mother would have wanted you to help your father, wouldn't she?'

'Of course I'll help. But Alida knows how everything is done. I think she should give us a hand.'

'Why are you waiting, Alida? You heard me: Michiel will do everything for me.'

'Will the Kleinbaas manage?'

'I think so, Alida. You can tell me what to do.'

Here is the suit and tie, she says. Here are the shoes and socks. She pats the underpants. Fresh towels are in the linen closet. The shaving kit is laid out on the washstand.

'Oubaas can lift himself if you put Oubaas's arm around your neck. You must use the Palmolive, Kleinbaas, other soap doesn't agree with Oubaas's skin. And Oubaas likes the water lukewarm, not hot. The blue wash cloth and sponge are Oubaas's. And then, after you dry him off, there's the chamomile lotion in the blue jar. That stops—'

'I will tell him what to do, Alida.'

She nods. 'Kleinbaas can call if Kleinbaas needs me.' She demonstrates how to operate the intercom. On her keyring she carries an electronic buzzer: if she's not in the kaya to answer the intercom the buzzer vibrates and she comes from wherever she might be. 'What about Kleinbaas Michiel's ironing? Everything in that suitcase must be creased. And lunch? An empty stomach in church has never been a good thing.'

He lies that he ate something along the way. Maybe she could iron his shirt? From the stoep a dog looks up and watches as they walk the length of the passage. Michiel unzips the case and unfolds his white shirt as she comes to stand beside him.

'This is all, Alida, thank you.' He rises from his haunches. He wants to tell her that it has been many years since anyone did his ironing. He has done it himself since basics at Saldanha Bay. *Boot camp*, he has explained overseas. Glassman: *basics and boot camp* — euphemisms for young men trained not to feel so they can kill without thinking and live on, without feeling. *If Kleinbaas hangs his clothes neatly — shake out the creases like this — Kleinbaas will cut his ironing time in half. Hang the browns' shirts by the shoulders, like this, with the clothes pegs on the thick seam so Kleinbaas doesn't get a silver mark on the material once it dries.* With a steam iron Ounooi got for him at Kloppers in Bloemfontein the day they took him to board the train with hundreds of other eighteen-year-olds. When he came home on pass from the officer's course and then from Namibia with his balsak of dirty browns, socks and underwear taut as a drum, Alida spent her Saturdays washing and ironing.

'I'm barely here and you're already spoiling me, Alida.'

'A little spoiling never killed anyone.' Discomfited at her choice of words, she looks down at his suitcase. 'What about the tie, Kleinbaas? Let Alida press it.'

He again goes down on his haunches. Two ties are draped over the set of clean clothes for tomorrow's return. 'Blue,' Kamil said as they packed, 'if all's as good as can be under the circumstances. Lilac for a bit of activism if you need them all to go to hell.'

Still on his haunches he holds up both. 'Which one? You choose.'

'Oh, the purple, Kleinbaas. Like the jacaranda. Ounooi's favorite, Kleinbaas.'

'Alida,' he says quietly, rising, 'I don't want to trouble you, but I must ask you a favor. Can you please . . . Could you try to stop calling me *Kleinbaas*?'

She receives the tie from his hand as though taking charge of a fragile treasure. She lays it neatly across the shirt in the crook of her arm and keeps her gaze on the garments. Even in this dim light he can see her blush.

'I will try, Kleinbaas Michiel.'

'How do you cope with all of this? Will he not drive you insane?'

'I was two years old when he was born. I changed his nappies and I wiped him then and I'm changing his nappies and I'm wiping him now. Now, at least, I can wipe myself.' With a glance up at him she leaves. He watches as she turns left to pass through the dining room. Her shoulders stoop. She is much too old for this work. Any work. He listens to her heels on the wood — reminiscent of Ounooi's — and waits for them to go silent on the kitchen linoleum. He anticipates the squeak of the screen door. Instead there is the rattle of keys as she unlocks the new kitchen gate. He pictures her crossing the back yard, along the footpath lined with wild iris, to the laundry. She places a white handkerchief protectively over the tie, smoothes it, sprinkles water from the enamel jar, before the iron hisses down against the lilac of raw silk.

The bathroom they used as kids has been refurbished and its wooden floor replaced by large white tiles. A new bathtub on ball-and-claw feet stands beneath four large square windows. The windows are open, letting in light and air, bird and children sounds from the garden. He notes the solid chrome handle that must have been fitted to the blue and white tiles for Oubaas. The linen closet has made way for a shower cubicle of frosted glass with a fleur-de-lys pattern. Somewhere during the years of his absence the old man must have relented and allowed the renovations Ounooi always wanted. He remembers Oubaas watching the bookkeeping with a hawk's eye. Money was spent as long as it was saved in equal measure and as long as he had the final word — at times even on the income generated by Ounooi's bottling industry. He had gibed at her suggestion of bringing in an architect to update the outmoded kitchen and dank, dark bathrooms. Only new plumbing and heating for the winter were allowed. Other than fresh white paint, the interior had remained as it had been since the owners who bestowed the name *Paradise* had left.

Ounooi was allowed most other things she needed or desired: she traveled across Western Europe, Greece, Turkey, Israel, Taiwan and Uruguay with members of the congregation. Oubaas 'surprised' her with a new Mercedes every five years while he drove the same Datsun bakkie until it came apart. And Ounooi dressed well — too well — *everyone thinks your mom is a snob with her clothes and books.* The sons traveled the length and breadth of South Africa and Namibia (South-West Africa, then) on sports tours. New rugby togs as needed for the younger two, tennis rackets for Peet. Church suits. For each an honors blazer for sport and academics. No hand-me-downs. What was outgrown or discarded went to the compound. Things outworn in Ounooi's closet were either sold by Alida for her own purse or she tailored them to wear under her housecoat or to church. Later, when Karien and Little-Alida were grown, Ounooi divided old or rarely worn garments between her two protégées.

He rinses the tub and opens the hot and cold faucets to ensure the water is tepid. He stands in front of the mirror above the washbasin. The mirror, flecked from years of water and steam, he knows for certain is that of his youth. Odd that amid the changes this was not replaced. An oversight, or Oubaas idiosyncratically closing the purse before the remodeling was done? Though he doesn't feel tired his face tells a different story. At home he and Kamil would be asleep now. He opens the cabinet behind the mirror to look for eye drops. He runs his hand across the graying stubble of his unshaven chin. He wets his hand and tries to clear the oily sheen from his skin. In the mirror he catches the reflection of the new bathtub. Into his mind drifts the image of him lowering Kamil into the water near the end of their touch-and-go days, Kamil hanging on by his fingernails to his white cell count of 39. They wait for the whisper of a protean miracle to turn into a hum then to cautious relief all through Eureka Valley.

Oubaas faces him when he re-enters the bedroom. 'Pa ready?'

'Gods. What I'm ready for is to join Ounooi. Heartbreak killed her, you know. You have a way with women, don't you?'

'Ounooi had a stroke, Pa.' Still, he knows, the arithmetic of one's own responsibility is rendered doubtful by voices that explain events from vantages of their own. That, he imagines, is why on her trip Ounooi left good enough alone. Efficiently, respectfully and without getting involved he will get this ritual behind him and go home. 'Come, Pa, let's get this done.' He takes hold of the wheelchair's handles. He wonders whether the orange fabric on the grips is the handiwork of Ounooi or Alida. When he catches his father's smell he instinctively averts his nose. Slightly sour, moldy, melded with camphor that has seeped into unwashed flannel. The smell of old age and bedridden young men. How could Ounooi stand it? She, with roses on her dressing table, attuned to every nuance of sense and appearance. She of the white cotton blouses, baggy cotton jackets, the slightly longer than fashionable beige skirts, the silver and white gold – never yellow gold – earrings. With Virginia Woolf framed on her desk at school. How does elegance live with this before its eyes, in its perfectly shaped nostrils and beside it in bed? Had she, in the years of his disease, regretted having married a man so much older than herself? He feels his heart lurch. He steers the chair alongside the tub and steps around the footrest. Even when they are clasped to the armrests Oubaas's hands tremble. He looks up; what Michiel reads in the blue eyes is contempt. Clearly the insistence that his son – *this* son – be the one to bath him is not some grand gesture of reconciliation. No, this is born from a disdain still simmering all these years later. This is not a mother's funeral;

it is to be a father's final showdown with a son. For this he has been lured to the farm.

'Let me help Pa with the pajamas,' he offers, stooping, reaching for the shirt's buttons. Motionless the old man watches as Michiel's fingers clumsily go to work. The stale smell is now inescapable. He tries to hold his breath. The proximity to the other man's face makes him self-conscious of not having washed for a day and a half, of having brushed his teeth without enthusiasm in the plane's cramped restroom an hour before landing. It is possible that part of the reek comes from himself.

Oubaas's sunken chest is blue-white and veined. Like Roquefort. His breasts sag. The nipples are pronounced, like those of a pubescent girl. Even as he tries not to look closely, Michiel does not fail to register the pallid folds of skin beneath the thinning gray hairs of the belly. What muscle is left in the arms can no longer be discerned. In the precise pattern of a farmer's tan, in a V from neck midway to hairy chest, sunspots and moles discolor the skin as they do on both arms from above the elbows to the hands. In the folds where the chest meets the soft upper arms, the skin is beige, veined blue, with the bruised yellow wrinkling of old apple.

'Can you raise yourself, Pa, so I can take these off.' Michiel tugs at the pants. 'Or must I lift you?'

From strength he wants witnessed, like an adamant boy, Oubaas hoists himself on trembling arms, hovers slightly above the seat, allowing Michiel's fingers to slip into the elastic band of the pants and in one motion drag them down to the ankles. With a soft exhalation Oubaas sits back down. Michiel pulls the brown slippers and socks off along with the crumpled pants. He feels his eyelids sting. He turns his back, folds the pajamas beside the shaving kit and places the slippers beside the washstand.

'This bathing business is unnecessary,' the old man mutters.

Michiel looks at the reflection of the naked man in the wheelchair. 'Shall I just use the washcloth, Pa? We can at least wipe you down before you dress.' Neither speaks. Through the windows comes again the *koer-koer* of turtledoves and the constant piet-my-vrou. Up in the mountains a baboon barks.

'You must go and call Alida.'

Michiel turns. 'I can do it, Pa.' The words come without his thinking. 'If you'd like me to.'

The old man nods. 'Roll up your sleeves. This can be a messy business. You were never one for facing the mess you made. Now you're going to live in China?'

'I'll only be there for a week, Pa. The company I work for is opening a new office.'

Folding back his sleeves he goes on to one knee. When he leans forward he feels their shoulders touch. Oubaas's arm searches to find its way around his neck. Michiel reaches back, finds the fingers and draws the hand down so that it rests on his collarbone. His hand, across his father's, takes in the trembling of the fingers. Already he senses how light the old man is. What have time and disease left undone to the behemoth before which they quivered until deep into their teens? He feels the body tense against him. 'Feel the water, Pa. With your other hand.' The old man reaches down and stirs the water with his fingertips.

'Dis reg.' The water is fine. 'Little-Alida has been to China too. She told your mother it's the filthiest place on earth and that they eat dogs.'

'I'm going to pick you up, Pa, and lift you in. Ready?'

'I *can* stand, Michiel, if you help. I take you around the neck and you take me around the waist.'

'Will it not be easier if I lift you right in, Pa?' He does not say: I have lifted weights every other day since first carrying another in to the bath of our own home. Your sour breath, the baby finch curled in its nest and the stale musk of night sweats on warm days are familiar to me. Like unwashed feet that smell of dried peaches. He slips his free arm beneath the skinny white legs. The body in his arms tenses. With only a slight heave he lifts and in his ear he hears a soft grunt.

'I've got you, don't be afraid.'

He goes back down on to his knee and brings the body to above the bath. 'We're going in, okay?' He feels the nod in his neck, the scrape of stubble against the fabric of his shirt. Slowly, feeling the buttocks come to rest in the bath, he releases the legs into the water. With his upper arm sliding up behind the neck and shoulders he lets the head recline against the back of the tub. The extraordinary lightness of a grown man released into water. Oubaas sighs, his eyes closed.

'Okay, Pa?'

'Uh-uh,' the old man grunts. Against the white enamel the head is at last at rest; still. Also the hands, adrift on his stomach, are placid. He inclines his head slightly to Michiel, who is kneeling at the tub. The eyes, when they open, are soft; the blue lightning dispelled, as if its presence was always, since childhood, only a figment of his youngest son's pained imagination. 'You can use the cloth for my body. Ounooi used the sponge for my face.'

He will begin at the feet. He meets his father's eyes, sensing that something between them has altered. For ever, or only here, while the declining patriarch is drifting at his son's mercy? With Glassman he has speculated whether the old man suffered from a kind of bipolar disorder. Could the outbursts at his boys and at farm workers be given a neurological rather than psychodynamic diagnosis? Had there been the right pills, back then — any of a dozen mood stabilizers favored by Kamil's students at Berkeley — might their entire lives have been different? But how to account for the selectivity of his rage? Never, in Michiel's memory, was the physical or verbal violence directed at Ounooi or at Alida. Oubaas could clobber a worker or any of his sons, shout or growl at incompetence but be as friendly as summer dawn the instant Ounooi or Alida came near. Or Karien; all those weekends and holidays here. What was it in Oubaas that women — even Mamparra and Adam's wife Liesbet — were spared? 'No,' Michiel concluded in Glassman's chair, 'my dad suffers from more than biochemical imbalance or misfiring neurons. Whatever it is is mixed in with the delusions of raw white South African male power. You have to have grown up there to know what I mean.' And Glassman laughed out loud and said: 'Michael, I'm from Texas.'

'When we've finished washing,' Oubaas speaks, his gaze still on Michiel, 'you can fill the white Tupperware bowl from under the sink with very hot water. Then you shave me in here. That's how Ounooi did it. Less water all over the place if we do it while I'm in the bath.'

Kneeling at the tub, Michiel takes the feet between his hands. The toenails, hard as shells, are yellowed but neatly trimmed; scrubbed. Is this how he was with her, when they were alone? Was it the obscured vulnerability, or frailty, that she fell in love with, and that held them together? From the first courtship to the later routine of their Sunday afternoons, had gentleness been reserved for her, to be part of their lovemaking, or in the calm lethargy of afterwards? Michiel looks up at the face, the closed eyes, head to one side, the weak neck with its sinews, the mouth sagging at the corners. Like one of the ancient turtles in the Solomon Sea. You look up and see them against the incredible blue. They glide down to look, wondering at you there in their place. Might this fugitive moment contain something of what the religious call grace?

He rinses suds from the feet. The ankles are covered in a patchwork of elevated blue, purple and red knots; against the softer white skin around the Achilles tendon varicose veins fan upward in fine embroidery. Michiel bends the left leg, soaps shin bone and knee, then the calf with its one vein bulging diagonally from behind the knee's fold towards the shin. He brings the knee down, struck by the softness of the calves, their fleshless, empty feel. Nothing is left of the browned muscles that expanded and

31

contracted as Oubaas strode ahead between neat rows of mielies and sunflowers.

'If it takes you this long to come home again, I too will no longer be here.'

He wrings the washcloth. Oubaas's eyes remain shut. Is this, after all, your way of 'reaching out', as Benjamin said?

'You are quiet,' Oubaas murmurs.

You and I have never had much to say to each other might be the most truthful response. Silence has always reigned between us. As a boy I tried constantly to read you to know what you thought of me and wanted of me. I twisted myself in knots to please you; embraced an unyielding vigilance I'm still trying to unlearn. You spoke more to me – at me – as you sent me packing than in all the years before. But Michiel does not now wish for truth. Instead, he will say something respectful. Something to acknowledge whatever might be happening here; grant his father and this moment the benefit of the doubt. *Honesty will do*, Kamil might say. *Truth is sometimes too much.*

'I'm thinking, Pa, how life brings us to unexpected places.' He lathers and washes the diminished thighs, rubs the cloth closer to the protruding bones of the hips.

The old man coughs once. And then says, 'Next unexpected place you'll be is my dick.' He guffaws and Michiel chuckles, unable to stop himself from laughing. Oubaas's laughter comes from his belly, his head thrown back. His chest rises and falls. A soapy cascade over the tub's side drenches Michiel's jeans. Still smiling, Michiel returns his eyes to Oubaas's face. What he sees now cannot be mistaken for mirth. The mouth is open, with the lips drawn into a snarl, the eyes stretched to bursting. The face is contorted and there is no sound from the throat. The arms bring up the hands, somehow manage to place them, again doddering, over the open eyes, leaving visible only the mouth's soundless gape.

'Oubaas?' For an instant Michiel thinks it is a seizure. Then a drawn-out note, like that of a muted oboe, comes from a lost place within the old man's chest. A gasp for breath and the note has turned into a wail. His chest heaves. There is another gasp before he sobs into the tremulous cup of his hands. Michiel cannot bear to watch. How long it continues he will not remember. What he will remember is that he sat down on the bathroom tiles, the wash-cloth still in his hand. That he may have stuck his fingers into his ears. That quiet eventually returned and that only then did he rise back on to his knees to see a vein standing out on his father's fore-head, his eyes and cheeks glistening, the eyes now bluer than ever, the defeat in them terrible.

Then Oubaas speaks. 'How much time is there?' He looks from Michiel up to the ceiling. 'Will we not be late, Peet?' Michiel allows the slip to pass and glances at his watch. There is no need to rush. He resumes: hips, belly, chest, neck. Perhaps inferring from the path of the washcloth his son's reluctance, the old man says: 'I manage my own private parts. Hand me the cloth. You need only guide my hand.' When he is done he instructs Michiel to take the bottle of Denorex from the washstand. 'It's for dry scalp,' he says. 'Your mother rubbed in coconut oil and let me sleep with it in my hair. She blamed my smoking. Said it dehydrated me. So I stopped smoking, but I still get the scaly scalp.' Michiel places his hand beneath Oubaas's head and, using the enamel jug from the wash-stand, wets the thick gray hair. He lets the head rest against the tub again while he pours the strong-smelling brown liquid into his palm. Then, rising to sit on the tub's rim, he rubs in the fluid, his fingertips massaging the lather into the scalp. With the jug full of clean water he rinses three, four times. Now the blue sponge for the face. From the closet underneath the basin he takes the large Tupperware bowl and fills it with hot water. He spreads shaving cream on his father's chin, cheeks and throat. He takes the razor from the washstand. Seated on the rim, he begins to shave the gritty stubble.

He meets his father's gaze.

'How could you leave her when she was pregnant?'

He returns his eyes to the task at hand.

'That was not how I raised my sons.'

If we were the way you raised us, Michiel could say, there would be nowhere on earth for us to live.

'This could be your last chance, Peet.'

'I'm Michiel, Pa—'

'The razor won't do the job. People will know you tried and failed. The law will be involved again. More serious than AWOL.' Michiel sees the glint back in the blue eyes. 'But you could push me under. I assure you there is not much fight left in this body.' He is smiling. 'You can say you left the bathroom to fetch something. When you came back I had blacked out and drowned. The last will and testament is in town, at Malherbe and Partners.'

The haste with which the old man has gone from despair back to here takes Michiel by surprise. He feels his own breathing shorten, anger rising in him. He rinses the razor. Steadies his father's chin with his free hand and then carefully drags the razor down the cheek. Then the swish of the caked blade being rinsed again. He repeats the downward stroke along a wider path, closer to the ears and sideburns.

'There were times, Pa, I wished you a taste of your own medicine.' When he at last speaks his voice is calm, resigned even to his own ears. 'Some kind of revenge. But that desire went, with time, Pa.' He has felt himself relaxing, concentrating on the razor, even as he weighs each word. In the bathroom's quiet the stubble coming away from skin resembles the tiny crackle of a wave drawing back from the beach. And when I saw you on the stoep, Pa, in your pajamas in the wheelchair – this he wishes to say – it came to me that revenge couldn't satisfy me now. The pictures Ounooi brought said nothing of the chair or the tremor. She chose to present you as you must have been till a few years back. In reality you have grown too old for me to get back . . . at you, Pa. Old and weak and pitiful. Revenge may be a dish best served cold, but delayed too long the festivities no longer seem worthwhile. *Die kool is die sous nie werd nie.* The cabbage is not worth the sauce, he hears himself saying, but he says nothing. He empties the bowl's dregs in the sink and gets clean hot water, catching sight of his warped reflection in the chrome faucet. He looks into the mirror and notices his red eyes before again sitting down on the bathtub's rim. And at heart, old man, I always loved you. Is there a way to force these words out?

The blue eyes are still on him, waiting for him to go on. For a moment they stare at each other before Michiel looks away, his attention back on the razor. With his fingertips he removes the shaving cream that is massed in the ear's shell. When I hiked back to the farm in disgrace I came because there was no other place to go. Never, even as a child, had I known such loneliness.

'Jissis,' Oubaas interrupts his thoughts. 'A man halfway through his thirties who still cannot explain himself. Stand up for yourself! Is it possible that you are even more pathetic than I remember?'

'Even today, Pa, when you will not allow me to mourn my mother. Even—'

'I asked you here because she loved you! Perversions and all. Get me out of this bath.'

'Is there no mercy in you?'

'Mercy! You sound like a woman, for Christ's sake. If you must be this thing you are, can't you at least pretend to have balls? I have nothing to say to you. Get me out of here. Call Alida. Go to the intercom . . .' Then he seems to change his mind and, with his face to the windows and with a volume that is astounding from so frail a chest, lifts his head and bellows, twice, three times, the name of the woman who raised him. From outside, into the chamber's quiet, comes the sound of doves, as if nothing in here has happened.

An hour before they leave for town he enters the dusky living room across from his old bedroom. The shower has left him invigorated, as if from a good night's sleep. His suitcase had been moved from the passage and placed at the foot of his old bed, the left of the two singles. On the closet door his jacket and pants hung neatly alongside the ironed shirt. The tie – creaseless – was draped over the shirt's shoulder. Down the hall he hears Alida, still busy with Oubaas. It has now been decided that she will, as originally planned, accompany the old man and the prodigal in the rental car.

The living room's new sliding doors are shut. New armchairs. The old settee and chaise longue have been re-upholstered. *I am writing in English so Michiel doesn't have to translate and you can share the news from home.* Her letters, read aloud in bed, to Kamil with his head on the pillow beneath the silk tapestry of the Green Tara. *If the two of you were here you could help decide where to put the couch. I convinced Oubaas to pass on to Alida the dreadful old La-Z-Boy he now rarely uses. I have been showing everyone pictures of your apartment's tasteful furnishings.* Mohair blinds and lace curtains. On a new coffee table is a mass of calla lilies (from up at the spring, he knows), the long green stems bright through the clear glass vase. Where people gathered this morning for tea and cake it is now spotless, all evidence of mourning cleared. The room is cooler than the rest of the house. When he sees Ounooi's beloved Maggie Laubscher in its gilded frame, the Pierneef etchings and a number of new Claerhouts in pastel, he thinks of his own bedroom's walls. Stepping back across the passage he hears the familiar creaking of the one infirm floorboard. Things he drew and painted in primary school and that Ounooi had framed are no longer there. In their place are etchings and charcoal drawings by Karien: a horse's nostrils flaring; a goat and kid on the footpath at the cave's mouth. Whence her thing for farm animals? He notices too that the wagon wheel with small lampshades that hung from the ceiling has been replaced by spotlights aimed into the room's corners. In place of metal frames, large sash windows allow in more light and the curtains have been replaced with blinds. On the beds are duvet covers with blue and white motifs of African masks. On the foot end of his old bed, neatly folded, is still the kaross of blackback jackal skins inherited from Grandpa Ford. Someone — Alida? — has placed a vase of callas (arums, they're called here, he now recalls) on the three-tiered bookshelf with the small collection of books, beside the desk.

He re-enters the living room. His movements behind the long sofa are reflected in the gray of a new, widescreen television set. Were they here, together on the blue sofa, the last night? On racks below the screen are remote controls and a satellite decoder. *Oubaas is mesmerized by sports: he watches everything — rugby, European soccer, the Tour de France, water polo, you know how he loves all team sport. Strange, he's never taken to American football. As you both know I have my own little indulgences: you go girl!* Kamil and he had been surprised at how up she was on recent films, British and American popular culture. She'd watched, she told them, the 1998 Clinton–Lewinsky hearings in real time. *Ridiculous: the lewdness of it all.* Flipping channels in their apartment she'd chuckled at coming across *The Bold and the Beautiful*. She watched *Days of Our Lives* so she could pass on to her students in her adult education project what was coming down the pike to what they were watching in South Africa. 'If I tell those women I saw it in America, my street cred will skyrocket!' On the farm, even with the satellite dish, they didn't receive current episodes of the soaps (which she didn't watch anyway) nor *Oprah* (which she did, religiously): they were always a season or two behind the US.

The yellowwood floor is covered in the blue, cream and deep magenta kilim she had shipped back from a trip to Turkey in the early seventies. The rug arrived without the English text of the weave's story that had been promised by the merchant. She had traveled by bus across the Euphrates and Tigris to Urfa, the birthplace of Abraham, close to the Syrian border, and then to Mount Ararat, 'further east than Moscow'. From Istanbul she'd gone to

Israel. *My Middle East tour*, she called it. Behind her desk is the wall covered top to bottom by books. A life's reading ordered alphabetically, not by genre as are his and Kamil's. A, top left, down to bottom right Z: Aristotle, Blake, Chekhov, Dante, Eliot, Flaubert, Gogol, Hamsun, Ibsen, Joyce, Kipling, Lawrence, Melville, Nietzsche, Ovid, Proust, Rousseau, Sartre, Twain, Voltaire, Woolf, Yeats, Zola.

Did Alida or Benjamin clear her paperwork for this morning's gathering, or did she herself file everything the night she died? He looks at the photographs: the family of five in black and white, taken by the town's photographer, on the chaise longue. Framed by silver baroque curlicues, Oubaas smiles broadly. His thick dark hair is parted at the side and swept back with Brylcreem. In a dark suit, he has Benjamin on his right knee, Peet on the left. Michiel stands beside Ounooi. She, bare knees inclined to one side, is dressed in a crimplene miniskirt. Two of the three boys have teeth missing. Their faces glow. Their short-back-and-no-sides do not hide thick brushes of dark hair. In London, then in Australia, he'd let the school/army cut grow out and hadn't allowed a sharp object near it for years. When he met Kamil in Sydney it reached below his shoulders. Once the thinning became too obvious the buzz cut was Kamil's idea and Kamil's responsibility to maintain.

He hears giggles from the garden, a name called followed by running footsteps and a dog's bark.

Peet. In color. His head, in profile, is inclined as the Chancellor touches his shoulder. Who would not recognize the then South African President's skewed grin? Beneath Peet's cap and the wing of dark hair over his ear the features are more pronounced than they have ever been in Michiel's memory. A deep groove extends from beside his nose to the corner of the black moustache. A few days before fishermen will find his body. Michiel's eyes go to his brother's tie and white shirt collar, above the V where the black gown and the two hoods come together. The photographer's flash has cast a shadow where the shirt collar stands away from the throat at the Adam's apple. How much weight had he lost? Oubaas and Ounooi must have noticed. Ounooi, your genius for seeing only what you wished. From Peet he learned how to knot a tie. Like other boys, and Benjamin, Michiel marked his school tie's flip side, one small pen-mark for each cut received, and a bold line if the caning came from the principal. In all Peet's high-school years, the eldest, the quiet one, the disciplined, the academically focused, the four As in Matric, the tennis player who never allowed himself to be bullied or scorned into playing rugby, had received only two cuts and would have scoffed at the suggestion of scoring them on his tie.

And here we are. At seventeen in our honors blazers. A decent-looking boy/man with fading pink acne scars at his temples and an attractive girl/woman with her hair in braids, their eyes ignited with optimism. Gorgeous and Genius with capital Gs, Ounooi said. How could anyone not have been in love with you, Kariena? My girlfriend, lover, heart. Beside them, a more recent photograph of her and Dirk. On her lap a child, a mahogany child, laughing like happiness itself. Dirk slightly gray, but still the Adonis. Beauty alongside beauty. They must fuck like tigers. She is aging well. The white skin of memory is gone and she is darkly tanned, her arm copper beneath the child's little hand. The harder, angular edge to her face heightens the resemblance to her mother, Gerda Niehaus, the one-time Cherry Queen.

Benjamin: holding the rugby ball, captain of the school's First XV, captain of the Free State under-eighteens at Craven Week. All-rounder, first at *everything* they did outdoors on land or in water. Everyone's best friend. No, buddy. Early on it had been accepted that either Michiel or he — or both — would take over Paradys. With time Michiel seemed to lose interest, taking more to books, especially once the middle brother's skill with all things agricultural and his penchant for profits grew evident. Then, in high school, Benjamin made clear that more than being a farmer he wanted to make money. Paradys alone could never do that for him. He wanted to build an empire like Harry Oppenheimer. Or Rhodes. Or Anton Rupert with Rupert International: *Rembrandt van Rijn: every cigarette a masterpiece*. Paradys's cherry orchards and livestock would be but one project in his towering future. Midway through his two years of conscription he joined the Permanent Force for the minimum period; it makes financial sense, he said. As an infantry lieutenant in the Angolan War he completed a degree in commerce through UNISA.

The first and only family portrait without Peet: both remaining boys in uniform between Oubaas and Ounooi. Framed in the church's Gothic entrance. Benjamin in the khaki jacket with the two silver pips; Michiel, in whites, the gold looped bands of the ensign's epaulettes on his shoulders. Ten weeks before he would be relieved of those.

Glassman: Your late brother got away with college while you two went into the army? Michiel: They allowed for you to go either after high school or once you had your degree. Glassman: Those were your choices? Michiel: Unless you went to jail, or left the country. Glassman: You didn't choose college like Peet? (Name pronounced as an American or Brit would, without the Afrikaans diphthong.) Michiel: Two kids in college at the same time would have been expensive for my parents. Peet was the brain. He was born to be a lawyer, like all the men on my mom's side of the family. Glassman: Why did you choose to become an officer and go to war in a foreign country? Why not be a pen-pusher or drive a truck? Michiel, some sessions later: There was no decision, no choice that I remember making consciously; it was as easy as breathing. Michiel, another year later: I was too embarrassed not to go. Too ashamed not to be an officer. Glassman: Shame masquerading as pride? Michiel: I didn't see it like that at the time.

'Kanu! Pulane!' He looks up. It is almost his mother's voice, from the garden. 'Get in here and wash those grass stains off so you can put on your shoes.' From the perfect white South African English accent he knows it must be Little-Alida. Lerato. Her voice continues with what sounds like a warning, in seSotho, a language Michiel barely understands. A child protests, also in seSotho, and then the voice he remembers calls out: 'Kanu, I am not speaking again!'

And here is Benjamin's family. His two kids and Giselle. *Your brother, just like Oubaas, chose an English-speaker. A real accountant, though. Runs their investment business with him. Wonderful mother. Strong woman.*

He sits down in Ounooi's chair. He lifts another framed photograph: it is the day after he collected her in the snow from JFK. A city tour that included the harbor ferry trip. The snow has been swept into heaps beneath the Statue of Liberty. Ounooi is wrapped in the winter coat with the faux fox-fur collar he and Kamil had bought for her at Nordstrom's. *She may not have anything warm enough for the winter — come on, Michael, surprise her.* Drawn low over her ears and gaze is the velvet hat — *think Annie Hall* — that caught Kamil's eye as they were already in line to pay for the coat. Michiel, bundled and hatted, smiles directly at the camera. His arm is around her, his gloved hand pulling her to him. How radiant she looks — they, together — in the winter sunshine. All that matters, really, is that they had this at least. Within hours he will register the omission of himself and Kamil together, here, on her desk, and will pardon this almost at the instant of realization. Why provoke the old man's ire? For now, he is moved by her smile, by the two of them reconciled in their shabby way, amid the other tourists, with Manhattan's skyline rising regally across the water.

At the sound of loud laughter he stands up from her chair and parts the lace curtains to look across the stoep to the lawn. A smartly dressed girl and boy are trying to get the bull terriers to stand still for long enough to place crowns of honeysuckle on their

41

heads. The dogs drop their necks, pawing at the nuisance. From the direction of Peet's rondavel comes a woman in a black pantsuit. She is slender and tall, like her father who died in a Welkom mine. She speaks into a cellphone, gesturing with a key. Over her shoulder she carries a black leather purse. Braids swing as she speaks. Hand on hip, head shaking vigorously, she accents the air with the key. Alida's only child, a few years older than Peet. Ounooi taught her to speak English and Afrikaans without the (black) African accent. Unbeknownst to Oubaas, Ounooi used the bottling business as security at Volkskas for Little-Alida's first student loans. At the end of her first year at the Jo'burg College of Education she won a scholarship from Anglo American to attend Wits. She dropped the education major and read for a degree in civil engineering, graduating summa cum laude. Ounooi's one disappointment was her protégée's decision to marry instead of applying for the Rhodes scholarship. *Of course I initially thought the girl was pregnant.* It was the early nineties. Time of the first bigger changes. Ounooi begged her to reconsider. But by then the prodigy had a mind of her own and the influence of the white woman who had taught her flawless English had waned. Ounooi attended the wedding. In a hall of three hundred guests, she was one of only a dozen white people. In a recent letter: *Little-Alida is here from Jo'burg while her wealthy businessman husband visits his family in Lagos. This man loves the twins and is an exemplary father to the two who are also here for the Easter weekend. The son becomes more precocious with each visit and the little girl now suddenly wants only to be a ballet dancer. She goes everywhere on tiptoes.* He cannot take his eyes from the woman on the lawn. At the sound of the key in the sliding door she looks up. He smiles when he sees that she has recognized him. With the phone still to her ear she opens her mouth wide and lifts her hand and wiggles her free fingers at him.

'*Kleinbaas* Michiel Steyn!' she exclaims, closing the phone and crossing towards him standing behind the bars. 'The gate key is attached to the sliding-door key,' she says, coming up the stairs. Once the gate is unlocked they embrace as naturally as if they have done this their entire lives. Will she, like him, think later that this is the first time they ever touched each other so deliberately? When she speaks again (in English, he notes, not in their Afrikaans of old), the tone is quite different. 'Mom said you were coming. I am terribly sorry about Ounooi, Michiel.'

'Thank you . . . I'm so glad *you* are here.'

'How can I not be?' She waves the children closer. 'Come and say hello to Michiel, you two,' she calls. 'He's Auntie Beth's son from the United States.' The girl comes closer, but the boy tarries. 'It's good that you've come, Michiel. It's something Ounooi would have wanted.' The boy entertains the dogs with a stick while the girl comes towards them carrying the flower crowns. She is no more than six or seven years old. Her arms go around her mother's hips, her eyes glued to Michiel.

'You must be the jewel in your mother's crown,' he says and the girl turns her face into her mom's hip, peeping at him through one eye.

'Stop being coy.' Lerato juts out her hip, trying to loosen the child's grip. 'A real little flirt, this one.' And then again to the child, 'Introduce yourself, my girl.'

The child lets go of her mother and extends her right hand. 'My name is Pulane. I'm pleased to meet you.' The voice is tiny.

With the child's warm hand in his, Michiel goes down on his hunkers. 'I am so pleased to meet you, Pulane. I heard you made your dress yourself with fabric from Timbuktu.'

'It's from Truworths, not Timbuktu!' She giggles. 'Mommy bought it for me!'

'Well, I was told you design and make all your own clothes.'

'You're mad!' The child laughs and extracts her hand from his, pretending to swing the crowns at him as she leans back against her mother. She is a pretty child, a beautiful child, with almond eyes

43

slightly slanted up towards tiny ears, skin much darker than both her mother and grandmother with braided hair tied at her neck. 'I bet you don't know the dogs' names!' she says.

'This one, mmmm . . .' he feigns mulling over possibilities, 'is called Portunovascotiakokkadoodledoo.'

Pulane shrieks with laughter. 'It's not that! Her name is Isabella!' She looks up at her mother. 'And what about that one, over there with my brother?'

'Mmm . . . Must be Versaikreaturasomnambulatakolombangara.'

'No, no, no! Mommy, tell him. His name is Grootman.'

'Kanu!' Lerato yells to the boy throwing a stick into the orchard for Grootman to fetch. 'Did you not hear? Come and say hello. We'll be late.' To Michiel she says, 'I have things to drop off with the cousins in the township before the service.' She and the children are staying over, but she is set to leave before dawn for a meeting and to get the kids back to school. For an instant he pictures the five of them in Alida's kaya: the Anglo American executive on the tiny extra bed that was hers when she was a child, and now the two children, maybe sharing a mattress on the floor. Is this how they slept before Peet's rondavel was opened to them? Or did she and the children take rooms in the hotel that surely, now, must cater to clients of color? Is there a chance that the manor itself has been allowed her in the years following who and what she has become? He cannot bear to ask.

The boy stands breathless at the foot of the stairs. He is dressed in a cream-colored suit with brown leather shoes, his hair very short against his skull. He has his grandmother's high forehead, the same confident bearing of set shoulders and light brown skin. At least two inches taller than his sister, there is little to suggest he is Pulane's twin or Lerato's son.

Michiel steps on to the lawn.

'I'm Michiel.' He extends his hand. 'I've heard a lot about you.'

The boy says, 'Pleased to meet you, Michiel from America.'

Then, aiming for an American accent, 'I'm Kanu Mahabane-Okonkwo from Gauteng, South Africa.'

'Pretty good, actually,' Michiel comments.

'We're going to the Winter Olympics next year and we're going to ski,' Kanu goes on.

'I've promised them,' Lerato says. 'Salt Lake City. A week at the games and then lessons at Tahoe. Give me strength.'

'That's not far from where I live. We've skied there.'

'Ounooi loved San Francisco. It's a wonderful thing that you and she—'

'How fast do you go on skis?' Kanu interrupts and Lerato tells him to behave. Then, 'Actually, it's time we take off. You two, wait for me in the car. Open the windows so you don't roast like chickens.' She hands Kanu the key and the children run off, calling goodbyes and the dogs darting alongside.

'I'm hoping his energy levels stabilize around the mid-level as he grows older. Do you remember how Benjamin could never sit still? This one is just the same.'

'Benjamin has calmed down?'

'Giselle has worked some magic on him.' She laughs. 'That's right, you haven't seen them yet, have you?'

'We've spoken on the phone.'

In a gesture he remembers from Alida, when she was touched, expressed sympathy or gratitude, Lerato places a hand on her diaphragm. 'This must be a terrible shock to you. It was, to all of us.' Her cellphone rings again and she turns off the sound. 'I'm putting it on silent,' she says, 'before I forget to turn it off and it disrupts the service.' She drops the phone into her purse. She inclines her head towards the car, which squeaks as the remote control opens the doors. 'They adored Ounooi. She never let us leave here empty-handed: koeksusters, bags of dried fruit, natbeskuit. Kanu is mad for the natbeskuit. And cartons of cherries. I don't need to tell you that I loved your mother. She was a generous human being.'

Your world, today, he thinks as she speaks, must be a world apart from this farm. Where do you find the language to say of the baas's wife 'I loved her'? And what of Oubaas? What does a woman like you think of him? 'Thank you, Klein——' he stops himself. 'Sorry, Lerato.'

'Everyone here still calls me that. Mom tries. Mostly from grandiosity, so that her child's name corresponds with the occasional picture in the newspaper and on TV . . .'

He accompanies her to the car, from which loud music blasts through the open windows. Kanu is in the passenger seat and Pulane is in the back, already strapped in.

'Turn down that thumping!' Lerato calls, wagging her finger at Kanu, whose head pops out at them. Then to Michiel, 'I can feel my flat hand on his behind before the day is out.'

The boy adjusts the volume and lifts himself head-first through the open window. 'Do you like Brenda Fassie?' he asks.

'I'm afraid I don't know who that is.'

'Mommy, he doesn't know Brenda Fassie!'

'Enough, Kanu. Sit back and get your shoes off my upholstery. Fasten your seatbelt, or would you prefer to stay here with the dogs while we go to town?'

Kanu pulls his shoulders back through the window and sits down, jutting his jaw towards the windshield.

'Great tie,' Lerato says, reaching as she gets into the car, running the silk between her fingers. 'Sien jou oppie dorp.' See you in town. The Volvo moves through the gate with the dogs bounding ahead and then falling back. Kanu's head appears through the passenger window again and he yells: 'I'm going to ski with you in America!' Michiel waves and the car comes to a standstill. He sees Lerato tug the boy by the shoulder back into his seat. He imagines her admonishing him to fasten his seatbelt before the car moves again, down the gravel road.

His hand slides down the raw silk. Isabella and Grootman

make their way back, sniffing at things along the way. He now remembers the old homestead entrance, before the electronic gate was installed. River rocks cemented into tall pillars on either side of a cattle grid. Miemie comes to see them off. The three of them with Ounooi in her old Mercedes: Little-Alida walks down the gravel road dressed in her black and white school uniform, barefoot. Carrying her books under her arm, she steps to the side of the road as they pass. She waves. They wave. The grass, bleached beige, is matted by frost. The Mercedes will pass around the koppie and Little-Alida will turn right on to the footpath that will take her through the acres of leafless cherry trees to the black farm school on the Oberholzer farm. It must have been a five-kilometer walk. And five back, rain or shine. Michiel is in Standard Two, Benjamin Standard Three and Peet already in high school. The Malutis are snow-covered. Little-Alida, running against the cold, is about to turn into the orchards. Ounooi honks.

Slowing the car, she says to them: 'I cannot live with myself if that child has to run to school in this weather.'

Benjamin, on the back seat, protests: 'Ag, Ounooi! We're going to be late for school if we first have to drive all the way around to drop her off.'

Ounooi, reverting to English: 'If you want to feel what it's like to be late for school, I'll drop you right here, Benjamin.'

'Good idea,' Peet says, turning in his seat to look back at Benjamin. 'Give the big mouth a taste of walking. Maybe he should go barefoot.'

'Open your door, Benjamin,' Ounooi says, 'and move over so that Little-Alida can get in.'

Benjamin has moved across the seat and sits pushing his shoulder into Michiel. Peet engages Little-Alida on what is being taught in her class in comparison to what is being taught to her standard at Generaal Reitz Primary. At the farm school the other children stand back as the Mercedes enters the dusty schoolyard. Little-Alida says *thank you, Ounooi*. (The voice he hears now in his head, he realizes, is the tiny voice of Pulane.) Benjamin says nothing. He is furious at his mother and remains leaning against Michiel.

'Stop squashing me into the door,' Michiel moans. They are pulling away when Ounooi instructs Benjamin to return to his side of the back seat.

'Ek sit nie waar 'n *meid* gesit het nie. Ek gaan nie na kaffer ruik as ons by die skool aankom nie.' I'm not sitting where that *kaffir girl* sat. I don't want to smell of kaffir when we get to school.

The car stops. 'I beg your pardon?'

At hearing Ounooi's tone Benjamin moves away from Michiel.

Ounooi, still in English: 'Repeat what just came out of that mouth, Benjamin.'

'I don't want to stink,' Benjamin mutters.

'What I heard was the following.' Ounooi, now turned around in her seat, repeats word for offending word Benjamin's sentences in Afrikaans. She goes back to English again: 'Now, I have warned you three a thousand and one times that our family does not use that language. I don't care what you hear at school; in our family we do not speak of people like that.'

'But I don't want to smell like her. Everyone will laugh at me. Just go, Ounooi, we're late already.'

'Get out of the car, Benjamin. If you don't want to smell like Little-Alida, get out and walk to school.'

'Oubaas says kaffir when you're not around, Ounooi!'

'I don't care what your father says behind my back. You know my rules. Get out or shall I come and help you out?'

Benjamin begins to cry. 'Ounooi is choosing sides for a kaffir girl against me!'

'The hours it will take you to get to school will afford you ample time to contemplate what you have said and why I will not tolerate such sentiments.'

'Let him sit in the front, Ounooi,' Peet intervenes. 'I'll sit in Little-Alida's place.'

'I'll sit there,' Michiel offers. 'He can sit on this side.'

'You two stay out of this. Get out, Benjamin. Not even a bucket of crocodile tears will keep you in this car today.'

Defiant, Benjamin throws open the door. Ounooi tells him to take his book bag from the trunk. If she finds out he hitched a lift from one of the farmers his pocket money will be docked for a month. Still crying, Benjamin slams the trunk. On the dusty soccer field the children stare at them. Ounooi drives off. Michiel looks back at his brother striding forcefully into the veld, probably towards the path along the river. Surely Benjamin has learned his lesson; surely their mother will now stop the car? Ounooi turns on the radio and listens to the news on *Radio Today*. She does not stop. Peet turns in his seat to look quickly at Michiel: this is a part of Ounooi we do not know, his eyes say; but do not worry, little one, she still loves all three of us.

When Little-Alida began attending high school in the township she got a lift every morning, on the back seat beside the two youngest Steyn boys. Once Peet went to university she sat in the front. More than once Benjamin got into fisticuffs (the score growing on his tie) with whomever at the white school called the Steyns *kafferboeties*. Kaffir-lovers. Was that Lerato's earliest taste of a snazzy car? He could laugh out loud. *What do you call a kaffir that drives a Mercedes?* he remembered this morning in Jo'burg's traffic. *A thief.* To have been here to witness the counting of the old words: for that he would have wanted to be in this country, on this farm. Is it *schadenfreude*? Does that have an equivalent in English? *Gloating*; not quite. In Afrikaans, *leedvermaak*, if he remembers correctly. *There is a difference*, Kamil's father, the one-time communist, is fond of saying, *between those who are on the side of the oppressed and those who merely hate the oppressor*. I have returned, Michiel thinks, as little more than a voyeur. No longer a participant but in a brief walk-on part as a spectator, a member of the chorus. *South Africa's Miracle* he sees and hears in the media, the phrase of both earnest and self-congratulatory dinner-party conversation. A miracle, he knows too, fraught with a thousand and one challenges obscured by Lerato and her bright children driving in a new Swedish car past the path she once took barefoot to school. He knows (how can he not?) the statistics of HIV infections and AIDS-related deaths. Of hundreds of thousands of people streaming into the cities and into squatter communities — *informal settlements,* as he has lately noticed online. The nation's unemployment rate somewhere around forty percent. Black Zimbabweans are now crossing into this country, where twenty years ago it was the former Rhodesia's whites.

He knows, as he has for years, that his home — whatever a home is — is no longer here. It is not only his work and Kamil that keep him in North America. Nor their circle of bourgeois friends comprising techies, doctors, designers, lawyers, Anglos, Latinos, Japanese-Americans and one of the Pauls on the ground floor who is African-American. Not only the circumscribed safety and normalcy of Eureka Valley, where men can hold hands and kiss outside the walls of subdivided Victorians they rent or own partly or wholly. It is also that BART runs on time and that they get by without owning a car; that as long as you're not working for a dotcom your job feels secure. That you can walk up Market at midnight (despite the homeless) or take Muni without unwanted surprises in a mood that will take generations to establish here. And he knows too much of starting over: the alienation and awkwardness, the first decade's pervasive nostalgia that demands constant beating back; circumlocution in a fudged accent from behind a pane of glass thick between you and the new world.

He glances at his watch. With the dogs at his side he enters the scent of spring beside the sheds and Alida's kaya. Excited voices carry down through the blossoms from the compound. Behind the white of cherry is a pink banner of apricot trees in late bloom. Then apples. Oranges. Lemons. At the base of each tree the grass is trimmed back from round soil retention walls. Plastic irrigation tubes feed the trees from the spring against the orchard's highest point, below the stables and dairy. The pipes connect each tree, turning the orchard into a grid of symmetrical squares. From here comes the fruit for jams, preserves and marmalade, with all preparation overseen by Liesbet and Mamparra. At long tables in the shed there are cooking pots on the flames of gas stoves and women in blue overalls peeling, chopping, boiling, stirring and stewing. He again wonders about the farm's future. After all these decades, surely Liesbet and Mamparra manage the bottling on their own? But they're both getting on in years. And Alida cannot possibly be of help, not with the caretaking of Oubaas now piled on top of her domestic duties. Will Liesbet manage the marketing? The bottles, unless things have changed, have always carried Ounooi's signature on the neat white labels that read 'Fruit of Paradise — Vrugte van die Paradys'. Each lid is decorated with a blue and white paper doily, held down by a blue elastic band. Harvest year written by hand. The farm stall on the main road was initially staffed by Little-Alida and other farm women. In the mid-eighties, Liesbet and Mamparra were held up at knifepoint there. Pietie, who'd been courting Mamparra to no avail for decades, and was concerned for her safety, convinced Ounooi to close the stall. She had been meaning to reopen once things again seemed safe, settled down. Instead, as new kinds of crime soared, she began marketing to Woolworths and coffee shops in the bigger towns, even as far afield as Bloemfontein and Johannesburg. From the jams and preserves she supplemented her own travel, clothing and housekeeping allowance. In rare years of a meager cherry crop, it was the income from the jams and preserves that shielded Oubaas from having to knock on the Land Bank's door. In the US, Ounooi told Michiel about plans to have an extension added to the ron-davel. She was planning a bed and breakfast. Recent years had seen an explosion of visitors both local and from overseas, especially around harvest time. Benjamin, Ounooi reported, was in fact trying to convince Oubaas to build extra rondavels up near the spring, for the views. The town now has a week-long cherry festival – yes, still with the Cherry Queen contest but now grander, with the winner and her two princesses waving from a red cherry-shaped float ahead of a parade of other floats down Church Street.

Over the sound of the doves and a sheep's bleating at the kraal, he hears the drone of a bakkie on the compound road. Again voices, louder now, in seSotho and Afrikaans. What sounds like a call to action, followed by laughter. There is the tinny honk of a tractor after its engine starts. Then the put-put as it idles in neu-tral. Here is the locked gate through which the workers come in the mornings to report for duty. Eight small houses. Same as always. Facebrick with red tin roofs to suggest a quaint uniformity with the house and outbuildings. The fence around the compound is not quite as high as the one around the homestead and orchard. Not electrified either. The trailer is hitched to the tractor, with a dozen or more formally dressed people seated on the rim and others inside the bed. Some women wear hats. Small children, in their day clothes, wave from the open doors of compound homes. The adults are on their way to the funeral. He assumes the work-ers are now allowed inside the church. No longer the separate Dutch Reformed Church in Africa. When Peet was buried they were not invited to the service, but allowed at the burial on the farm.

'Move it, Pietie,' he hears a woman's voice. 'We're first stopping at Pick n Pay.'

Michiel starts down the fence. He is aware of the engine's revving followed by the gentle putter of the vehicle's descent. If he reaches the cemetery he will be behind the oaks and may go unnoticed. He is not inclined to speak to the workers now. There will be too many greetings and pleasantries. He hastens his step to evade the jollity of the nearing voices. He cannot retreat into the orchard: if someone were to see a man – even a white man – half hidden in the trees it will lead to bigger commotion than if he were to simply greet them and get it over with. He hears the tractor slow as it begins to pass him. He recognizes Pietie at the wheel, dressed in his Sunday best. Pietie lifts his hat and Michiel raises his hand. The tractor is about to move on when a woman's voice from the back of the trailer goes up: 'Dis mos Kleinbaas Michiel. Stop die trekker, Pietie!' This is followed by silence and then a chorus of welcome and condolence. Some do not know whether to show surprise at seeing him, or to gravely comment on the reason for his being here. He waves a general good day. Adam alights and comes trotting towards the fence. Others want to come too, but are admonished by Pietie to stay put.

'Sorry we're not all getting off, Michiel,' Pietie calls. 'These women took all day to get dressed. They must want us to get caught in the rain.'

'Dag, Adam,' Michiel says, carefully taking the hand that has come to him through strands of electrified wire.

'Dis goed om die Kleinbaas weer op Paradys te sien.' Good to see the Kleinbaas again at Paradys.

'Careful, Adam,' Michiel says as he guides Adam's hand back through the fence.

'We only turn them on from six at night till six in the morning.' Then he adds, 'We have made a good place for Ounooi to rest, Kleinbaas.'

Despite Pietie's chiding a woman wearing a red hat has slipped off the trailer and comes uncomfortably on high heels towards them. Voices go up for her to return. Michiel recognizes Mamparra before she reaches the fence. The nickname was given when, as a young girl, she mislabeled the jars of an entire harvest: peach became apricot, cherry apple, mulberry fig. Instead of *Summer 1961* she wrote *Summer 1861.*

'Michiel!' she exclaims, both arms coming through the fence. Like Pietie, Mamparra called the boys by their first names and also rarely used 'Ounooi' and 'Oubaas' as the other workers did. 'It's me, Mamparra! Don't you remember me?' She smiles from beneath the red brocade, the tail feather of a pigeon attached to the front fold by a silver brooch in the shape of a starfish.

'How can anyone forget you . . .' He leaves off the name as she takes both his hands between hers. 'I still hear you singing the cherry lines.'

'Our loss is too big, Michiel,' she answers. She draws back one hand and from her bra brings a handkerchief to her eyes. Through the fence comes the smell of cheap perfume, a rose scent. And Vaseline? Calls again from the trailer.

Michiel waves to faces he remembers. He greets Liesbet, Adam's portly wife, by name. She had a reputation for a fiery temper and left the farm more than once, only to return months later from wherever she had been.

Adam helps Mamparra back up as hands reach down from the trailer. There is more solemn waving, the quiet turning to stare as the tractor drives off and Grootman runs along the inside of the fence.

In his palm, Michiel finds the familiar smell of Lifebuoy. *July bent at the doorway and began that day for them as his kind has always done for their kind . . . black hands smelling of Lifebuoy soap . . .* the phrase with the smell. Five double-spaced pages of his dissertation on little more than that one sentence. Here, not only separate from the house and the white world, but also from the woman in the black pantsuit and the Volvo. How does *she* relate to this part of the farm and these people to her? And Pulane and Kanu to the compound children? *The former house niggers,* Kamil might make the comparison. *The house n-word,* before tenure. Which of these women who walk miles up and down lines of fruit trees beating tins to scare off birds and baboons have dreams of a boardroom? Working in the big house — *that* might constitute the farthest reaches of imagination. Who imagines themselves cocooned in fleece, waving little flags among the nations of the world under stadium lights? How much of imagination, too, is dulled by our station within the hierarchies of ownership, labor and unemployment? On his way here he stopped for gas, to pee and buy a Diet Coke (*Coke Light*, he saw it is branded here) at an Ultra City near Winburg. Walking from the car to the men's room, the cafeteria and back he made at least four moral choices before eight upturned hands, four pairs of eyes. Somehow those signified something different from the requests, threats and familiar jocularity of the homeless on Powell below International House. Here, unlike there, he felt responsible beyond the gesture of giving or not giving. When he gives there — and he does, often — a note stuffed into the pouch, dropped in the bowl, placed in the fingers, he is merely being kind. This morning (all four times; expressions agog at the uncreased notes fresh from First National at the airport) the meaning of receiving too seemed different. Here, the surprised *dankie Baas* alleviates nothing of the giver's sense that not enough is being done. This too, he knows, has in time become part of why he lives there. At a certain point the moral responsibility of here (where so much of him belongs, is owed) exceeds the returns. But then not four moral choices, really. At least five. Six if you tally driving a car and pulling up to the pump. Does the purchase of a gallon of gas or a can of Diet Coke, Malik would say, in the United States or India or in Occupied Palestine not already constitute moral choice? Perhaps less obvious than reaching into one's wallet for a coin or a note to drop into an expectant hand, but none the less a choice with effect? And Rachel will say: For god's sake, Malik, can you stop terrorizing the boys for one minute? Where would the two of us be without the liberals? Not happily picking oranges in Jaffa, I tell you.

From beneath the line of pear trees he looks at the cemetery. Isabella sits at his feet, staring up at him. He rubs her nose, feels the wet snout finding his palm. The grass has been cut back from each gravestone and the outlined rectangles of the oldest graves. Through the oaks, dappled sunlight plays on the freshly weeded ground. The tree trunks have grown thick enough to crush the rusty wrought-iron fence so that it leans inward. Family lore had it – Michiel still hears Ouma and Oupa Steyn – that the four oaks were planted during the Anglo-Boer War by the last Afrikaner owner, in memory of his wife, daughters and infant son who died in the concentration camps at Aliwal North. With the Boer men on commando, Kitchener's soldiers swarmed the countryside, took women and children hostage and burned farms, homes, livestock and crops to the ground. *Scorched earth*, the English called it: it was here, in the koppies and vlaktes of the Orange Free State, that the strategy was first used . . . 'Bullshit! *Thalatta, thalatta!*' cries Malik. 'Scorched earth is as old as Western civilization – have you not read Xenophon on poisoned wells and crops destroyed? They died of dehydration! And that's how the Romans eradicated Carthage; leveled it and wiped it from maps before they carted in bags of salt to blight the earth so nothing would ever grow there again. William the Conqueror took the salt lesson from Carthage and nothing grew over miles and miles of northern England for years so that when there was no food the starving broke open their own families' skulls to eat their brains. Edmund Spenser, prince of poets, sings the praises of England erasing the livelihood of the Irish in Munster in the sixteenth century. England gave the Virgil of his times a vast farm stolen from the Irish, not by the sword but by starvation. And what of Sherman during the American civil war? How do you think Kit Carson forced the Navajo off their land? And why do you think a million died when the US invaded the Philippines? It was because of what they did there,' Malik says, 'that Twain, the greatest American writer, refused his seat on a podium at Harvard beside Teddy Roosevelt . . . Have you people never heard of napalm, just two decades ago? Of Guatemala, a decade ago? If they don't teach you history anymore, what kind of teachers can you be?' The Boer men were forced into surrender; ancestral farms were up for grabs. An Englishman – Horwood – was able to buy this land for a sixpence. When it came back into Afrikaner hands the first Oubaas Steyn changed the spelling to *Paradys*.

A mound marks the open grave for Ounooi, beside Peet and a newer grave that must be Ouma Steyn, who passed while he's been away. His eyes linger for a moment on the simple black marble headstone and slab of his brother. From this side of the fence he cannot read the inscription, but he sees that someone has placed fresh sugarbush in a vase there. When Michiel left, the earth had not yet settled and the sinking and dissolving grave mound was still the only marker. The officers' mess tent. A sweltering December day on the border. Malaria has appeared in the local kraals. The OC, Lotter, comes in from the ops tent. He asks his young platoon commander to step outside. They stroll along the river-bank. Papyrus sways in the current; pink and yellow water lilies drift on the crystalline river. The rains are months late. Elsewhere in South-West and Angola it has rained, but not here. Patrol boats hang quietly from the jetty. Across the river are the baobabs, their colossal stems swollen by the water of two, maybe three thousand years, their truncated branches like roots against the blue sky. *Bad news from home. I'm sorry, Steyn. Your eldest brother has drowned. You leave this afternoon with the victuals convoy; compassionate leave. You'll be back up here for New Year.* And there you are, Peet. Your friend Leon placed your graduation hood on the coffin. Our mother could not hold herself upright that day so Benjamin and I did. He feels his throat constrict. When he later saw Leon in Sydney they had dinner and went sailing on the harbor. It was shortly after the real changes began here and Leon was in Australia to assess the worth of a Roman

Dutch law qualification and graduate degree in Latin over there. Michiel goes down on one knee and his hand reaches for Isabella's head. He takes the satiny ear between his fingers. At some point he will have to allow himself to weep. It will be the first thing Glassman asks when he gets back: *And how did you mourn?*

He heads for the dam and Isabella trots ahead. Had there been more time he would have liked to pass by the stables to see the new horses. When he reaches the water Isabella is up on the diving rock, looking across the glassy surface. Miemie used to do the same, scaring the life out of the Egyptian geese before they could fly off. She was up here with him the morning before he left. He was naked on the dam wall, legs dangling in, weighing options as thoughts of Karien — *I can't bear the thought of you near me again* — bumped against despair and the impulse to escape. This is where Oubaas found him. He stood on the sawed-off eucalyptus stump, looking down on his son's head of short army hair. Michiel dropped his hands to his crotch, vulnerable below the man who owned the dam, the orchard, the farm. The world. He looked up; his father looked away. Michiel tried to broach the idea of going overseas.

'You're going back to the Defence Force.'

'I can't go back, Oubaas. Not to Salisbury Island. Oubaas knows people. Oubaas knows the Minister of Agriculture. Oubaas can at least help organize a transfer for me. To another base. Port Elizabeth or Simonstown.'

'I will not acknowledge this thing and what you are. Be a man, for once. Go back for your national service and face yourself. After that we can talk.'

'I'm facing myself right here, Oubaas. I don't need to go back to the army to know who I am, Oubaas.'

'Then you will not set foot on this farm again. That's life, Michiel. You play by the rules or else you don't play at all.'

I am the rule the game depends upon, he thought years later, wishing he'd had the wisdom and strength – the knowledge of the machinations of good and evil – to have said so that day.

He hears Alida call. Over the tips of white blossoms that slant downhill like a snowy slope he makes out her shape on the stoep. With his hands around his mouth he calls 'Ek kom, Alida.' He walks back with spring in his nose and Isabella ahead of him, leaping at butterflies, chasing grasshoppers. There is still the sound of turtledoves. And the hum of bees swelling in his ears, different, he realizes now, without the voices from the compound. Hot sun on his short, sparse hair, warming his scalp and the nape of his neck. The mood, the feeling is that of when almost everything and everyone rests on a Sunday afternoon. On the stoep Alida, dressed and coiffed, stands like an aged sentinel beside Oubaas. From beside the wheelchair Grootman lifts his head at Michiel and Isabella's approach.

All the way from the farm clouds have been gathering in banks. Before the sign bidding visitors welcome in Afrikaans and English to *The Cherry Capital*, an antenna shaped like a supersized fir tree towers over karee and acacia. He has been driving at a snail's pace, less to take in the scenery than to diminish the time he would have to spend standing around at church. Not only to delay looking into faces of long ago and hearing the awkward pleasantries of mourning: there is ambivalence, dull excitement felt in the stomach and leadenness of arms and legs, coupled with dread at facing Karien. *I bear you no grudge. About tomorrow I know not.* And the husband. And Benjamin, with his perfect family. Being reintroduced into blood's mysterious loyalties under these impossible conditions. How to face the Chosen, the one in three who did not betray a single expectation?

Kamil leaned across the bed: *It's your brother; I'm not sure it's good news.*

Ounooi. In her sleep. In bed beside Oubaas. Service scheduled

59

for late Monday afternoon. Early enough for the interment at Paradys to be in daylight.

They sat with their backs against the pillows under the White and Green Taras. Kamil recollecting the visit and the woman from Michiel's stories, now dead. Michiel's own mind initially numb, then overtaken by the blitz of memory.

'I have to go.'

'Of course you have to.' Kamil's hands going around Michiel's.

He began calling while Kamil researched fares online.

The operator at American Airlines apologized for the 'bereavement policy' that requires an official death notice and the passenger's birth certificate as proof of kinship. A call to Benjamin, the paperwork faxed and within hours he was booked (Visa card, online) for later the same morning. Nothing available on SAA from Jo'burg to Bloem. He'd rent a car in Johannesburg. Cellphone contracts were changed to enable calls to and from the southern tip of Africa. Kamil would inform Ling at International House. Cancel Glassman, or could the appointment be moved to later in the week? Forty dollars and the key in an envelope under the doormat for America — normally Michiel's task on Mondays.

'How do you feel?' Kamil, elbows on the kitchen island, hands beneath his chin, his bushy eyebrows joined in a frown.

'You do Xanthippe's water. I'll do the week after Beijing.'

'How do you feel about going back, like this?'

'I haven't had time to think.'

'Yeah, but how do you *feel*?'

The town's entrance has a new gas station where, under thatched shelters, women sit on blankets displaying curios, baskets, beadwork and Basotho hats stacked in precarious cones. Minibuses with Lesotho and Free State license plates line the roadway. Pedestrians gather on pavements and congregate in the street; a man dashes to grab a child about to run into the traffic and hurries off laughing as the little one's legs pedal under his arm; two youngsters stand arguing, one on the white center line, the other mid-lane with his back to the oncoming traffic.

'Die moedswilligheid self. Gebruik jou toeter, Michiel.' Wilfulness incarnate. Use your horn, Michiel.

He slows, gears down and brings the car to a standstill. From a car behind comes an impatient honk. One of the boys in the road meets Michiel's gaze, his eyes speaking scorn. Michiel lifts his hand, extending an apology. The companions saunter towards the minibuses. There goes the reason to not adopt a male child of any race, nationality or creed: to have that leer, terminally hip and fatally cool, strutting in through your front door because it belongs in your home: what for?

'So is hulle mos deesdae,' Oubaas says. That's how they are these days.

On the roadside before the first homes wooden giraffes are for sale, the most impressive as tall as five feet. Could one be wrapped and flown safely in cargo? The figure would provide height in front of the balcony's bare wall and the squat Buddha. A gift for International House? *Listen*, he hears himself saying, his fingers tugging at his earlobe, *the giraffe is very tall. No, tall, not toe-ru. Tall.* A Japanese girl giggles and claps her hands: *Gi-ra-f. Perfect.*

Homes give way to school, municipal offices, business center and church, then once more a block of shops and finally more homes as one leaves town. Far down the street they can see Paradys's tractor and trailer turn into the Dutch Reformed Church parking lot. Gardens here have been cut off from Church Street's sluiceways and pavements by fences and hedges. A house he remembers with a tin roof now has tiles. The gables and sprawling lawn of the Erasmuses' Cape Dutch home is separated from the street by a shoulder-high white wall, its entry an arch with a sign advertising *Bed & Breakfast*. At the high school children in sports gear circle the field and huddle on the pavilion steps. A boy with a javelin dances and runs, brakes as the projectile sails forth. Girls, no more than thirteen, one light, one dark, prepare for the high jump. The dark girl takes a wide berth, turns and flies backwards – way higher than the bar – her fists pumping victory even before her back touches the mat. Inside freshly chalked lanes a tangle of adolescent limbs, with among these, too, hues disallowed here in another time. Were this field and the number of black people on the highway in air-conditioned vehicles a yardstick for seven years of democracy, things would seem well underway.

Alida's cellphone rings. 'No, Kleinbaas, we're almost here. Things got a bit busy . . . we've just passed Generaal Reitz. We see the church.' His own phone is plugged into the travel adapter in the socket behind his old desk. He looks at the time: ten minutes before the service is due to start.

Oubaas, having barely spoken since they left the farm, now asks: 'You know that she married Dominee Dirk after you left?'

'Ja, Pa.' His eyes follow Oubaas's trembling arm and finger that point to a sign advertising *Moosa's Haberdashery and Eastern Fabrics.*

'*You* will derive particular pleasure from knowing there is now a koelie shop in town.'

He looks back down Church Street and suppresses an impulse to fire back something about the turmeric taste of all good Indian cock. *Mindfulness,* Kamil will say, *each word a butterfly's wings at Machu Picchu that stir the Gulf Coast hurricane.* And Malik, snorting: *This obsession with language is like raking for a needle in a haystack while the barn is in flames. Another new-agey postmodern deflection. As long as you can tell your story you're meant to be okay.*

'Did you go in at any of the other towns on your way here?' Oubaas asks. When Michiel shakes his head Oubaas says: 'You won't find a white face there. Nothing has seen a coat of paint in years. They slaughter goats and cattle right in the town center – even in churchyards – for whatever sacrifice or witchcraft their gods demand. Every main street now has some or other *boy* name. Everything's gone to the dogs.'

He recognizes Lerato's car in the packed lot. Pietie has parked the tractor and trailer against the farthest privet hedge and lawn where pied crows squabble over some kind of carrion. Paradys workers, some carrying blue and white Pick n Pay plastic bags, are crossing the lot towards the entrance.

'Park at the little gate.'

'It's for the wheelchair, Kleinbaas. There's a ramp at the handicap space.'

Mamparra has handed over her shopping bags and is headed for the rental car.

'There's your brother.' Oubaas tilts his chin towards the vestry.

Michiel sees Benjamin, dressed in a dark suit with a woman at his side and two children following from the doorway.

'Get out and greet your family. Alida, get the chair and bring it round.'

'Let's first get Pa out of the hot car.'

'Your aircon has been on, Michiel. I won't melt. Thomas can give Alida a hand. Gods, and here's the mad Mamparra too.' Mamparra has come from behind and bends forward, peeping in at Oubaas from beneath the hat-fold and starfish half over one eye. 'Astrante bleddie meid.' Cheeky bloody black girl.

'Will you manage, Alida?'

'Kleinbaas can just open the boot.'

He searches for the lever under the dash. Taking the jacket that Alida passes over the seat he alights into the muted organ music and glances from other funeral-goers.

'I'm at my post, Michiel,' Mamparra says at the trunk. 'This wheelchair can get too much for poor Alida. Her strength isn't what it used to be.' Then Alida is there, her eyes narrowed, addressing Mamparra curtly in seSotho as she reaches in for the folded wheelchair.

'Dag, Broer.' His brother with arm extended; blue eyes behind frameless glasses; graying temples; a firm grip. 'Meet Giselle,'

Benjamin continues in English. 'Come – Thomas, Bianca – say hello to Uncle Michiel.'

With her arms around the children's shoulders Giselle guides them forward. The boy, with light acne at his hairline and a sliver of one curly bang peroxided white, must already be a teenager. The girl is perhaps nine. The children reach out their right hands and in near unison say, 'Pleased to meet you.' No trace of an Afrikaans accent. The girl, Bianca, returns Michiel's smile, so that he notices her mouth and the shape of her teeth, so much like Ounooi's. Thomas makes no effort to hide his skepticism and has already stepped back to his mother's side. You then, the boy's pale expression seems to grumble, are the uncle from America; the one who broke Grandma Beth's heart. Whose name is never spoken in Oupa's presence. Giselle steps past the children and hugs Michiel. She is a short, handsome woman, with translucent white skin. She is dressed in a long-sleeved silk blouse and tailored navy blue knee-length skirt. Her ears are diamond-studded and there are gold bands on the fingers of both hands. 'It's good that you've come. Our joy is only marred by our sadness about Ounooi.' Beneath the sincerity is a no-nonsense bearing. He imagines her efficiently working numbers, calculating profits as she shifts about shares, overseeing a sizeable domestic and garden staff while making time, as any good mother of her class would, to chauffeur her children between a dozen after-school activities.

Benjamin comes to stand in front of Michiel. Michiel feels his brother's arms go around him. Now, in Afrikaans, Benjamin says: 'She would be grateful to know you're here. I am too. Thank you.' With their arms still around each other Michiel says: 'Dankie, Bennie, vir jou . . .' he gropes for the word then, unable to find it, says, 'Dankie vir jou kindness.'

Alida and Mamparra have Oubaas in the wheelchair. Mamparra takes hold of the handles while Alida, down on one knee, straightens out the old man's jacket and pulls down each pant leg. When

Alida rises Mamparra turns the chair to prevent her from taking over and the old man sways in his seat.

'Okay, you two,' Oubaas says to the women fussing behind him, 'Thomas will take me into church.'

'They'll ring the bell for Grandma when we're all inside, Oupa,' the boy says as his hands grip the orange handles. The red sandstone building sits like a colossus, its finger pointing to a god somewhere in the bulging heavens.

'Looks like a storm,' Benjamin says, his eyes cast up, allowing Michiel to notice the chin still chiseled despite some weight, the suntanned skin and the gait still throbbing with the stuff that makes a rugby captain, and an army officer who throughout life never breaks rank; whose gentle balding merely cowls his supreme confidence.

'The shame is that Mevrou isn't here,' Mamparra whispers to Alida, loud enough for all to hear, 'to see her family together like this.'

'She can see,' Alida counters.

'I mean in the flesh,' Mamparra whispers back. '*I know* she's with Jesus. Praise the Lord.'

In the gloomy foyer Michiel feels the organ's vibrations through the carpeted floor. Pick n Pay bags with handles knotted into tight blooms are half hidden beneath an oak table in the corner.

'You sit with us, Alida.' Benjamin signals for Alida to fall in behind Thomas. The boy will steer the wheelchair to the front but Benjamin wants Alida beside Oubaas, should she be needed when the pallbearers exit. When Michiel gestures to Giselle that he will walk at the tail, Bianca steps around her mother, smiles again at Michiel and takes her place in front of him. In spite of the cropped, dark hair and the intensity and directness of his niece's eyes, he sees her, unmistakably, in a photograph he recalls of his mother as a young girl.

Pews are tightly packed with extra chairs placed in the aisle. At the back sit the Paradys workers. He nods at Pietie and Adam. Even as he keeps his gaze down he glimpses the robed choir and the organ-pipe stalagmites on the balcony. Heads turn. Over Giselle's shoulder he sees the small casket, almost insignificant beneath the pulpit. Amid the preponderance of white faces he finds Lerato. He winks at Pulane and meets Kanu's eyes. The boy puts on a solemn face as his gaze fastens on someone behind Michiel. At the front pew Alida again takes charge of the wheelchair. She looks to Benjamin, who whispers for her to take the first seat beside the aisle before the rest file in. Michiel senses a presence behind him and looks back to find that Mamparra has tailed the procession. The space remaining between his niece on one side and the uncles and aunts on the other offers place for only one, leaving him and Mamparra awkwardly huddled. He extends a hand uncomfortably to his uncle, who motions for the others to move down. Benjamin too has leaned forward and whispers for everyone to slide closer. With Michiel and Mamparra seated the pew is uncomfortably tight. Tucked between her and Bianca, he has to cross one leg over the other. He lifts his arm, squeezed against his niece, on to the backrest behind her.

In the Beginning was the Word: the pulpit cloth is the same blue velvet as it has always been, with the same verse embroidered in gold. The casket of unstained pine, with rope handles, rests on a fold-out chrome stand. On the coffin's lid are a single sugarbush protea and the two circles of honeysuckle, interlinked. Wreaths, then, not crowns. For a moment he imagines the real casket kept elsewhere and the pine box here merely a simulacrum. He had anticipated an impenetrable dark vessel, lacquered, with cornices and stainless-steel handles, the length of its surface covered in roses and lilies. Something imposing. His brother's casket somehow his mother's. He tries to conjure her, head on a white pillow. Is there funerary make-up on the face she so rarely chose to adorn? He sees her with her neck thrown back, laughing again, on their balcony. On Sunset Beach, her hair coming loose in the wind, *God, I love the ocean!* He reaches farther, to where he tiptoes into their bedroom. His hand goes to her shoulder. He whispers *Ounooi, I had a bad dream* and climbs over her, to sleep till morning's safety between her and Oubaas. Behind a pane of unvarnished pine. No longer thousands of miles of ocean and two continents' reach between us. *Through everything.* In the inside pocket of my coat is a card. A silver dollar. Kamil says to say *farewell, Beth, travel safely; the river is wide and you need a coin to place in the palm of Charon.*

He blinks as he receives the program passed to him by his niece. *Elizabeth Ellenore Steyn, née Ford, 4 February 1938–8 September 2001* in bold italics above a watercolor of yellow and orange sugarbush. Bianca touches his hand. He lowers his head, feels her breath against his cheek.

'Mommy says the program's picture was painted by Karien.' He nods, having guessed as much. The spaces between the notes coming from the organ are punctuated by the click of pedals and the breath of pipes. He allows himself to hear the Beethoven String Quartet, and to acknowledge who would have seen to it that Ounooi's face remained free of make-up. He can no longer keep his eyes from the balcony.

Her hair is in a French plait and her neck is bowed over the keys. Her shoulders and back are covered with what looks from down here like a beige cotton jacket. Here we are then, he thinks. You and I. How many hundreds of days you have been in and out of my head on other continents, mid-oceans and skies. Shall I share with you the dreams, the anger and guilt? If I were to genuflect before you, could you guess the hours I have talked of you on a black leather chair in Berkeley? Shall I tell you how I have spoken to myself in your voice?

Ounooi had neglected the piano for years, and when neither her sons nor Little-Alida showed interest or aptitude for playing or for singing the instrument was dusted, wrapped in blankets and sent by bakkie on permanent loan to the musically talented girl who was in grade one with Michiel. Her father, Constable Opperman, had divorced Gerda Niehaus, the famously beautiful and passionate receptionist of the town's largest butchery. Until high school, when another and then another set of parents divorced, Karien was the only one in the A class from a 'broken home', the brain from day one right to her smiling face on the *Volksblad*'s front page: seven distinctions for Matric and an eighth for art as an additional subject. In primary school Michiel's gifts to her were packets of Simba potato chips and an occasional ice cream during break. Hers to him, friendship unconditional. No surprise in high school when Ounooi more assertively – possessively – took the girl under her wing. *In all my years, this is the sharpest mind to pass through my classes. Boy or girl. She is going to be a nuclear physicist or a professor or anything her heart desires. Genius with a capital G.* That the girl and her youngest son had developed a crush on each other provided further impetus. Karien worked Saturdays and holidays in the pharmacy. With her wages she bought simple silver earrings and, for church, baggy clothes in beige, white and khaki. She began putting her hair up so that anyone could see who she was emulating. She began visiting the farm, away from her own mother and the town: weekends on the horses, up at the dam, or on the living-room kilim doing homework and reading to each other . . . *my skinny hands light a candle for you, because you became my friend, because at break you fetch me from the library, to join for songs in the hall, because you remain my friend in spite of the dandruff on my shirt and my nylon jersey, and because you have come to love me, despite the ripe pimples crusting on my cheeks, because you explain math to me in the afternoons, and sometimes run your hand through my clean hair, see how my candle trembles for you, it says thanks and prays for you* . . . At the long dining-room table Karien got to know Peet. She heard more of the Fords, her mentor's family, where three generations had been men of the law. When Peet followed suit, he too became Karien's idol: his intellect and quiet wisdom was what she aspired to, his adult detachment so in contrast to Michiel's tactility. When she had more to say to the eldest brother than to him, it did not bother

Michiel. Quite the contrary, for Peet was the first man he ever
loved. To Ounooi's delight, being a lawyer or advocate became
Karien's ambition. The year Michiel went into the navy, she went to
Bloemfontein on a full scholarship. There, at the start of her soph-
omore year, he saw her a last time. He had rehearsed a story. But
when he got there it was she who informed him that his name had
been in a newspaper. She shut the doors to the residence lounge —
illegal for a female unchaperoned in male company: *I'll explain to the
house mother the biological impossibility of falling pregnant when one already is.
Your whole life has been a lie; we will have to start from scratch if we ever do, as
if twelve years of school and we never happened. I can't bear the thought of you
near me again.* Words to that effect. Around her lips was a white welt
in her pale face. He hadn't seen her really angry before. She did not
weep. He did. *But what about,* he started, only to be cut short by *I can
take care of myself.* And then, as he prepared to leave, the *coup de grâce*:
'If I'd chosen Peet and gone with him this would not have happened and he wouldn't have drowned.' He hitchhiked from there to
what awaited him on the farm. Ounooi. Oubaas. Dominee Dirk.
When he found no resolution there he went to Peet's friend Leon.
Then to the loneliness of London. To self-pity and remorse. He
trudged through Bayswater's winter gloom to find a telephone.
When the distant voice said *Emily Hobhouse Dameskoshuis, goeienaand,*
he asked for her; it's an international call, he said and waited, listening to his pounds ticking away. He heard the receiver hung up.
He called again; no reply. He tried the private number he'd used
before; the receiver was slammed in his ear. He sent a registered
letter by express mail. He again called the private number. He
would reiterate what he'd said in the letter: *I will pay. With what I
inherited from Peet. Come to me in London. We can solve everything here.* Her
friend answered. Karien had left university and was 'being taken
care of by decent civilized people who really love her'. He found
a hotel reception job that came with a room. The work was illegal,
but reasonably paid. When not on reception he holed up, smoking

the tiny room blue, staring out on to the square with its bare trees. Karien, what are you doing and what about this thing that is ours, together? Where are you, while I am in this dark city with its gray Thames, ceaseless traffic and dull blue faces? Months passed before he received reply, Poste Restante Bayswater: *I took care of it myself. What I know today is that I have no need to hear from you or see you again.* He borrowed books from the hotel library. The weather had improved by the time his hair was growing over his ears for the first time in his life. He walked the streets and sat on park benches to read. He found Forster's *Maurice* and read Woolf and about her and her circle. Anger welled in him. At night he pounded the pillow till there was a tapping from the other side of the wall. Angry at last, he longed to say: you and my useless mother, what cheap fakes, living in that backward country like baboons! You know nothing of Woolf and what she stood for. Do you know what she would have done under these circumstances? You who do not even know the names Vita Sackville-West and Lytton Strachey and Dora Carrington. And your infatuation with Peet; you fool, Karien, you're clueless, aren't you?

Cap low over his forehead, he attended a lecture at the Commonwealth Institute. He heard the voice of a black person from behind a lectern for the first time: a condemnation of his country's State of Emergency, a plea for international sanctions and in support of the sports and cultural boycotts. Seated beside him was an elderly black woman. She said hello before turning aloof at hearing his accent. They again found themselves beside each other, waiting at the Underground. She asked what he had thought of the lecture. He said it had been informative, though sanctions would result mostly in black people's further suffering. Was he in London for his 'gap year', she asked. He didn't know what a gap year was. He was working before university, he said. To study? English or history, he answered, dreading a question about the army. She wanted to know where he was from. The

Free State, he said. Oh, she smiled; she herself was from Brandfort, near Bloemfontein. And why are you so far from home, he asked. 'I work for an NGO.' He didn't ask what an NGO was. 'With your interest in history I'd like to send you something worthwhile about the Free State. We're both from there, after all.' Reluctantly he gave his name and that of the hotel.

The manila envelope at reception had no sender's name and no return address. Neither a writer nor a book he'd heard of: *Author, Statesman, Editor, Journalist, fluent in seven languages, the first black South African novelist: 1876–1932. This book is an exposé of one of the most far-reaching pieces of legislation in South African history.* The epigraph was from the Song of Songs: *I am Black, but comely, O ye daughters of Jerusalem, as the tents of Kedar, as the curtains of Solomon. Look not upon me because I am black, because the sun hath looked upon me: my mother's children were angry with me; they made me the keeper of the vineyards; but mine own vineyard have I not kept.* Inside, a brochure advertising another lecture. Between switch-boarding and checking in new guests – using Karien's letter as bookmark – he read the book cover to cover that same night.

Where, he wonders, wedged here between his niece and Mamparra, had he disposed of Karien's missive in the frayed envelope? He remembers his name in her script, the stamps of Jan van Riebeeck and the airmail sticker of a white springbok on blue. Perhaps he threw it out years later, during the clean-up when he was leaving Sydney for the Solomons, or from there for San Francisco and Kamil.

The church bell is ringing.

Sixty-three slow chimes, he knows. How many has he missed?

A child coughs. In the middle pews a throat is cleared.

The vestry door opens and there is the husband; robed; once jet-black hair now salt and pepper, but still all there. As are the looks. He has paused below the pulpit stairs with head bowed, hands clasped together where they emerge from sweeping black sleeves. Michiel is aware of the knot in his own stomach, a pulsation in his hands and legs. How is it that the residue of anger still remains? He looks back at the coffin. He searches unsuccessfully for an image of Ounooi *not* on the couch beside the young dominee here, in the vestry. The frown on her forehead is all that belies her calm elegance. She has made the appointment for herself and her disgraced son. In Afrikaans: *You know I joined the Dutch Reformed Church when we got married mostly for your father's family. You've been away* (she does not say, in the army) *but you met him in December* (she does not say, at your drowned brother's funeral). *He's not a conventional conservative dominee.* Here she takes to English: *He has a contemporary angle on things. He preaches in the township. He is broad-minded and educated — I've seen his bookshelves. He will give the most sanguine advice. Go and tell him everything.* She does not say: *Go and confess the unspeakable.* Since Michiel's undue appearance on the farm — his next pass is two weeks off — Ounooi has not spoken of what her youngest son has done or what she knows (without saying she knows) from the paper. Under other circumstances she may have savored the texture of in flagrante delicto. She'd come out on to the stoep at Miemie's excited barking. Michiel was on the bottom step with the one sports bag he'd taken from the officers' mess, the dog's head in his lap. *Michiel, my darling, I'm so happy you're here.* No hint of shock or disbelief so that at first he thought she could not know. Then — even before he saw the cutting slipped half under ledgers on her desk — Oubaas came in from the kraal. His father's jaw was set as if it would never again move and no word again pass his lips, while Ounooi merely cocked her head at her youngest's claims of calumny. When she took him to see the dominee her face remained implacable, making him wonder years later whether this was from a state of grace or delusion. It is the young dominee's first placement following national service. The district is gaga over the handsome new shepherd who has brought understated style and new blood: guitar, piano and tambourine are allowed in church; the ranks of the youth group have swollen; he speaks of cautious reform: there have been consumer strikes in town and the *Europeans Only* signs on the white side of the station platform and at the post office are regularly being vandalized. He is unmarried. Not a mother in town does not publicly wish her daughter for him, or secretly for herself. So far he has confirmed one set of youths in this church; a few years earlier and Michiel and Karien could have been his confirmees.

The handsome, almost-gray man has ascended his throne. When the congregation sits the front row squeezes back in together. Dirk's arms become wings: 'Dearest Beloved in Jesus Christ,' he starts, his voice thoughtful, soothing as Michiel remembers, with nothing of the righteous oratory of the generation of ministers with whom they grew up. 'We are gathered here as it has been ordained by our Heavenly Father that our beloved sister Beth Steyn be taken from us.' He lowers his wings. He smiles down at the front pew offering compassion for each individually. 'While the death of a beloved is a great loss that brings deep sorrow, the Lord himself gives us solace and comfort.'

Only years into analysis had Michiel found language to express the recollection of his own desire in the vestry that day. Without saying it yet, he had also become aware of the erotic glimmer between him and the man who listened to him weekly. In what he told Glassman, Michiel still saw the dominee's lips move and still heard the young preacher offer nothing to moderate his expulsion from paradise. *The church is clear on these issues. The Word tells us it is an abomination. But I do not believe it is for us to judge. Does God not also say, love the sinner and hate the sin? I suggest you return to the army and ask them to refer you to someone; in the army with me were men who were cured of such urges by psychologists. I can call the base chaplain, who will provide you with spiritual guidance.* Interfering with the phrases in Michiel's ears was psychic excess, images of his own cock disappearing between the beautiful dominee's soft lips, his fingers caught in the thick black hair. Kissing the full mouth and taking Dirk's cock, raised from its matted black nest, into his own. Fragments of fantasy realized, he imagines now, here in the pew, in the organist's life. Unless her particular brand of attraction and pattern of romance extended into marriage too, beyond the brothers Steyn.

'Heaven and earth shall pass away, but my words shall not pass away.'

Christian holidays in the mountains above Vancouver. There were gifts and carols for Nawal's children, though no tree. In the garden with the little ones, before they were put to bed, Kamil and Michiel caught snowflakes in their mouths.

'Love,' Rachel uses a phrase repeated by her son, 'is made of only a small part of what we feel and a very large part of what we do. It's best understood as a verb, not a noun. That's the truth erased by the fiasco of romantic love.'

'But what of desire, Rachel?'

'That's the biggest fucker.' Malik laughs loudest of all.

'Was it lust or love that drew you to Malik?'

'Pure lust,' Malik chimes.

'Lust alone would not get a nice Jewish girl like me to fall for a Jaffa Philistine. We were communists. I liked his ideas. His passion for what we believed in. Socialism was going to solve the problem of Israel and Occupied Palestine.'

'Come on, Rachel,' Malik winks, 'I'm a sexy shegitz.'

'You were nominally good-looking by Arab standards.'

When Kamil drives Michiel to San Francisco International, somewhere before the airport off-ramp he says: 'It must have been Xanthippe's feed. Beth wanted to know what kind of lizard it was. A leopard gecko, I said, from Afghanistan or Pakistan. Why burden such a small creature with such a heavy name, she asked. I told her about the snapping when we first got her. Somehow we went from Xanthippe to Rachel and Malik out of Palestine into Canada. Beth said she would have liked to meet them.' Airplanes were taking off over the long arm of San Francisco Bay. 'She assumed I was raised Jewish because of Rachel. She asked whether I spoke Hebrew or

Arabic. When I told her none of us had been back she had a lot to say about cultures abandoning their roots. She thought rituals kept people together and that modernism and migration were making everyone the same, also in South Africa. She was dismayed that no trace of your accent remained. She wondered what was left of the Indians here. I think she'd wanted to see natives in ceremonial dress, like at pueblo dances. I lightened the moment by saying I'm as much Jew as Arab, at least as far as one old ritual goes.'

'You told her that?'

'She said you were all circumcised.'

'She used Peet's name?'

'Just "all my sons". Something like that. She asked how often we fed the reptile. I wanted to say "every other night unless we're annoyed with each other", but I held my tongue.'

'There is additional sadness today in the knowledge that this is not the first time we gather for this family to say farewell to a loved one.' Dirk speaks of how as a young dominee he helped bury the eldest Steyn son. Solid, reliable, loving, fair-minded and brilliant Peet. Mostly above the alliances and loyalties of the family's daily squabbles. Something gentle and undefended. A tendency to listen rather than speak. Like the rest of the family his eyes were blue, but with nothing of Oubaas's or Benjamin's tendency to be triggered to ice or fire. Not like Ounooi's either: while hers were kind, she looked at people at an angle just above their eyes. When Peet looked at you, you felt as though he was observing a thing of infinite wonder, maybe holy, something you never saw in the mirror. *Thou*, his eyes said, rather than *you*. What he loved in this brother Michiel feared in himself. The capacity for kindness and the love that drew him to Peet, the gaze that made the beholden feel almost beloved, was what frightened Michiel if it was seen in himself. What was admirable in his brother he considered a fatal flaw in himself. In Berkeley, session after session would be dedicated to getting at that, to picking at the Gordian knot a bayonet on parade had begun but failed to quite undo. Why are they called Gordian fans, he asks on the dive boat hovering over the wreck of the *Kasi Maru* in the Solomons. *Gorgonian*, someone corrects. Perhaps for the hair of the Gorgon sisters whose stare turned people to stone. 'Like the veins in Gorgonzola,' Kamil says, lifting a yellow scuba tank on board. Inwardly Michiel smiles, a window opening to let in the skinny man in the baggy red bathing trunks fussing to clear his glasses on a damp towel. He is allowing himself a glimpse of them together, fingers and limbs intertwined on a city sidewalk. Under a cover of cloud rise the green slopes of Kolombangara's extinct volcano. *Kolombangara*, a word Michiel loves without knowing its meaning, merely for its texture and sound. In turquoise water corals and crenellated fans turn the rusted ribs of a war disaster into terraces of color and darting life. The boat rises on a swell and Kamil's hairy olive-colored arm shoots out to steady himself. He stumbles forward on deck, says, 'Oopsie' and lands on his butt. Michiel recoils. His stomach lurches with the boat's rise and fall. He stands to offer a hand to Kiko, who is in the water beside the boat.

And what of Benjamin? The middle brother's character radiated everything Oubaas wished for. That was Benjamin's luck, which more often than not the other two were grateful for: that Benjamin accepted himself as the ready repository of their father's every ambition meant that at least some of what may have been demanded of them frequently was not. Benjamin rattled off inventories of sheds and storerooms, assessed the annual harvests from individual trees without glancing at a logbook as efficiently as he could slit a sheep's throat. His ardor for the farm was no greater than Michiel's, but of a tangibly different nature: Michiel thrived in veld and kloof, on morning runs with Ounooi and in each season's flamboyant transfiguration. Benjamin — alongside Oubaas, with whom he regularly locked horns — oversaw the daily workings of the farm. He spoke seSotho almost as well as English and

Afrikaans. He confronted his father in ways Peet had no impulse to do and Michiel was too timid for. Cowed by Oubaas's temper and scorn, Michiel's adolescence became a state of hyper watch-fulness: swallowing down his fermenting resentment he tried to do precisely as his father instructed. Peet, on the other hand, heard Oubaas out and then followed his own head regardless, taking whatever censure came his way. No argument on Paradys reached the pitch of those between Oubaas and the Chosen. Cut from the same cloth, they were like bulls aware of each other's strength, the older knowing only time kept the younger from bringing him down. One either killed the other or abided by – or got off on – the violent camaraderie.

Michiel remembers the family's return from a holiday. Peet was back at university. They were somewhere in the Transkei. What did Benjamin say or do that compelled Oubaas to pull the car to the side of the road? 'Vandag bliksem ek jou hier in hierdie kafferstaat, mannetjie.' Today, mate, I'm going to knock the shit out of you here in kaffir-country. With *I'm waiting for you, Oubaas*, Benjamin was out even before the car rolled to a stop. Oubaas was already undo-ing his belt and left the driver's door open; stone-faced, Ounooi leaned over to shut it behind him. She and Michiel looked towards the windshield. 'Marry a savage, my boy, you end up raising at least one more.' Rare words critical of her husband. There was the thud of what could only be a fist. Ounooi and Michiel's heads turned. A single motion and Benjamin swung Oubaas round, twisting his arm up, between his shoulder blades. Glancing at the car and find-ing Ounooi's eyes on him, Benjamin abruptly averted his gaze. He lowered his mouth to the old man's ear. Oubaas stood with his chest heaving, jaw locked and eyes glued to where tarmac disap-peared between verdant hills. A young man with his herd was coming closer on their side of the road. A car passed, slowing for the cattle. Benjamin stepped around his father. They shook hands. Michiel read from his brother's lips *I love you, Oubaas*, a phrase that would be inconceivable coming from his own. Side by side father and son returned to the vehicle. The cowherd raised his hand as the Mercedes, climbing back on to the tarmac, drove slowly by. 'What did you say in his ear?' Michiel wanted to know, later. 'The day you pin him like that is the day I tell you.' The verbal outbursts continued and Michiel still heard reports of occasional smacks to a laborer's head. But never again did the old man lift a hand to any of his sons.

Michiel and Benjamin boarded the military aircraft on Grootfontein's runway. In the uncomfortable nets, dressed in browns, grief separated them from the bonhomie of those going on pass: conscripts, members of the Permanent Force, a few who had joined for short service and one wounded while burying his own side's landmine. If they had spoken they would have expressed quiet incredulity at what had happened. All three of them were strong swimmers. Since they were toddlers their days had been spent at the dam. Six feet of water without a shallow end: either you clung like a terrapin to the side or you swung your arms and kicked, and swam. Had Peet been caught in a current? But then there had been the beach holidays at the Kei when they went in, fearlessly, way beyond the breakers: if a current takes you, don't fight or swim against it, go with it, eventually it will bring you back to shore, or someone on the beach is bound to see you being taken. At some point Benjamin said: 'I don't know how Ounooi will get over this. Or if something happened to another one of us.' And from that came the idea that Michiel be transferred from the border, away from the war. Benjamin had contacts. And if he couldn't secure his brother's transfer they'd get Oubaas to put in a word with the Minister of Agriculture. 'With your brain for statistics you will know, Benjamin,' Michiel half-heartedly countered, 'that the odds of a marine dying in an intelligence camp in the bush are a thousand and one times smaller than being run over by a drunk driver somewhere inside the country.' *A marine,* came Kamil's mock ecstasy when, weeks after they'd first met, Michiel broached his military past. *I've had a marine in my bed! What a thrill! What on earth will Mom and Dad say?* And Michiel's explanation that their corps had not been the killing machine of its US counterpart: no major military operations, rarely casualties. Instead, their work involved harbor patrols inside South Africa, or on rivers in Namibia. (By the time he reached Sydney he would never have said *South-West Africa.*) Only rarely were members of the local population (LPs) brought in for debriefing and interrogation by intelligence officers. *What kind of interrogation?* That happened on one side of the camp. I had nothing to do with it. *How could you not have known?* It wasn't part of my job description. *Ignoring,* Kamil said, *differs from ignorance in that it is harder work.* Don't you ever get off your fucking moral high horse, Michiel wondered. 'Everyone knows we're not winning this war,' Benjamin said. 'The shit gets closer to home every year. And Paradys is right next to Lesotho. Our guys are already in the townships around Cape Town and Jo'burg. Think of what happened in Rhodesia: the next front will be the farms inside South Africa. Some fucker trained in Moscow will plant a landmine on the farm road, right where Ounooi runs.'

Large drops thud on the church's tin roof, followed by distant thunder. They are to sing the Lord's Prayer. Whispering that she knows the words, Mamparra holds out her program to Michiel. Her thumbnail harbors a thin line of dirt, attenuated by what may be a fungus. When she leans away there remains again the flowery perfume. From the back pews, altering the hymn's familiar sonance, come the voices of the Paradys workers in flatter vowels, sharper, clearer diction, with the choir, harmonic from the balcony, invigorating the congregation's dragging; three separate units of sound melding. Each declaration has somehow been retained in his brain, as though sung by him weekly without interruption: *Geheilig sy U naam, U koninkryk kom, U wil geskied* . . . Hallowed be Thy name, Thy Kingdom come, Thy will be done, on earth as it is in heaven . . . Thy and Thou, the intimate forms; *U*, the formal, distant from me and from hell. The thin threading voice of his brother's friendly child. He looks down on to her short brown hair, notices her strong jaw moving with the words. What was it with the son? Thomas. More than suspicion: a *display* of distrust. Mamparra's high soprano returns from boyhood, the pitch almost dissonant against and over the sound around him. Instead of shaking her tin of stones or beating on the empty coffee can she walks the cherry lines singing. A thousand and one songs, at times joined by other women: Sotho, Tswana, English, Xhosa, Afrikaans and Zulu. From their saddles Karien and Michiel reach into the foliage, stuff cherries into their mouths, the next sweet sphere already at their lips before the previous stone is ejected; they pit them in their mouths and with a red fleshy mass in their hands lean forward, allowing the horses' lips to receive the sweetness; and there, inside the racket of cans, is Mamparra's song. She led the Apostolic revival among the Paradys workers. Till late on Saturday nights the singing from the compound — *He is the King of Kings, the Lord of Lords, his name is Jesus* — until TV kept the farm's weekend sounds from the living room. On Monday, Mamparra would be hoarse. *Revival, Michiel. Ag, it was beautiful. Jafet gave his heart to Christ when he heard me speak in tongues. It's only Pietie and Adam still holding out. But Jesus works in mysterious ways. You know, where two or more are gathered in His name* . . . The farm's clown. Once, with school friends there for the weekend, they summoned her from the compound. They offered tips for her to prophesy in tongues. A posse of white teenagers on chairs, while the black woman stands with her hands as if in prayer on the polished red cement floor. Before she can prophesy, she says, she must receive the spirit, then preach Jesus' infinite love and forgiveness. *No, kak, Mamparra, no preaching today. Just do the tongues.* The boys guffaw, fall into their own mimicry — *unlabara fo Cristu losparrafat indragarrahsandi* —

till Ounooi appears on the stoep to put a stop to it. When compound gossip brought news that Pietie had quietly and without show given his heart to the Lord, they thought Mamparra would at last accept his proposal for marriage. Still she resisted, for the umpteenth time saying she knew too much about men to allow one across her doorstep. He reaches for a handkerchief, realizes he has neglected to bring one.

What layer of disconsolation has he entered? Or is it the grief of all memory repeated in the superlative? Never over and done, only done over. He went to Glassman for the first time after he'd been living with Kamil for a year. 'You're going out?' Kamil asked. Just a quick drink, he answered. Kamil: So you won't be home tonight? He: Why are you pissing on my battery? Kamil: Walk out that door and I suggest you stay in whichever bed you find yourself. He: What do you mean? Kamil: Rachel had it in her to stick with a philanderer but I don't, knowing it's someone else's gunk clogging the shower drain. Not knowing which words from you at least try to be true. Not knowing what you were thinking when you said, 'I'm going to buy bread.' Looking at photographs of us and not trusting who it is, there, beside me. I thought this ended in the Solomons, but you're like an animal. *Allow yourself to feel what your doing does to me.*

In that moment the world lost its color. Life without the diminutive man who till then hadn't given ultimatums seemed drawn in outlines of black and white. Standing in the doorway, Michiel protested: 'You want some middle-class heterosexual ideal for us.' 'I want a relationship.' 'We have one.' 'If the kind you need allows you to rut with everything you scent on the street, then take your bags.' 'Men like fooling around a bit, Kamil, for god's sake.' 'Men like spraying Agent Orange on villages and trees. I have better things to do than spend my life cleaning up that mess.' Michiel stepped back inside the apartment. He closed the door behind him. And grudgingly agreed to a 'few sessions' with the shrink Kamil had seen while in graduate school at Stanford. Behind the chair in which Glassman sits in his Berkeley office is a framed black-and-white photograph of Derek Walcott beside a print of 'Love After Love': *The time will come When, with elation, You will greet yourself arriving At your own door, in your own mirror, And each will smile at the other's welcome* . . . I'm here because Kamil Kassis — he was one of your clients, remember? — thinks it will help us stay together. Glassman: How long have you been partners? Michiel: I hate that word. I've lived with him for a year. Glassman: What about the word 'partner' causes discomfort? The few sessions ran, initially, to two years. With the urge to flight reasonably contained ('integrated' was Glassman's word), he terminated. Until the touch-and-go days when Michiel, baffled, enraged and fearful, recommenced the weekly trek. Glassman: When acute trauma has not been reasonably integrated it superimposes itself over future experience — new trauma in particular — without the psyche knowing what's occurring. Do you want to leave because he's dying, or because you know the devastation of abandonment? How do your brother's death, Karien and leaving your country figure in losing Kamil? With Glassman's help he would see Kamil through the ravenous conclusion of disease: sarcoma, the final night sweats, dementia. To help nurse their son, Rachel and Malik came from Vancouver for weekends. A few times Nawal too, without her kids. When the miracle drugs appeared Michiel continued the weekly crossing to Berkeley. As the intensity of the touch-and-go days wore off, his mind began drifting back here, to what and whom he'd left behind. Relaxing at last into what felt like a future for the new millennium waves of nostalgia washed through him: a youth of near bliss, unmarred by any of what he knew to be truer. Without wishing them, images came of him and Karien reading to each other before their lips and tongues meet; of his mother smiling as he, in his school uniform, walks by her classroom. In a dream an always-faceless Lieutenant Govender inaudibly explains algebra to a much older Michiel as they pass on horseback through landscape that could be Paradys or the Australian outback. In one of many dreams taken to Glassman he is on the Plains of St Augustine, where he and Kamil traveled after a visit to Mesa Verde: rows of gigantic ears swivel together in spectacular choreography, relaying sounds and signs from space while he crosses fields of sunflowers mouthing his own name. Online, he found himself regularly reading news about South Africa. Then, eighteen months ago, Glassman asked whether he had ever considered re-connecting through more than memory. Michiel: We went over this when I first came to see you. I have no need for them in my life. It's over and done with. Glassman: The process of personal integration is of course never-ending. Eventually there was the single-paged letter, handwritten. And Ounooi's response, a few weeks later: *How marvelous to hear from you, Michiel. What a superb idea for me to visit, and what perfect timing! With me retired and a good part of the bottling done by mid-December, I'm a free woman!* Her response as though his silence had lasted no longer than the natural interval between regular letters and phone calls. One more letter, in which he included her ticket. She was due after he would vote for the first time as a US citizen: his candidate (Kamil voted farther left) lost to the born-again Christian son of a former president whose other son was the governor of the state that narrowly decided the contested election through intervention by the conservative Supreme Court. Kamil, before Ounooi's arrival: Your mother keeps an orchard and bottles fruit, she raises three sons and a husband, she runs as many miles as you do every day, she reads and keeps abreast of new literature, does flowers for church and helps the community while she takes care of her appearance? Please enlighten me, as one English teacher to another, when and how does Superwoman find time to grade essays and exams? Michiel: Servants.

Mamparra's voice swells towards the high notes of *for ever and ever*, before the *amen*. When they sit, Michiel again crosses his legs, feels sweat in the small of his back.

'How,' Dirk asks, looking over them solemnly as they sit before him, 'does one assess the meaning of a life?' Do the minister's eyes – for no more than a second – find Michiel's in the front pew? A lash of lightning and a clap as it strikes somewhere close cut off Dirk's words and all eyes go to the windows. Again the patter of drops on the roof, before it stops, as if waiting. Rumbles and flashes in the gray. The sky cannot hold. *Our sister dances from the mountains of Moshoeshoe . . . she has unfurled her gray kaross, her bracelets flash and her beads glitter, the cattle and the big game look up, they flare their nostrils as the voices of the smallest creatures sing: it is the dance of the rain, look, our sister, she has come . . .* Will the interment be postponed and the body be returned to the morgue? 'Beth Steyn – Ounooi as she was fondly known to us – led a life centered in her family and her work. She married Dawid Steyn soon after arriving in town as the much-beloved English teacher at Generaal Reitz High. This marriage of more than forty years was in many ways exemplary. Characterized by an abiding love and fierce loyalty, it had another ingredient that underpins most healthy unions: respect for each other's differences. Beth was an intellectual, a voracious reader who enjoyed travel. Oubaas Dawid' – Dirk looks down, smiles at the old man – 'believes the world ends where Paradys meets the N2 and that the world's Great Books are the *Farmer's Weekly* and the *Landbou Weekblad.*' Laughter from the congregation. Bianca leans forward and looks down the pew to Oubaas; she turns her face up to Michiel, her eyes sparkling directly into his rather than above his brows. 'Beth's joy and pride in her three sons was constant and unyielding. And she loved not only her own children: more than once she stepped in to take care of others' children in need. Sometimes their acute need. And no one in this town needs to be reminded that her life was dedicated to education. She had an unflinching belief that humanity's future depends on education.' *Let me tell you two about education, Rachel says, when we fled to Israel from Berlin, Germany was the most educated nation the world had ever seen. What a clincher, Mom, Kamil counters, please send word to Rwanda and to the Mission.* 'Beth's Standard Nine and Matric classrooms were places well known for tolerance and the free flow of ideas. The seventeen-year-olds I have confirmed over the years have challenged me frequently thanks to what went on in Beth's classes. Even after retirement, she did not sit back. The adult education program she started in the township . . .'

She was our favorite. What style that woman had. Always willing to listen. Managed to not alienate anyone in this right-wing town, regardless of her ideas. I always thought she was a real bitch. Signed for her servant's child's bank loan, the manager told me. Hush-hush. Ukushisa oku leli sonto kukhipa umkhovu etsheni angazi umuntu uyophuma nini la. We will miss Auntie Beth. Sailing into the township in her Mercedes-Benz like she was Joan of Arc, bid jou dit aan. I salute you, Ounooi, for what you gave me. Modimo ha o roriswe bana beso ka ha re kopane mona betsong la ona. A better woman than your time allowed. May it be that you had no pain. Miesies, you never wanted us to say Miesies, Ounooi was okay. I feel the rain in this knee of mine. Say after me, the rain in Spain falls . . . I still have her copy of Cry, The Beloved Country, *with her name in it. Wife of my life, how do I face every day without you? My child was saved because you believed in him, told him it was okay to cry. Mos gedink haar eie hol ruik na laventel. Washing on the line! Tonight we're sleeping on the bare mattresses. Inene akwaziwa nto ngemingcwabo ngaba Bantu. Kuthe cwaka ungeva nokuwa kwesipeliti esi! Bafe behleli xa bebonke endaweni yokufa komlungukazi. Now we'll see what becomes of that farm; she was the power behind the throne, that one. Without you there, Ounooi, things will be tough. Lekker in daai manor gebly met al die leë slaapkamers. Queen Bee of Paradys. Never said a word about the dead son, just smiled. Long-suffering. If you hadn't stopped me, I'd have been married with three snotnoses living on the wrong side of the tracks. And the other one, the one she called 'her traveler', you know he ran away from the army, sitting there now, too late for tears. Ho na le se etsahalang lehodimong. Na ekaba maru le lehadima di tla tlisa pula? Moffie. All that platinum jewelry probably goes to the daughter-in-law. Or to the Grand Lady Lerato. Good-looking dressed-up black bitch has forgotten where she comes from. Kaffer-naaier. It's genetic, the stroke thing — she was health personified. Still wanted to run the Comrades. No, some work was done on that face, I'm sure, on one of the so-called trips; how else do you lose a child and still look so good? One of the few white people here who tried to be part of the solution and not the problem. Laasmaand se rekeninge. That she never left the old goat, that's the question. Drove straight past me where I was walking along the highway into town. He's a proposition, a man like him won't stay single long, invalid or not: there's money. She was the role model, everything we wished to be. All the young farmers wanted to marry her. Their cars were lined up outside that little house at number nine Cross Street. Lives in San Francisco that one, you know what I mean. Re a o leboha Morena Jeso. Re lebohela lerato la hao. Die voortreflike familie Steyn. If you have money like that, of course you can afford to be nice to everyone. Success begets success. Sy was 'n goeie ma. Wonder how the two sons get along. Without her there still wouldn't be electricity in the compound. Never looked you in the eye, always over your head when she spoke to you. Benjamin, there next to their maid, he's the backbone of that family. A multi-millionaire. All three kids very clever. I'd give my left foot for that farm. Perfect family.*

Michiel bows his head. He sees her with him waiting for Muni: a young African-American in US Navy step-outs is ahead of them, closer to the stop. Ounooi is commenting on the performance as she holds the play's program and the Borders plastic bag of books in one hand. She shakes her head at the increasingly delusional behavior of Blanche DuBois. Something in Michiel gives; he speaks over her so that she steps back, away from his violent whisper: *You read all these books, you stand here prattling about a literary character in denial, you rattle off phrases from Shakespeare and quote Brecht in German. But they have never made you see anything of your own life. Words, words, words that entertain you but do not affect you one jot! Well, let me relieve you for once and all of your denial, your own delusions about your sons. Listen, you elitist snob. Let me inform you about Peet.*

Michiel, please. Stop. At the mention of Peet's name she has stepped back, turned her shoulder to him. Her eyes, below a frown, are on the GAP window display, as if there were something distracting there.

'You will hear me out,' he almost hisses, stepping up to her, bearing over her as she leans away into the window.

Peet's coffin weighted by roses and lilies descended between layers of fake green carpet. His bosom friend had driven up from the Cape. A mere week earlier Peet and Leon had celebrated their graduation at the Lanzerac in Stellenbosch with Ounooi and Oubaas. As the mourners departed, it was with Leon that Michiel and Karien went up to the dam, through the orchard where women in blue overalls were back on aluminum ladders picking mulberries for jam and figs for green fig preserve. From the black pipe the stream of spring water tumbled like quicksilver into the cement dam. Lilies wreathed its base, where seepage kept the soil moist all year round.

'Last time he and I were on the farm we swam up here,' Leon said. Michiel heard himself and his brothers splashing, struggling, pushing heads under, someone crying, stomping home hollering, 'I'm telling Ounooi', and calls of 'cry-baby', on tire tubes, racing, wrestling, shouting, stinging each other with a wet tennis ball, sjambokking each other's legs with rolled-up towels, naked, in early adolescence, dangling from the sides, seeing whose erection looked biggest from above the water's surface, who could come first and then fleeing each other's tendrils like frogs' eggs, he and Peet (in dark glasses) and Karien (her face shaded by Ounooi's sun hat), in bigger tire tubes, floating with books open in their laps. As Leon speaks Michiel looks up, takes in Karien in a dark dress she must have borrowed from someone at university, her face grief-stricken. 'It was a beautiful dream, with graduation behind us and most guys thinking of the army next year.' Leon had decided to delay national service by continuing with an honors degree in Latin. Peet, always the plaasjapie, had been up at cock's crow. They walked far that morning, on the beach. 'I went back for breakfast but he stayed for a swim.' Leon looked down into the water. 'Every hour since then I've asked myself why I left him.' His eyes found Michiel, then Karien: 'For the rest of my life I'll regret it.' Peet's shirt and shorts were found where Leon had left him, his footprints visible from the bundle down to the wet sand. Other people were on the beach now. Scores of other Maties. They began calling around; everything was closed for the public holiday. Sea rescue came and the police. Their group searched the beach. Others went out on paddle skis and surfboards. 'At sundown I called here. Oubaas wanted to come. I told him to wait, there was nothing they could do. Helicopters and boats had been fine-combing the coast.' At noon the next day a fisherman found the body in a tidal pool, in the direction of Gordon's Bay. 'He was undamaged. No evidence of a shark. A simple drowning.' Leon leaned his forehead on the dam wall and sobbed.

On the flight back to the desert Michiel relays this to Benjamin. Later still, he would think it may have been at the recall of *a simple drowning* from Leon's lips, that a seed of suspicion might first have been planted, undetected till he himself left the farm near the point of skipping the country. He is on the train to which Ounooi has taken him. Oubaas left the house early and did not come to say goodbye or see him off. Neither parent knows that he has his passport. 'You're a strong young man,' she says as the train pulls into the station. 'Call us when you get to Durban.' As far as they know he is en route to Salisbury Island, going back to confront humiliation once more. On the train he replays his lies to the scornful Oubaas, the voiceless Ounooi: 'They set us up. We weren't doing anything. He was a friend from the officers' mess and I shouldn't have taken him to a whites-only beach. I made a simple mistake.' When *simple drowning* overlays *simple mistake*, two phrases rub against each other like primitive sticks, raising a suspicion that till then has been unimaginable. He will think he must see Leon again; want to hear Peet's story away from the farm, away from the state of grief in which both *simple mistake* and *simple drowning* might have had to stand in for *simple truth* as *simple truth* would have been unbearable. Unspeakable.

Whether through reckless postponement of what awaits in

Durban or whether in search of the final impetus to use the passport, he goes overnight to Cape Town. He travels through vineyards
to the mountains of Stellenbosch. In a place of blinding white Cape
Dutch architecture he finds Leon. While students mill in the
bleached courtyard of *Die Ou Hoofgebou*, Leon and he talk in a narrow
classroom with low oak desks engraved with a palimpsest of names
and illegible graffiti. When Michiel reveals himself as effectively
AWOL and decommissioned, Leon opens up. Glassman: About
your brother being gay? Michiel: And that he'd known for two years
that he was sick. Finishing his LLB kept him from going insane. In
those days there was nothing except to wait it out. Glassman: How
did you feel? Michiel: Threadbare. Like nothing could hold me
together. I wished he'd spoken to me. As much as his death, his secret
life seemed unbelievable. The morning on the beach, Leon had
known. They'd been discussing it for months. He had to force himself to keep walking, to not turn back. If Peet had been unable to live
with it I couldn't. By the time I bought my ticket to London I was
certain that I was sick myself. That I would die, away from home.

Unspeakable and unspoken to anyone but Glassman and Kamil.
Till the night on the winter-wet streets of San Francisco. Away
from Paradys, all those years later. When Michiel says to Ounooi
what he, in his own disgrace, went to find out from Leon.

Peet did not drown.

With her back to him Ounooi raises her arm with the program
and the plastic bag. *Don't do this*, she says.

*Drowning as we use it in English implies an accident. Selfmoord, Ounooi, if
you want the Afrikaans.*

She swings around with her forearm covering half her face. She
stares at him, her eyes bewildered.

To drown oneself is suicide.

Her gaze is disoriented, her look unfocused. She shakes her head,
turns, seems to half-stumble, her cheek squashed and distorted against
the window.

You will never forgive yourself for this, she whispers.

He walked into the sea because he was dying, he smirks, choosing words for their spite, *and there ain't any denying that!*

She throws her head back, covers her face with one hand and raises her other arm as if holding him off.

Later, but for still seeing the sub-lieutenant in uniform, he will be unable to remember the street and pavement around them. People must have seen and heard.

No, your eldest was not hemophiliac or a mainliner. Let me present it in terms Benjamin would use: you and Oubaas had a sixty-six and two-thirds percent success rate — two homos out of three. Now he snorts: *When it comes to real Afrikaner farm boys that ain't half bad, Ounooi. You raised two of us. That statistic in my world is a mark of pride.*

'Then why . . .' she whispered, turning wet eyes on him, shaking her head, pleading, 'why use it against your mother like a blade?' She was tiny against the glass window, as if an old woman had entered the display of eternal mannequin youth. Within a few minutes she had shrunk to look as if everything that had never happened to her had happened now, all at once. The glimpse of her a decade hence pulled him back into the present, horrified at what he'd done. Their trolley had arrived. The young officer, ascending the step, looked back with a frown — shall I ask the driver to wait? — and Michiel waved him on.

He stood with his back to her. When at last he turned to face her again Ounooi's shoulders were upright and she was smoothing back her hair, once more clutching her purchases and theatre program beneath her arm. She wiped tears from her cheeks and from around her eyes. The exhaustion on her face dissipated as she tried to smile at him. It sounded at first like bravado when she spoke, her voice cracking even as she managed the smile and said, 'The rain has let up and it's a magnificent night in one of the great cities of the world.' A laugh escaped her lips. 'So much for Twain bemoaning the weather. Old curmudgeon. Let's walk.' She looked towards the

Embarcadero and then pointed up Market. 'All the way until we see
the rainbow flag and then right, yes? Kamil's been generous to let me
have you all to myself tonight.' She came close to him, looked up
into his face, on hers barely a trace of what had just occurred.

She slipped her arm through his for the walk south. He can
recall their reflections in lighted display windows, past the homeless emerging from beneath plastic huts and past the hawker selling
Guatemalan fabric from the sidewalk, through the stink of urine
and excrement rising from sewers after the rain. They paused in
silence, each with their own thoughts, for red lights to turn green;
passed cross-streets all the way up to the Castro. When they
reached Safeway he glanced at her. Her cheeks shiny with tears, a
slight quiver in her bottom lip.

'Ounooi,' he said, clasping her arm tighter to his side. 'I'm sorry.'

'I've grown used to your accent and that everyone calls you
Michael,' she responded, clearing her throat, looking ahead. 'But I
wish you wouldn't use the word *ain't*. It makes you sound like a
poor white. A hillbilly. You are the principal of a language school,
after all.' They stepped from the curb. She still did not look at him
when she asked: 'Would you be offended if your mother asked just
two questions?' Then a quick glance up at him.

He shook his head, shamefaced.

'I would like to know whether you have this disease. And, if you
do, what can I do to help?'

He wavered before answering. 'Kamil is positive. I'm not. He's
on the medication and to all intents and purposes as healthy as I
am.'

'You are men enough to take care of each other. He is a good
man.' She clasped both hands together before running an open
palm down his back.

'Ounooi, I was dead wrong to say the things I did to you.' Her
eyes found his and she brushed aside his apology as though it were
uncalled for, as if she were mystified at what he was referring to.

'When we get home I trust you'll join your mother for a glass of Amplexus.' Then, winking at him, 'I won't say no to some of those sweet Chilean grapes.'

'It's time,' Glassman says, checking the clock. 'We've gone over and my next patient is waiting.' Michiel lifts his coat from the arm rest. He passes the check with the thirty-five dollars co-pay. The other hundred is covered by the International House health plan. 'I hate the word patient,' he says, looking directly into the face he knows so well. 'And why is that?' Glassman asks, peering over his bifocals. 'It implies that the people you see are sick or crazy. I think it's nothing more than the human condition,' Michiel says, rising. 'An interesting point to revisit next week,' Glassman replies, smiling.

Dirk is introducing the mayor, Sam Thabane. This is the man under whose guidance Ounooi started the township adult literacy project. Not much older than Michiel, he positions himself to one side of the coffin. A former exile – Sweden, Holland, Canada, Tanzania, Russia? – sent here, rather than to parliament, by the new government to mend rifts fueled by the state in the black community during the turbulent late eighties; information Michiel recalls now from Ounooi's visit. He wears a loose green cotton shirt with a motif in yellow and black, with white embroidery around the long sleeves and buttoned neck. 'I met Beth Steyn in 1991, soon after Sharon and I returned from Zambia.' There is an easy confidence to his bearing and he speaks without notes, his voice deep for so slight a man. 'She wanted our help in reopening the municipal swimming pool. We remember that the pool was closed and filled in by the previous council in a last-ditch attempt to cling to the old ways.' Michiel notes the erasure of agency: no one person stands accused. It may as well be Ounooi herself speaking. 'Beth and her friends Sally Devon and Dominee's wife Karien wanted to raise funds to have the pool dredged, patched and reopened to the

public.' Only the *decent* are named. 'They believed that the younger
our children play together and learn to swim together, the sooner
the town will heal. We never got that project together as the transition demanded our attention on other key priorities. Beth put her
shoulder to the wheel in surprising ways: she raised funds for the
children's shelter, she joined the Women's League to lobby the state
for seSotho-language books in the Langenhoven Library. And even
before she retired, she and Karien Burger founded the Women's
Literacy Program. For most, it was the first time our people sat
at the same table.' So far the words white and black have not been
uttered. 'There is a lot more I can tell you about Beth, but let it
suffice to say that she was a rare human being. A few months ago
she came to my office; we bumped into each other in town after
that, but I think it was the last time we spoke formally. She wanted
to know what she and others could do to promote dialogue about
what was happening with HIV and AIDS. Up to four people a day
are dying in our hospital alone. The same is true in Zastron and
Wepener and Smithfield. Silence is killing our people.' Michiel's
heart swells. Ounooi, my hero. Beloved, through everything.
'One of the things that irked Beth, in particular, is the way funeral
homes exploit the formerly disadvantaged. Our people are buying
into the idea that only the biggest, most expensive funerals will do.
When I walked in here today and saw this coffin,' he lifts an open
hand to the casket, 'the simplest and least costly vessel to be buried
in, other than a mielie sack, it seemed to me that this might be
Beth's bequest to us: in death also she has chosen to model something of our shared humanity. If this coffin is good enough for
Beth Steyn it is good enough for any of us.' He pauses, then looks
at the front row. 'To the Steyn family I say, your terrible loss is, in
many ways, a loss to all of us. Beth knew that we are only human
through other humans.'

Then this, too, is what Michiel has missed out on. The daily.
The ordinary. His mother's humble contribution to reconciliation.

Truth, he thinks, she had her own brand of, like all of us. How much has Sam Thabane had to leave unsaid? Of suspicion and privilege, of the rich white woman's philanthropy? Of himself, perhaps not yet invited to sit on the re-upholstered sofa in the Paradys living room? Of the anger and despondency that might have driven a boy named Samuel, probably as a teenager, to join the swelling ranks of exile? Was he born and bred here; at school with Little-Alida? Did he wade the Caledon into Lesotho as his forebears had been forced to decades earlier? *Look at these exiles swarming towards the Basotho border, some of them with their belongings on their heads, driving their emaciated flocks attenuated by starvation and cold. The faces of some of the children, too, are livid from the cold. It looks as if these people were so many fugitives escaping from a war, with the enemy pressing hard at their heels . . . How comforting to know that once they crossed the river these exiles could rest their tired limbs and water their animals without breaking any law.* Under what non-funereal circumstances and in what form will that story still have to find public re-articulation? Have histories been revised? This, he thinks, is at long last the new being born, dragging its afterbirth along with it, scratching its head to figure out a way to imbibe the past or otherwise see itself perish. And he has chosen to remain apart from it. *Exile.* He thinks of the word as belonging in the realm of politics and coercion. To the lives of Malik and Rachel. And Sam Thabane. It has never been appropriated for himself, for whatever he is it does not make him the blood kin of exile: a bourgeois émigré, an expatriate like the Australians who went troppo in the Solomons. He left here with a white skin, a thousand and one choices, change to spare and only personal scores he wasn't sure he wanted settled. Still, if he ever musters energy and time for a PhD that could be a thesis topic: *Representations of Exile in South African Non-Fiction.* Or a comparative study: *South Africa and Palestine: Exile and Land: Sol Plaatje and Edward Said.* The latter would please Malik no end. What Rachel would say: *Your title already puts Kamil's petty bias on display. If there is a people who have a body of exile literature to fill the Empire*

State Building it is the Jews. Malik: *At least they'd have a building.* Rachel, smiling, leaning in to take hold of her husband's knee: *Surmay Arrasak! There are times I think my mother had a point . . .*

London spring. At times things seemed bearable through cracks in the glass behind which he felt he'd been living. Lying on his bed he reread Plaatje: *A pitiable spectacle, however, was the sight of those who had been evicted from the centre of the Orange 'Free' State. It was heartrending to hear them relate the circumstances of their expulsions, and how they had spent the winter months roaming from farm to farm with their famishing stock, applying in vain for a resting place. Some farmers were apparently sympathetic, but debarred from entertaining such applications by the sword of Damocles — the 100 Pound fine in Section 5 of the Natives' Land Act — they had perforce to refuse the applicants. The farms hereabout are owned by Boers and English settlers, but many are owned by Germans, Jews, Russians, and other Continentals.* Though in Matric he'd received an A for history along with an A for English, his memory held nothing of the 1913 Land Act. And if he'd heard and forgotten, or disremembered, it could not have been presented like this. And had it been, he is not sure it would have made enough of a difference. Not then, not there, with Paradys beneath *Kleinbaas's* feet. But reading it alone, from the confinements of flight and the distance of the stuffy Leicester Square room, receiving it from the hands of a black woman, with no one to interpret or rationalize, no conscious threat or incentive to goad understanding in the turbulent wake of what he'd left behind, enabled him, made him willing to take it in and see clearly the avarice and cruelty of it all. He now saw a tawdry A standing anchored in violent erasure. As he read, at times drifting into reverie, things from outside classes and books resurfaced. In art, Karien wanted to do something original, *not just any old frottage of leaves or old coins.* There were the petroglyphs above the entrance to the Bushmen's cave. And that thing that must surely be the fossil of a shell in the cliffs. They could make an adventure of it, sleep beneath the overhangs. Ounooi put her foot down: her fourteen-year-old charge was not sleeping out in the bush like some pioneer girl. (Did she say *voortrekker* girl?) A picnic at the waterfall, yes, but if they were not back before dinner she was sending Adam out to search for them. Up they went, with tracing paper, colored pencils and charcoal. Below the cliffs they tied the horses so the animals could graze. They scrambled up the crag that must once have been a footpath. Karien spread the transparent paper over the figure in the rock that resembled a nautilus; then over patterns that could have been random marks, or messages maybe, or representations of stars (is this not the Southern Cross?) or herds on the veld. Battle formations? Who says it was Bushmen; why not earlier hominids or whoever came before? From walls in the sandstone cave and up against fire-stained overhangs framing the entrance she traced ochre and red eland, blesbok, figures seemingly on the hunt or at war, some with erections, accentuated buttocks and powerful calf and thigh muscles. This looks like a cow hide, splayed open. A group playing instruments like sitars. What if this was their church, if under this cliff they made sacrifices and took communion through blood? They peeled off clothes, their screams, as water struck their bare skin and scalps, echoing in the kloof. Stretched out on a rock in the sun, they kissed with tireless tongues and did in any number of ways what wouldn't result in pregnancy or the loss of Karien's virginity. Before the end of high school they would give up on the idea of virginity and Michiel bought his first French letters (they would not call them FLs or condoms) in Bloemfontein. When Karien was alone behind the pharmacy's cash register she herself rang up the contraband. They dressed and rode down the mountain aglow with sun and laughter. Beside the orchard was the calligraphy of ancestral gravestones to explore. It had been years since anyone was buried on the farm, the last being Oupa Steyn. Grasshoppers skittered from rosebushes gone astray as they stepped on graves rank with the rot of oak and coiled in brambles, unaware of what lay beneath their feet. Places marked only by narrow upright stones and some with illegible script or numbers Michiel knew were casualties of the concentration camp, tangled in grass and what at some point must have been yellow creeping roses. There were workers' stories of the cemetery haunted by balls of light sweeping the hillside after rain. Another, that generations of cobras or puff adders nested behind the stone of the first English owner. Adam and Pietie had killed a clutch of vipers during the digging of Oupa Steyn's grave. Cat-foot, noisily scaring off whatever might lurk there, they kicked open a path to the more imposing gravestones: *William Horwood, 1860–1922, From Paradise returned to Paradise.* When Karien started on the graves of his own great-grandparents Michiel, smelling her and the waterfall on his fingers, sank down behind Groot-Ouma's worn angel with its one broken wing. With a hiss he shot out his arm; she screamed, jumped up, pencil piercing the tracing paper. She had to redo the lettering: *Hermiena Katarina Elisabet Steyn, 1890–1945, Survived the Sorrows of Bloemfontein, Woman and Mother.* The place was giving Karien the heebie-jeebies, but he wanted to see what the older markers had to offer. On these, also weather-worn, eroded by time or engraved too superficially to offer defined frottage, she had to use charcoal. *Moshe*— (the last letters of the name leaving no impression) and then, *Mohlakwana 1849–1898.* Probably a faithful servant of the earliest Afrikaner owners. More names, dates indecipherable or appearing only in part, though not even an illiterate could not recognize what must have been an entire family of Mohlakwanas. At dinner they reported their find. Could be the mad Mamparra's ancestors, Oubaas said. That's where the nickname came from, Ounooi explained, the alliteration of m's and the assonance of a's to make Mamparra Mohlakwana.

On Leicester Square dates and the mendacity of family lore came to matter. How was it that the first white man's death on Paradys was engraved as *1922* when there was already a Mohlakwana more than two decades before? If the humble, overgrown graves were from before the period of which Plaatje writes, there was a chance — an excellent chance — that the land had belonged to the Mohlakwanas or that they'd been tenants or share-croppers there before and until 1913. Rushed through the new Union Parliament, the Land Act prohibited black farmers from selling their land to other blacks and disallowed them familial inheritance of land. Blacks were thus forced to sell to whites. Even sharecropping by black farmers was outlawed. For a black person to own and run livestock became a crime punishable by law: gen-erations of sharecroppers were forced to either leave white-owned land or agree to become servants overnight and sign over their live-stock. Tens of thousands of farmers and sharecroppers were set adrift. Was it through a law of criminal prohibition and appropri-ation — legalized theft — rather than the concentration camps and scorched earth that old man Horwood first got his hands on the land he named Paradise? But on that day in their teens, in the after-glow of the mountain, at the long table with seating for Oubaas and Ounooi and for three sons and three future daughters-in-law and grandchildren, neither Karien nor Michiel brooded over dates. His bemusement came from the discovery that black people were once buried alongside white, his pride from anticipating that Karien's simple charcoal rubbing of the snail-like creature in the rock was sure to be the best in the class.

And here Mamparra Mohlakwana sits against me, melded to me and I to her, he thinks. The woman who had one child, who they called Geel. Yellow. Unmarried despite Pietie's persistent courtship. Their forearms and legs touching. Hers washed in the communal compound shower, his behind the glass cubicle in the revamped manor. His hand, with Kamil's ring on the ring finger, rests on his thigh beside hers. He stares at her hand clutching a crumpled Kleenex and gets fixated by the growth beneath the thumbnail. The sweat of her labor is in the calcium of his bones, in his powerful lungs (*lungs of an eighteen-year-old*, their GP says, *despite the years of smok-ing*) when he runs from the Haight to the bison paddock smelling the salt and kelp of the Pacific: every step, every breath, what she has done most days of her life is in him. *Astrante bleddie meid.* How much of what has propelled her into the front pew, seat of prime mourning with the family, is feigned absent-mindedness? Resistance, Kamil teaches his students, is the secret of joy. From what distance do names and words, sorrows and pictures tumble through *her* cheeky memory? He imagines a Mohlakwana on the koppie that September, looking towards the Malutis, telling a story to a smart man come from far, pen and notebook in hand, to record a great tragedy of expulsion and exodus. Did a Mohlakwana's words go by ship with Sol Plaatje to petition in vain for intercession by the great King George? And what became of Geel, Mamparra? Did Ounooi see to it that her shed-worker had only the one child or was it necessary to control only the manor-servant's fertility? More than once he sees his mother — it was never a secret among her friends — mashing the tiny tablet between spoons for Alida's porridge: a steaming bowl of Quaker Oats with milk and sugar, ready when Alida arrives housecoated from the kaya to pack lunchboxes for the boys. Only yesterday, it seems. Today in Zimbabwe white-owned farms are being given over to black war veterans. Veteran not of guns but of cheek, songs and mislabeled preserves in peacetime, has Mamparra's time come? He has read of domestic workers here whose fingertips no longer have prints, scuffed away in washing white people's laundry. Who now separates delicates from brights for Lerato's family? A fingernail soap-and-brush-scrubbed for a funeral, fungus as remembrance of cherries and horses, of charcoal moving in a young hand over tracing paper.

After they had buried Peet, with Leon retired to a bunkbed in the rondavel, when the house was sleeping in woe, Michiel and Karien lay on the living-room sofa. In the rawness of that night they spared no thought for precaution. Tears warm in each other's necks, they fell asleep and woke the next morning, their nakedness covered by Michiel's kaross that had not been there the night before. They looked at each other with big eyes. At breakfast they searched faces for clues.

'It wasn't me,' his brother grinned on the flossie as they flew back to Grootfontein. 'Busted you are, this time.'

Michiel was back in the Caprivi only for a day when the order came: a transfer to *SAS Salisbury Island* on the morning of January 2nd. His last letters to Karien and to his parents were submitted for censorship to the base 2IC. To Karien he wrote: *Who cares about giving up the danger pay: I'll be only seven hours' drive from you.* And to the farm: *I'm sure the navy will give me harvest leave to help in November and, who knows, they may even let me klaar out a few months early.* The coming year would be a breeze after the past one of basics, officers' courses (*I'm gonna go into Angola, I'm gonna kill old Sam Nujoma . . .* they sang as they ran with staaldak-webbing-en-geweer) and the monotony of the quiet riverbank base. After national service (the term they all used, without irony) there would be university. For the moment Karien's scholarships were location-specific, though maybe she'd do her LLB in Stellenbosch: they'd go to the Boland's mountains and vineyards, its oceans and the country's foremost Afrikaans law degree. That her studies and brilliant career would determine their *domicilium* – a word she began using in her letters to him – was never in dispute: there was, after all, they joked, the small matter of her genius with the capital G.

Although on other continents some of what he'd pictured for himself would come to pass: half a degree from London, completed in Sydney, paid for with earnings from his employ as hotel receptionist, waiter, maître d' and English as a Second Language instructor. Then a respectable masters from the University of California system on scholarship through the good offices of his association with Kamil. But for Karien everything, each brush of color that was him and her together, the capital G's future on their shared and on her own infinite canvas would be irrevocably altered within little more than a few weeks.

More rain had fallen in the Angolan catchment area. Brown and swollen, the river lifted patrol boats high on to banks. Flotsam sloshed between the jetty's wooden planks. Papyrus heads that had been swaying over the glassy flow two weeks before were submerged. Water lilies bobbed, gasping pink lotus-lips for light above the milky chocolate. Malaria had been contained in camp. During Michiel's absence his tent-mate, Lieutenant Steven Almeida, contracted the dangerous cerebral strain, *Plasmodium falciparum*. The camp's sickbay was out of quinine and, fearing the worst for his Portuguese-speaking intelligence officer, the OC had allowed Almeida to be taken downriver and across the border to a barebones clinic run by Red Cross nuns. Following time in the nuns' care Steven was back. The lieutenant with the enormous brown eyes was still weak and remained in bed under his mosquito net. At the clinic he'd been cared for by an Angolan doctor. A black woman, no less. Terrorists or not, Almeida said, Angolans are the world's most beautiful people and the doctor at the clinic no exception. *Lekker kommunis-poes geproe saam met die kwinien* — had a good taste of communist cunt along with the quinine, the officers joked. *Pity it was wasted on that one.* Michiel had more than once heard whispers in the camp that *the Porra intelligence lieut was too soft, a bit effeminate, AC-DC,* and though he'd grown fond of the man he took at least some almost unconscious care not to be seen around base in his tent-mate's company.

Almeida was born on a coffee estate in the Angolan highlands and left there as a boy, one step ahead of the rest of the Portuguese community that pulled out overnight. Still fluent in Portuguese, he was sent to the operational area upon graduating from Wits. He'd seen ops as deep as three hundred kilometers beyond the Namibian front: *No Passport Required.* The Kwando camp also housed recruits from among the local population and South-West Africa Territory Force who spoke fluent Herero, Diriku and seTswana. Locally spoken languages like Yeyi, Mbukushu and Kxoe, Michiel hadn't even heard of before. His platoon accompanied the base doctor and medics to local kraals and villages where the SADF offered basic healthcare. If his platoon found something suspect — a new arrival, an unannounced departure, a pot on a fire still bearing a forgotten Spanish-language sticker, a Cuban-issue bootprint left unerased — LPs were brought in for questioning. During the drudgery of his months here, there had been very little to report.

Awaiting transfer, he slacked off on inspection and patrol duties. With Steven still in bed they could be in each other's company without fueling camp scuttlebutt. He brought the convalescent's meals from the mess. They went at night to the officers' tented shower together. In the dim light, under the trickle of tepid water, Michiel turned his back to hide the evidence of his desire. Glassman: This wasn't the first time you were attracted to a man. Michiel: This was different. When I got back from the funeral I got a hard-on just looking at him. Glassman: Had your primary fantasies been of boys or girls? Michiel: Both, at first, around thirteen. Kamil says he knew when he was three, that the bisexual thing is still a kind of defense against who I knew I really was. Glassman: You had satisfactory sexual experiences with Karien? Michiel: The longer she and I fooled around the more I thought of going inside her while I wanked. Sometimes I'd find it was no longer me inside her, but some guy inside me or I in him; (now having to force the words out) Almeida was androgynous. His eyelashes seemed too long and his cheekbones too high for a man. His cheeks were red. He had a wide mouth and big lips. He shaved only once a week. I quit wearing underpants so I could feel myself swollen against the fabric of my browns. Glassman: Some part of you must have wanted him to notice? Michiel: The fear of another officer or *anyone* knowing — and he was a full lieutenant — was terrifying. Glassman: Don't even the most closeted among us, the most fearful and self-loathing, always leave the door slightly ajar, just in case the right person might see in, even only so we may chase him off?

New Year's Eve's merry-making would be followed by a screening of *Apocalypse Now*. The mob was drunk and rowdy. One of Michiel's troops had launched a fireworks display of mortar charges and Captain Lotter, adamant that the festivities should not spiral out of control, insisted a charge sheet be prepared for misuse of military property. There was a problem with the projector – too many lights on, generator overload – and the screening had to be delayed until all non-essentials had been turned off. Irritable from the afternoon's incident with the mortar charges and having seen the film once too often, Michiel returned to his tent once the generator went on the blink. Since early September the tent-flaps had stayed open to allow through any breath of air. Under the brown net draping the sides of the bed like a giant bloom, Almeida was writing a letter home, his pad pressed to bare legs. Michiel returned from the shower and crawled in under his own net, leaving off the light at his bedside. He lay in the dark, turned at first away from Almeida, then rolled on to his stomach to gaze through the double layers of netting at the man's profile. It was a desire that made what he'd felt for Karien seem a mere shadow of the real thing. With Karien sex, he would tell Glassman years later, was an extension of their fondness for each other. With Steven Almeida desire seemed to exist without context: it was beneath his skin and in the air, and his breathing changed even before there was the thought of touch. Their eyes met through the mesh. Almeida lowered the pen, resting its tip on the writing pad. A loud cheer went up from the mess tent. The projector was working again. Almeida rose, his erection outlined against his PT shorts as he slid from beneath the net to turn off the light. American accents and the rattle of choppers carried in to them through the open tent flaps, and on a warm breeze came the sickly-sweet scent of baobabs in bloom. Above the revelry from the mess Michiel could hear Wagner's 'Ride of the Valkyries'. There was the shisss-shisss of Almeida's mosquito net, then the creaking of his bed again taking his weight. Over swirling violins and trumpets Michiel took the rhythm of his own breathing from the other man's. In sync, with no other sound coming from either, they breathed for each other through the nets – over the rattle of gunships and bass growing louder, the clatter of Bren guns and explosions and the screams of people fleeing – touching only in breath.

The OC summoned Almeida from lunch. Detainees had been brought in during the night. Michiel bade his troops goodbye. *Durban by the sea a damn sight better than this desert; take me with Ensign; ag, please man!* He filled out paperwork and left notes for his replacement who was due on the same convoy with which he was leaving. Dinner – despite the chef's specialty chocolate and boiled condensed milk cake – was muted by hangovers and the absence of Captain Lotter, his second in command and the intelligence officer. Near midnight, when Almeida had not reappeared, Michiel made his way to the squat structure of brick and mortar that was the camp's one permanent building. The gate, normally without guards, was now staffed (manned was the word he used until Berkeley, where tongues are excised for using gendered terms) by members of his own platoon: the third shift of a rotating roster he'd drawn up that morning at the Captain's request. The building had served as a church and a school for local children, but at some point during the war its windows had been filled in, the only light now coming from up near the flat tin roof through small glass-covered spaces like portholes. Michiel passed the camp's doctor, who was returning to the sickbay: *Still here, Ensign? Tomorrow's D-day, Lieutenant.* Michiel knocked. 'Come in.' He opened the heavy metal door. Someone he didn't recognize and would for ever be unable to held a prisoner face down in a tub of water. An arm flailed behind with a hand clawing, the other dangling, limp. The head was wrenched up and he saw her mouth gasping, heard the garbling noise of her trying to make words. Whoever held the woman glanced over his shoulder – how is it that he could not have seen

the face that belonged to the white hand? — and gestured at someone behind a screen of sorts. Then the one holding down the
woman — did I never take my eyes off her? — must have pointed or
gestured, somehow waved Michiel away. He stepped back into the
shadows and must have closed the door. He started back towards
the gate, where he could see the glow of cigarettes. He heard the
door open and close, and a moment later Almeida was at his side.
They found each other's eyes in the dark.

'I'm leaving with the morning convoy, Lieutenant,' he said,
falling in behind the title he'd dropped months earlier.

'It's going to be a long night.'

'Is that—'

'I'm in an impossible position, Ensign. She hasn't told us what
we want to hear. I'm so sorry you had to see this.'

They shook hands and Michiel — now Ensign Steyn again —
passed through the gate, back to the tent where his packed balsak
waited. The baobabs' transient flowers had fallen after the previous
night's visitation of bats and moths, leaving a sweet stench that
made his nostrils prickle. For years he thought the smell misremembered, that instead he'd seen the white blooms glimmer silvery
in the full moonlight across the river. Constantly bothered by his
memory's vacillation between sight and smell, he'd recently found
a website that confirmed: December 31st, 1986, *New Moon*. If
he'd ever really seen baobabs bloom by moonlight it could not have
been then. He smoked one Camel after another, using the empty
mortar canister they kept between their beds as an ashtray. Kamil:
And then? Michiel: I never saw him again. Kamil: What became
of the woman, Michael? Michiel: I left with the morning convoy.
Kamil: Did you lodge a complaint? There must have been a form
to fill out. Did you not speak to the commander at your next
posting? Michiel: It was standard operating procedure. Some
version of this must have been going on in a hundred camps
and police stations all over Namibia and Angola. And inside the

country too. It was a state of emergency. I was living in a war zone, Kamil, not Disneyworld. Kamil: Didn't you at least want to know what they did to her? Michiel: I *saw* what they were doing to her. Kamil: '*What* were they doing to her?' Michiel stares at the man he has nursed through hell and back. He looks away. He shakes his head; notices the painting beside the TV that needs straightening and remembers that Xanthippe needs fresh water. He fears that their living room will never be the same after this. That the nameless woman will be here, between them, always. 'I don't know,' he says. 'I saw that they were torturing her. More, I didn't. I chose not to.' Kamil: But afterwards? I'm trying not to be judgmental, Michael, but you just left it at that? Michiel: I was transferred two thousand miles away, to a different country. Kamil, after a long silence: I hope you'll tell Glassman. Michiel: I've been talking to him about it for years. Kamil: Was it your beautiful tent-mate holding her down? Michiel: I don't know. I don't know. Kamil: It's odd that you never told me before. Michiel: Of everything, it's this thing I can speak about only in therapy. I wish I could tell you I was kicked out of the army for calling someone to account, that I left for reasons of conscience. Kamil: Do you think about it often? Michiel: Once a month, every other week, twice a day. Sometimes a year can go by. Then it can happen while I'm walking down the street. Or looking into a student's face – Spanish, Japanese, Russian – I can be saying, make sure your verb corresponds with your subject, this is what you must say, this is how it sounds when you pronounce it correctly in American English and there she is, in front of me, her neck muscles like ropes. In London I started dreaming about her. Glassman says that's normal. What's *normal* about anything, I ask. Don't tell *me* what is normal, it's *normal* that's the fucking problem that has me here every week at a hundred and thirty-five dollars an hour. Her eyes bulge from their sockets. Her hair is long, dreadlocks bunched in a white hand against her neck. It is a white hand holding her. Not one of the camp's black hands.

I think she's wearing a white cotton nightgown because I see her brown skin through the wet shine like mocha, as if her body has been submerged and is coming up from the water. Kamil tears up and says *Habibti*, good god, this is unspeakable, and takes his Michael into arms that have grown strong again.

Michiel has heard Rachel speak of the first skeletons of modern women whose collarbones and arm sockets can be seen to have changed when the earliest of homo sapiens began grinding cereals. Somewhere he has read (or heard, or seen on TV or the internet) that every cell of the body is replaced every few months. Within a short while we can no longer be said to be the same person. That's the marvel of the postmodern moment: pissed, shat and sweated out of all responsibility. But what of memory, held in bones and teeth way beyond the I's tenuous cohesion? How is it that from a million years ago, from Qafzeh and Skhul a hundred thousand years ago, from the Great Rift Valley and from Bossieshoek we can read femurs today and tomorrow as though they strode plains, bogs and hills only yesterday? We can explain the diet of Neanderthals, Paleolithics and Mesolithics. How much is left over to pass on the stories — by means of stable isotope analysis, he thinks Rachel calls it — through calcium that carries evidence of the drink, the injury, the nutrition imbibed or foregone, the puff on a dry tobacco leaf, the poison gas, the virus, every bite of animal, mineral or tiny red fruit passed, pitted or not, into the digestive system leaving a nano-microscopic etch from a time when a jaw shaved by a Gillette razor is still clad in flesh, skin and lips?

A black boy and white girl have stepped from the ranks of the choir and are standing beside the organ. Their eyes are on Karien. He imagines her offering words of encouragement. When the organ begins he recognizes the piece as Lloyd Webber's dedication to Irish victims of terrorism. Inserted right beside Beethoven. She could sing or play from the FAK as though from the sheet music of Bach himself. One child's soprano is taken up by the other. Voices intertwine in mourning, fingers, in his mind, searching the rubble of war. The chorus joins, humming in support only, but also part of the whole. He feels the hairs on his arms and legs stand on end. This unstoppable numeration. Where is the rain? If only he could get past these knees, flee the pew and escape the church. He breathes deeply. *Wat die hart van vol is, loop die brein van oor.* What the heart is full of spills from the brain. Or should it be spills from the *mouth?* The idiom forsakes him. Back only hours and he hears himself (does one hear thought?) in long stretches of Afrikaans. Language, come to collect its dues. For charges once impossibly reversed. Postponement means only for so long. Then we come face to face again.

Might the built-in telephone booth still be there beside the reception desk? A walk-in the size of a small pantry for the only public phone in the Salisbury Island officers' mess. Does it still take coins and can one still make reverse-charge calls? Collect calls, predating phone cards, cellphones, text messaging and internet technology. With the door closed you had complete privacy. From there you returned a call from a note left on the message board, with each word in letters formed so perfectly you could believe the note came from a calligrapher's hand. *What is it with these Indians and their perfect handwriting? The huge English vocabulary?* Were those floors also red cement? Do you see young Indian seamen in their blues guiding a Hoover to keep floors like mirrors? On a phalanx of ladders outside, with their elbows opening and closing like windshield wipers, shining windows with crumpled newsprint? Upstairs, the cabin looks down on to the harbor channel. On a quiet night, from your bed you hear the shushing sound from the wake of oil tankers passing by, and by moonlight you see letters indecipherable to a head bound by the Roman alphabet, entering and leaving the harbor channel behind dinky tugboats. You see crews on board; sometimes you wave, offering a casual salute over the short distance, a sign you think is universal at sea. From cabin doors between those of white, mostly English-speaking officers appears occasionally an Indian officer. Dressed in black longs, white shirts and cummerbunds, the base's naval brass along with you and your fellow platoon commanders are served dinner chosen from menus — entrée, main course and dessert — by the Indian seamen who earlier in the day shone up the floors and windows. You try to behave here as you learned was proper in a course manual titled *An Officer and a Gentleman*. You encounter female officers who live in their own section of the mess. From the manual: *Always walk on the traffic side of the pavement in female company*. How were Indian *officers* possible, Rachel wants to know. Kamil: *Dots*, not *feathers*, Mom! Rachel: There were women but I knew no Palestinian in the Israeli army. Malik: They knew better than to let anyone see their faces. You: I've been reading for years so I often can't distinguish what I know now from what I didn't then. Rachel: Most of us know nothing even of the way we write. When you blithely use a word, do you think of a sign with its roots buried deep in Syria and Palestine? You: Indians were brought by the British to South Africa as indentured workers to cut sugar cane. By the time of Reform in 1979 they'd been there for more than a century. Malik: History stirred as sugar into our coffee. You: The president who presided over Peet's graduation had been the *Financial Mail*'s Man of the Year for making a major speech warning whites to 'adapt or die'. A queer comic turned that phrase into adapt or *dye*. By the end of apartheid, sixty percent of the police force was black, so a few Asians in the navy shouldn't surprise you, Rachel. Malik: Complicity and co-option right alongside coercion. The small spaces that are made for people to breathe in any authoritarian system. Kamil, just back from an academic conference in Indonesia: I had a spat with a Malay professor who refused to call Islam homophobic because of the '*deep and authentic fondness*' that exists for some homosexuals in Muslim societies. Like the deep and authentic fondness men feel for the wives they beat, I said, and the deep and authentic fondness white kids feel for their black nannies. She shat her sari at the analogy.

The channels and mangrove marshes that existed on Salisbury Island long ago have partially been filled for railyards, dry docks, oil tanks, factories and the road criss-crossed by a rail track that runs from the city past two huge sugar domes. From here sugar is exported by ship the world over. The navy's ferry runs on the hour to and from the high coconut palms on the esplanade. In the dining room you sit for the first time at a table beside men who have skin tones substantially darker than your own. You begin to look forward to seeing Lieutenant Govender. When he is not there you register something you might concede is disappointment. You and he have had a beer together and played snooker in the officers' bar a few times. He has given you permission to call him by his first name: Sol. He pronounces your name Miegiel. Accompanied by the base's Presbyterian padre and Sonia, a Com-Ops officer, you and Sol drive in his car to a bar in the Maharani Hotel on the Golden Mile. Sonia is recently back from shore leave and a diving vacation in Mauritius. The way she describes what one sees under the ocean is electrifying. She and a friend are planning to save up and travel the world diving: anywhere they can get in, that is, with South African passports. While she speaks, you are wondering whether all Indian men's eyes are moist and dreamy like the eyes of this man from the town of Tongaat. Your two platoon killicks, Reddy and Moonsamy, are Indian too. You share (some) news about Govender and the Indians in your platoon on the phone with Karien.

At night, dressed in browns, it is your task as platoon commander to inspect your troops on their posts and in watchtowers between the silver tanks of the country's precious, dwindling oil reserves. Mindless work, you all agree: your men/boys patrol Restricted Areas for anything suspect, from limpet mines to the unauthorized movement of people or vehicles. Once a month you will take your platoon to a shooting range deep in the sugar cane fields for target practice and to brush up on urban warfare tactics. Your white troops take surprisingly well to their two Indian section leaders' authority. At nineteen you are at least six years younger than your killicks and the same age as your own troops. While keeping your distance – some of these boys were your peers in basics this time last year – you are fair and friendly. The troops, you know all too well, often sleep on duty unless warned by radio of your or the killicks' R-vehicle coming on rounds. Their laxness doesn't bother you: a terrorist attack seems out of the question on a military base that feels like a holiday resort. Your unit OC, a former Selous Scout, has been here since Rhodesia became Zimbabwe. In briefings you hear the acronym ANC from the base commander's lips. The ANC, as far as you know from newspapers and nominally from your own train-ing, is one of the new communist/terrorist groups becoming more popular and dangerous than AZAPO and the Black Consciousness types. Over time you have understood that an important leader is Nelson Mandela, imprisoned on Robben Island for a Moscow-backed conspiracy to overthrow the state. The Black Consciousness types have a hero called Biko-something-or-other. 'An A for his-tory?' Malik raises his eyebrows. You: Their names didn't appear in our textbooks. Malik: More streets on earth are named for Mandela than for any human being living or dead and you want to tell me you heard of him only when you were eighteen? Kamil: Dad, I ask American students what it means when a book is ded-icated to *sixty million and more* and not one – black, white, red or yellow – has a clue. Ask about six million and none *doesn't* know!

Your platoon has a rotating schedule to man a radar tracking station at Umhloti, an hour or so up the North Coast. Taking a lesson from colleagues, you at times fill out inaccurate information on your driving log to account for time during which you have in fact pulled the military's bakkie down a sandy track leading to a deserted beach beyond Umhlanga. Your life here feels like an extended vacation. If you could do follow-up camps here in years to come, what a blast! No danger pay, but every eight weeks the schedule allows you an entire week off. On the long beach you have lain naked on the hot sand, bereft over Peet. You are at a loss about this bottomless grief. You rage against his death and against the man, Leon, who went to breakfast instead of staying with the brother you loved. You can scream here, across the Indian Ocean or into the sand where no one hears. After another time off base with Sol — now without Sonia or the padre — instead of returning to your own cabin you go with him to his. *In the officers' mess!* Kamil exclaims. *If ever anyone was cruisin' for a bruisin' it was you.* Glassman: There was certainly an element of self-destructiveness already, then. You knew what you were doing was against the military — and some people's moral — code. You: It happened as naturally as breathing. It was heaven on earth. Kamil: In my own experience, 'heaven on earth' rarely lasts beyond orgasm. You: I wasn't thinking. Something more basic was at work. Glassman, some months later: And why is it that you could go to bed with the Indian lieutenant *then* and not with the white lieutenant a few weeks earlier at the camp in the desert? I even imagine a blind eye turned more frequently to such things in a war zone. You: You're trying to get me to say it was *because* he was black, or *not* white. You want me to say it was because of the extra thrill or that the risk to me was smaller because as a man of color his word didn't stand a chance against mine, even with my lower rank. Glassman: Perhaps a theory that simple is complex enough to explain why a white man from a constitutionally racist society would have sex with a man of color but not with a white. Kamil, later: An act of shame-based, racist desire, not of simple pleasure. Didn't you think an Indian officer's fall from grace would be much greater than your own? You: I wasn't thinking about anyone's fall from grace. If I had, I wouldn't have gone near him.

In the foyer you happen to scan the bulletin board. There is a message: TO: Ensign Steyn. FROM: Miss Karien Opperman. MESSAGE: Kindly call Miss Opperman A.S.A.P at her Emily Hobhouse residence. TIME OF CALL: 1300 hours. You have only one twenty-cent and one ten-cent coin and the reception desk is unmanned. At this time of day thirty cents will barely allow you to speak. You will call and if the money runs out you can ring back after nine, when rates are considerably lower. Karien herself answers. You can hear she is distraught and when the signal comes you barely have time to write down the private number where you can reach her in a few minutes' time. *Reverse charges*, she says before the phone goes dead. She speaks from the private room of the hostel's primaria, the house committee chairwoman. You have shut the cubicle door behind you. Nine weeks. There is no question of when: date, night and kaross are burned into your memory. You have slid your back down the wall. You sit on the floor with the receiver against your ear. Of course we will get married; it comes from your mouth. No, Michiel, we're too young. We're both still grieving Peet. This is too big a decision to make in the state we're in. But what is the alternative, you ask, perplexed. It is three weeks before your long pass, she says, we can do it then. Do what, you ask. The primaria and her boyfriend went through this in high school, she says. There's a nurse in Botshabelo. Jesus, Karien, you say, oh Jesus no, this is how girls die, we can't do this. It's not a wire coat hanger, Michiel, she's a nurse at the black hospital. She knows what she's doing. *Nee, Kariena, nee, asseblief, nee, moenie dat ons dit aan jou doen nie.* Michiel, we're not throwing our lives away because of one slip. I won't do this to Ounooi and you can't either. We're nineteen. I can pay for you to go overseas, you cry, Peet left me almost four thousand rand. I will come with you, my passport is in the Paradys safe, no one even needs to know we went. Michiel, I don't have a passport and we don't have time enough to wait for one. It's only done up to twelve weeks in England. Let's speak to Oubaas, you hear yourself, he knows people who can expedite a passport. Stop it, Michiel. Stop this right now . . . Once you have quieted down she finds it in herself to joke: Think of what we'll be giving up. Think of the capital G.

Michiel and Kamil stroll by men sunbathing nude on Baker Beach. They clamber across rocks towards the Golden Gate Bridge. This, here, beside the brutal channel – 2.3 million cubic feet of water per second – entering and leaving the bay twice a day is what they do on Sunday afternoons. Other than skiing in winter, it is Kamil's only exercise: he takes BART to Berkeley, doesn't run and cannot countenance the idea of a gym. While others have learned to use the words pecs, triceps, biceps and straight-acting as substitutes for physical and mental health, Kamil's contribution to his own physical well-being in the post touch-and-go days comes from nothing but the drug cocktail and a strict organically grown vegetarian diet. Kamil: She could have died. Do you think she might have known, in some way, that you and Peet were both gay? Michiel: The woman in whose room I called her knew the nurse and it had gone safely for her. Kamil: Still, a backstreet abortion. So reckless; a bit like Peet. Death rather than shame. And the layers of our complicity are breathtaking. Malik had a thing for a whole year with my Grade Six teacher, Miss Candles. We pretended it wasn't happening. Miss Candles gave me the best grades. Did your old man have affairs? Michiel: Thank god for small mercies, not as far as I know. Kamil: Then where did you get it from? Michiel: Christ, Kamil! That's how many years ago; why now? Kamil: I'm sorry. (A long pause as they clamber on, the waves rushing over the rocks, the orange-vermilion of the bridge now almost above them. 'Homosexual orange', Kamil terms it.) What do you say we have make-up sex on the sand? For you it will be like old times, Mike! Take back the beach! A healing moment! We'll give those tourists up there a big city welcome. Michiel, shaking his head, muttering: Fuck off, Kamil. Kamil bends to pick up a piece of driftwood as a tanker horn booms, the ship entering from somewhere across the Pacific, its name in Arabic script. *Khaliya Safin*, Kamil reads. Come, he goes on, we'll draw a line in the sand. Right here. It's all in the past. Done. Over.

The front pew makes way for the pall bearers. Passing his father, Michiel squeezes the old man's leg and meets the bereft gaze with tears dangling from the lashes like crystals. From the hands doddering in the lap, Michiel takes the handkerchief and wipes his father's cheeks and nose. He places the clammy wet cloth back in the terrible hands, folding the fingers closed with his own. It is when he straightens up to take his first step towards the coffin that he, without thinking, looks up. Half-turned on the organ bench, she is looking down over her shoulder. He does not avert his eyes, but when he tries to return her smile he feels his face contort and has to look down.

They lift the coffin from its bed. The pressure on Michiel's shoulder is no more than that of a light plank box. Like a single-layered container of tomatoes. With the smell of pine and honeysuckle in his nose, his gaze goes to his brother's shoes that direct their pace. The coffin is guided into the hearse by undertakers in black suits while the bearers return to where Bianca waits with Oubaas, alongside Alida and Mamparra, with Dominee Dirk in the arch.

First out are the Paradys workers. The women have recovered their groceries and some men have bags of mielie-meal or rice over one shoulder. They shake hands with Dominee Dirk then stop to greet and express condolences to Oubaas. To Ounooi's sons: 'Thank you, Kleinbaas Benjamin.' 'So good you came, Kleinbaas Michiel.' 'Welcome back, Kleinbaas.' 'Ounooi said it was a very big place there where you live now.' And to Giselle: 'We're so sorry, Nooi.' 'Ounooi was so proud to have Madam in the family.' Nods along with the designation 'Kleinbasie' for Thomas. 'Kleinnooi' for Bianca.

The first to speak to Alida is the mayor. To Michiel, introduced by Benjamin, he says: 'Sam Thabane. Glad to meet you. This is my wife, Sharon. Beth enjoyed her visit with you in the States. Welcome back.'

'What you said about her was moving,' Michiel replies, their hands still clasped. 'You were very generous.'

'She was a pillar of the community,' from the white woman at Sam Thabane's side. When Thabane takes hold of Benjamin's hand Michiel notices an extra movement in the handshake. Palms and fingers join, followed by an additional grasp about the wrist, then again back to the meeting palms. He notices the gesture repeated when Thabane greets young Thomas, and again with the Paradys workers congregated at the end of the line where they excitedly wait to shake their mayor's hand.

Many of those passing by Michiel knows or remembers from boyhood and youth. He is grateful for the long line that makes only cursory greeting and condolence possible. Aunts, cousins, second cousins, women and men who were children at school with him and his brothers. Here and there a name forgotten; all kind; pleased to see him or able to hide the fact that they are not. Members of the Free State Agricultural Union. Oubaas's old golfing buddies. Then there is Obie Oberholzer, from Diepfontein, whom Michiel almost doesn't recognize, with his wife and children, all blond-haired and brown-eyed, all oddly pink and obese. Had Michiel come across Obie anywhere else he might have walked right by the fat man he'd once thought an above-average looker. 'I'm so sorry about Ounooi.' And Michiel's response: 'She told me about your parents. One is grateful that my mother could go the way she did.' Obie nods and squeezes Michiel's hand before he and the pod of albino hippopotami move on. There are people from the township. Women from there who say, 'It is nice to meet you,

Michiel. Beth told us all about her trip to America.' Members of the Women's Auxiliary of the Anglican Church where Ounooi was a member. Of the ANC Women's League ('Beth wasn't a member, but a bridge between us'), teachers, a retired school principal from Michiel's days at Generaal Reitz High: 'Nee, kêrel, jy lyk perdfris daar uit Amerika!' Well, lad, you're the picture of health from there in America. The longer the line lasts, the less gravity there is to the interactions. It is a less white affair than he'd anticipated. He is greeted by youth and elders from the AAC, the AIDS Action Committee, one explains, and with a thumbs-up says 'sharp sharp' to Michiel before moving on. Lerato has gone down on her haunches to speak to Oubaas. She and the kids are near the end of the line, now consisting mostly of choir members. Inside the organ continues, unbroken: playing one last time for the woman she idolized. Then the forgotten caboose: Gerda Niehaus and Constable Opperman. When the mother's eyes meet Michiel's the coldness she wishes him to see is underscored by the white lines around her compressed lips. 'Tannie——' is all he manages before she has extracted her hand and moved to Benjamin, who is already greeting her ex-husband. Constable Opperman has stepped around Gerda to evade even eye contact with his daughter's betrayer.

Workers are piling back on to the trailer. Cars drive off.

It is now Dirk who comes to him. There is only a hint of awkwardness when their hands meet. 'Benjamin tells me you're here only till tomorrow.'

'Unfortunately I have to get back to work.' Michiel cannot bring himself to utter any of the recently repeated pleasantries.

'I must see to the locking up,' Dirk says, sensing the discomfort. 'We'll be on the farm. We're staying for dinner.' And then, before he turns to re-enter the church, 'Karien is looking forward to seeing you. If you'd like to wait a moment, I'll ask her to come and say hello.' Michiel nods.

Oubaas is leaving with Benjamin and Thomas. The boy wheels

the chair to the slick silver Mercedes-Benz. There, Michiel thinks, go the last three generations that will have it like this. Benjamin opens the car door and Oubaas's arm goes around Thomas's neck. When the old man lifts himself Michiel's own body braces as if he rather than his nephew is taking the old man's weight, helping him into the comfortable front seat.

Mamparra has not joined the trailer and is to travel with Michiel and Alida. He feels a child's hand slip into his. Bianca. Her eyes are shy, belying the guileless gesture of taking his hand. 'I'm coming with you,' she says. From the parking lot he hears his name called. It is Lerato, speaking through her car's open window.

'Is it all right if this one comes with you?' She points to Kanu leaning across from the seat beside her.

'Come, Kanu.'

'Gogo,' Lerato calls to Alida at Michiel's side, 'why don't you two come with me? Leave Michiel with his fans.'

Mamparra and Alida, approaching the Volvo, have to step off the pathway as Kanu charges by.

'Kanu!' Lerato stops the boy in his tracks. 'Do you want a hiding now or later? Come back to this car!'

The boy nods, returns to the car with pursed lips. He shuts the door he left ajar, before dashing back to Michiel and Bianca.

The only person Michiel has been waiting to see has appeared from the foyer. He sees her in the arched doorway. He passes the keys to one of the children and asks them to wait in the car. 'You better come soon,' Kanu quips, 'or else we're taking this skedonk for a spin.' The boy's mischief lingers as Michiel and Karien face each other with a dozen paces between them. Before either can speak, Benjamin's voice reaches them from the parking lot. The hearse is ready and waiting. Michiel asks his brother to go ahead. He will catch up at the tail. 'It will be slow going anyway,' Benjamin answers, 'we'll have the tractor and trailer to take into account. They're part of it.'

'Dirk will be out in a minute, Benjamin,' Karien calls from the arched doorway. 'He's closing up with the kids.' That is how Michiel hears her voice. An ordinary phrase to smooth the day's events. Then, to him, she says: 'The church can no longer afford a beadle.'

Here she is. *Through everything.* She raises her chin and walks closer, as does he. Her gaze is direct, a smile at her lips.

'Did you recognize the Beethoven?'

He nods and asks: 'May I give you a hug?'

'You never asked permission before. No need to in our middle age.' Their arms go around each other. 'You are the best hugger,' she says into his ear. 'Always were, you bugger.' Her laughter moves her body against his and he presses her tightly to him.

'Age sits well with you, Karien,' he says once they have let go of each other. The sides of her green eyes are lined by laughter, time and sun. How stunning the resemblance now to the beauty who a moment ago took and let go of his hand as if she were touching shit.

'I was looking down on your head from the balcony.' She steps back, reaches out, sweeps over the buzz cut.

'Better than a comb-over,' he says as a child's voice calls to her from inside the church.

'I must go. I'll see you at Paradys.'

'Thank you.'

She turns, then stops. Across her shoulder she asks, 'For what?'

For your kindness, for trying to make light of this. 'For the String Quartet,' he says. He sees the smile line around her mouth, the crinkle in her cheek.

With her back still to him he hears, 'Which number?'

'Fifteen. Opus one hundred and thirty-two.'

'Thirteen. Hundred and thirty-three.'

'No, Karien,' he smiles. 'It was not.'

She nods, pauses, and he sees the back of her long neck extend as she drops her head before stepping off. For an instant, and only from behind, one might think she was Ounooi, as a younger woman.

Kanu is behind the wheel, with Bianca in the passenger seat. An argument is underway about who is to sit beside the driver. The boy has made a strategic mistake and must now try to get the girl into the back. Michiel suggests she stay put till they get to the Paradys turn-off and then change places with Kanu. At the edge of the parking lot they wait for street traffic to pass. Kanu asks that the radio be turned on for music.

'It's a funeral,' Bianca protests.

'So?' Kanu asks. 'Mom says the goddess says life goes on.'

'We'll turn it on softly,' Michiel suggests.

'What goddess?' Bianca asks, turning in her seat to face Kanu.

'Mom says the goddess is who sees to *everything*. Dad says it's Halle Berry.'

'What nonsense!' Bianca exclaims, turning back to face forward. 'Isn't it nonsense, Michiel?'

'Well . . .' he says, staring in the rearview mirror at the church's sandstone walls and bell tower. There is a clock up there he doesn't remember from before, though he has heard it chime, even today. He finds the building beautiful, in spite of itself. Is he mistaken in thinking the architecture Romanesque? Or is it Gothic? 'Well,' he says again as he turns out into the street, 'there are a thousand and one ways to look at it.'

From the gloom of wind, cloud and thunder, with slivers of blue, the sky had spread its wings massively. Now there was only piffling yellow rain against the sunset: Jakkals trou met wolf se vrou — Jackal is marrying wolf's wife. In North America he has heard *the devil is beating his wife.*

From the canopy of oaks workers wandered up the hill and the family returned home through the orchard. He went to the dam followed by Isabella and Grootman. The dogs had hovered at the graveside, heads cocked as the casket went in. When the first sods hit the planks Isabella lay down, her eyes moving between the assembled people and the gaping ground. Grootman scurried through the shovelers' legs, getting in the way, yelping. Had they found her scent, Michiel wondered, through the pine.

Call now if u can. All well. Love, M. With one arm on the wall and the phone to his ear he heard Kamil's voice, clear, as if from only farther up the hill.

'I put your card with the dollar on the casket.'

'I miss you.'

'Me you too.'

'I have to teach in a sec. Glassman can see you on Thursday. And Friday, to make up for next week. Can you give me a thumbnail?'

'I'll tell you when I'm back. It's a funeral, so not the time for settling scores. The old man's very ill, more than Mom let on.'

'Have you seen Karien?'

'We spoke briefly after the service. Her son sang in church. Everyone's here for dinner.'

'Speaking of kids, you up for a snippet of domestic news?'

'What's wrong?'

'Tiny mishap this side of the Atlantic.' Kamil's little laugh. 'America called a few minutes ago to say she knocked the tank over. La Creatura Felice is loose in the apartment and America's too scared to vacuum for fear of sucking her up.'

'Tell her to latch the windows. She should stop up the front door and the balcony sliding doors with towels. Is the tank broken?'

'Yeah. I told her to do the laundry and the dusting. She can go early. Listen, I must run. Can I call when I get home?'

'Pretty soon I'll feel the time difference. For now I'm still running on adrenaline. I'll text you if I don't take a pill and crash early.'

'I'm thinking of you.'

He remained for a while at the dam, under the darkening sky, before strolling back through the quiet with the dogs for company. Outside the rondavel he came across Lerato.

'You don't want to eat with us?'

She rolled her eyes. 'We tried a few times. Between the old man wondering into whose eye to plunge his fork and my mom's discomfort, it's too tiresome.'

She is leaving in the early hours of the morning. Their goodbyes were made along with vague undertakings, prodded from Kanu, of skiing in Tahoe. Michiel will miss the boy's energetic provocations. On the stoep he spoke with Dirk and Benjamin while the kids were being herded to bathrooms to wash hands for dinner.

Gusts chase and collide in lace at the open sliding doors. Ten places at the long yellowwood table set with Ounooi's white Artzberg. Giselle and Karien help Alida arrange dishes on the sideboard where hot-trays keep food and plates warm. From the kitchen, over the sound of the oven door and the clank of pots, comes Mamparra humming the *Pie Jesu*.

The table the first Oubaas Steyn wanted in here was too large to fit through the doorway. Using Knysna yellowwood a master carpenter built it inside the dining room, never again to leave in one piece: till Ounooi's sliding doors came. How long before the heirlooms go, and to whom? Or will they stay, with the farm, if the place is sold? There is room for six places on either side of the table and one more at each end. The second Oubaas had a smaller family, the current being the eldest and only son. With Ounooi and his three boys they were five: Oubaas at the head, where he sits now, in the wheelchair. To his left were Ounooi and Michiel. On his right, Peet and Benjamin. The seating changed when Peet went to university, then again with Benjamin in the army, Michiel in the navy. Once her boys were gone Ounooi relented and agreed that Oubaas could watch TV while they ate dinner – from trays, neatly laid by Alida with blue tray cloths and white damask napkins: *my last stand against our complete descent into savagery.*

'It's easiest if we take each child's plate and dish up here,' says Karien. 'You all stay where you are.' Met with a chorus of 'I want' and 'I don't want funeral rice' and 'Alida made soetpatats just for me,' and 'I'm not *touching* that spinach'.

'Quiet!' Both Giselle's palms are raised. 'We'll take orders so no child goes to bed starving. Or, god forbid, has her plate soiled by this nutritious creamed spinach Alida spent half the day preparing for your ungrateful mouths.' A stern look is cast at Bianca, beside Michiel.

'I'm not having any of that either,' Michiel whispers to the child with her hands steepled over her nose.

Plates pass between the women at the sideboard. Loud drops thud on the tin roof, then stop.

'I wish the rain would make up its mind,' Bianca mutters.

'Oupa says there's one heck of a storm brewing.' Thomas, to Oubaas's right, has been glued to the old man ever since they left church. When Michiel meets his nephew's eyes, the gaze beneath the streak of white hair is quickly averted.

Beside Thomas sits Thabiso. Adopted as a toddler, he is near the same age and height as Thomas. 'His father died while his mother was pregnant with him. She worked in the manse from before I arrived,' Dirk told Michiel while they waited for dinner. 'When she passed away the laws had already changed and we could formally adopt.' Those were the early days of the plague, he said. Last weekend he attended or led twenty-three funeral services. And those are only the adults. Children are frequently buried during the week.

Next to Thabiso is Karien's place and then, elevated on living-room cushions beside Dirk, is little Palesa. Her fingers are splayed on either side of her place setting, her lips puckered and her eyes, full of anticipation, on Karien at the sideboard. 'We fetched her from Bloem when she was three weeks old. We didn't want to adopt from here again. How do we explain choosing one child over

another to the community? Karien carried her in a sling against her
chest for the first six months.'

'Alida, what about Lerato and her two?'

'You take first, Kleinnooi Karien. Then Alida will dish for the
rest.' A servant's sentence spewing meaning as much from the form
of address as from the omitted personal pronoun. But then would
the hierarchy not remain intact even if Alida had it in her to say: *Go
ahead, Karien. Once the guests have been served I will dish up for myself, my
daughter and my grandchildren?*

'The rain is near,' Karien objects. 'Let's do it now so you don't
have to get wet carrying it over.'

Michiel looks to Oubaas, then Benjamin. He sees the quick raise
of Dirk's eyebrows, the near-wink: *This is not my house. Not my place to
comment.* Here we all are, then, Michiel thinks, and she who soon
will sit on the board of Anglo American Corporation is out there.
How does she tolerate setting foot on this farm? How, over time,
was the current order arrived at and at which point in her climb up
the corporate ladder was she allowed from the kaya into the rondavel? There Benjamin sits without uttering a peep. The
machinations of transition, even on this one plot of earth, are stu-
pefying. Here sit two dark-brown children: unthinkable before,
unless invited to the kitchen as the white boys' pre-adolescent
playmates. Little-Alida, Lerato, did homework and extra English
lessons there too. No, my love, I *gouw* to *bed.* Give Ounooi a nice
long *go* and a nice long *bed,* not I *goh* to *bid.* Think of yourself as the
princess in *The Princess and the Pea.* Close enough in age to be companions to one another, the Steyn brothers seldom developed the
intimate companionship that could exist between black and white
children on farms until puberty turned black to labor and white to
Kleinbaas and Kleinnooi. Why did Ounooi, governed by class
more than race, as she eventually seemed, not stamp out this abomination when her little black princess began earning more money in
a year than Paradys has made during all the years of his absence?

Christ, she and her husband can probably pay cash for this whole set-up.

The drops begin to sound like the rain is settling in.

They hear Lerato in the kitchen. Kanu, a moment ahead of his mother and sister, appears in the dining-room doorway and goes at once to Michiel's side. They have come to help carry out plates ahead of what looks to be a cloudburst. From the roof comes a volley of thuds, a racket of blows.

'Hail.'

'Hail!'

'The cars—'

'Ben, the—'

The heavens open. Both dogs have darted in to shelter beneath the table. Eyes go to the ceiling and the doors, where the lace curtains bulge. Hands to their ears, children look to their parents. Kanu is somehow back beside his mother; both twins are clinging to Lerato, her mouth agape. All sound but the clatter from the corrugated iron roof is erased. Palesa screams soundlessly up into Dirk's face as he lifts her on to his lap. The noise is deafening. Michiel's arm goes around Bianca, draws her against him as mouths open and close as if in a silent movie. Giselle is behind Michiel, her hands sliding down her daughter's head, covering the girl's ears. Karien has stepped from the sideboard to behind her chair, one hand on Thabiso's neck, the other between Palesa's tiny shoulderblades.

Oubaas sits with his head bowed, as if in prayer.

Inconceivably the volume is notched up. The corner of Thomas's mouth twitches as he sends a grin to his mother. Karien bends, her lips against Palesa's ear: *hail my love*, Michiel reads her lips, *Mamma and Pappa are here, it's okay*, stroking the little head welded to her father's chest. Lightning flashes. A white stone ricochets across the table and a glass shatters unheard. Someone points to a hole in the windowpane. A bolt and whip; bright orange flares from the stoep. When Benjamin and Michiel shut the doors they see the top of a jacaranda in flames. A massive branch crashes, taking the fence with it. Thomas and Thabiso are now also at the window, their eyes aflicker from the inferno devouring the top half of the tree.

Slowly, over a minute or two, the noise lifts. Astonished, everyone remains where they are. The dining room smells of smoke. When it seems that the last stones have clattered from the roof they gather at the sliding doors, eyes riveted on the dying flames.

'The food is getting cold.' Oubaas sits alone at the far end of the table.

'Should Michiel and I check the damage, Oubaas?'

'Let's eat first,' the old man mutters, defeated. 'Don't let good food go to waste is what Beth Ford says.'

'Lerato?' Karien's open palm offers places at the table.

'What else is one to do after that? Find a place, kids.'

'That was something else.'

'The poor tree.'

'What happened?'

'Lightning, my love.'

'Will the tree die, like Grandma?'

'After dinner we'll take torches and go and look at what happened.'

Four more place settings are prepared. Drawers and cabinets slide open for knives and forks and napkins. Plates. Water glasses. A wine glass for Lerato. At last they're seated: Kanu between Michiel and Alida, Pulane beside Dirk. From the end of the table Lerato faces Oubaas. Dirk is about to say grace when the *Pie Jesu* comes again from the kitchen. Michiel and Lerato's eyes meet. They both look at Karien.

'Die hemel help ons,' says Oubaas. 'Is daai een *ook* nog hier?' Heaven help us, is that one *also* still here?

Pushing back her own chair, Karien dispatches Thabiso to bring an extra one from Ounooi's desk. They hear Karien in the kitchen: 'Kom, Mamparra, kom eet saam met ons.'

'Karien,' Dirk calls, 'please bring a plastic cup for Palesa.'

'I'm famished! Are we *ever* going to eat?'

'Bianca,' Giselle says, raising an eyebrow at her daughter, 'this is a most unladylike performance. We've spoken about this how many times? I want you to center, my girl.' She lays her hands on her own chest, inhales deeply and, still gazing at the child, says, 'Do you want me to guide you through some breathing exercises?'

'No, Mommy.'

Under the table, Michiel squeezes Bianca's knee.

Lerato clears space at her end of the table so Alida can lay an additional place.

Mamparra enters the dining room with a dishcloth over her shoulder, the red hat still on her head. She nods at Oubaas, looks around and folds the dishcloth as Thabiso arrives with the extra chair.

'Let's put your hat here on the sideboard,' Karien offers.

Mamparra sits down with the dishcloth in her lap. She smoothes down her blouse and smiles nervously at the children. Lerato takes the dishcloth and places it on the sideboard, with the red hat perched like a surrealist tortoise beside the hot-tray. She slides the napkin from under Mamparra's fork and unfolds it, smiles and lays it on her lap.

Oubaas's jaw is set; his eyes a smoky blue on the table

Karien winks at Michiel. Unbelievable, I know: Ounooi, are you here, rather than on the other side of your orchard, to witness this? Face to face, side by side, yesterday today and tomorrow. They bow their heads for Dirk to say grace as the rain at last starts coming down on the roof.

When did the hurricane hit London? September, October? He was attending night classes at the university. Hadn't had a haircut or shaved in months, so the face in the mirror above the small wash-basin was almost foreign to him. 'You could get rid of this,' one of the men said from the pillow beside him, tugging at the beard and ruffling the stringy fringe. 'Styles here are different from the provinces.' Soon he was able to soften his accent: no mistaking him for a conscript AWOL from the SADF. Answering the switch-board or checking in guests, he practiced what he thought was a London accent. He read and listened to the BBC and never dropped his aitches. When he brought back native Londoners from the West Heath he kept them talking before getting down to the other business at hand. If they obliged he repeated key phrases and asked for feedback. Once the visitor had left he wrote things down in his own phonetic script. Accents from Jamaica, Ghana and Senegal were of little use to him, though those who had them were his most frequent guests.

He went to another lecture at the Commonwealth Institute; if the woman was there, he'd return the book. From the brochure he knew the speakers would be South African academics and mem-bers of the African National Congress. The theme was *The Freedom Charter in a Future South Africa*. The document was unknown to him and it would be the first time he would knowingly rub shoulders with members of the banned organization. The place would also be crawling with South African intelligence operatives. He would listen and get out. Each chair had on it – in the outlawed green, yellow and black – a double-sided Xerox of the document. *We, the people of South Africa,* he read while waiting, *declare for all our country and the world to know: That South Africa belongs to all who live in it, black and white, and that no government can justly claim authority unless it is based on the will of the people; That our people have been robbed of their birthright to land, liberty and peace by a form of government founded on injustice and inequality.* The book woman was on the panel as a dignitary of the ANC Women's League. *This*, then, was the auntie handing out books on the Underground to naive Afrikaner boys spending their 'gap year' in

London: part, surely, of a carefully orchestrated campaign. Not disinformation – he believed every word of Plaatje's account – but a propaganda tactic nonetheless: slip testimony of black suffering into white hands and *voilà!* Another useful idiot waving banners at South Africa House, he sneered to himself.

The first speaker was introduced as an historian, banned from Fort Hare University. 'It begins way back,' the man said, 'when we walked out of the Great Rift Valley on two legs and a few of us strode into Europe and along the way turned white. But, like all history, that path is winding and too vast to cover in fifteen minutes. I'll start closer to where we are today.' He spoke in a soft voice and language almost poetic: in the face of extraordinary repression numerous organizations came together to draw up a document that would give voice to the dream of a united, democratic and just South Africa. 'The first meeting took place in 1954, in the little town of Tongaat.' For a moment he was thrown back as the town's name leapt at him. Hairs on his arms and the back of his neck bristled. He felt blood rush to his face. 'From there delegates fanned out across the length and breadth of the country to consult and to reconvene a year later for the process to be consolidated.' The state passed the Suppression of Communism Act, making illegal all activity aimed at the overthrow of the unjust system. Activists, lawyers, academics and trade unionists were arrested. Most organizations were declared criminal, their leaders and members banished or imprisoned. 'But even as our organizations remain banned,' the exile concluded in his gentle voice, 'as our members are kept under house arrest, gagged, and our leaders languish in prison, the Charter remains a guiding document for the country we envision.'

The People Shall Govern!
All National Groups Shall have Equal Rights!
The People Shall Share in the Country's Wealth!
The Land Shall be Shared Among Those Who Work it!

All Shall be Equal Before the Law!
All Shall Enjoy Equal Human Rights!
There Shall be Work and Security!
The Doors of Learning and Culture Shall be Opened!
There Shall be Houses, Security and Comfort!
There Shall be Peace and Friendship!
These freedoms we will fight for, side by side, throughout our lives,
until we have won our liberty

There was nothing feigned to Michiel's applause. After this came inputs on the Charter's specifics: the economy, a future constitution, women's rights (delivered by the woman of the book), education and culture. In a future such as this — although even its beginnings would be unrealizable in his lifetime — Michiel *could* picture himself. For the first time in months he was back, if not at Paradys, then at least somewhere else in that country. Was this outlawed organization, this *movement*, something he could belong to? Discussion and questions from the floor followed: What does 'sharing in the country's wealth' mean? Are we talking nationalization of the mines? Answer: Yes, nationalization, but in a manner conducive to investor trust. Question: Something akin to the UK, before privatization? Answer: Something like that. Question: All Africa's liberation movements have been supported by the Soviets. Do you see a one-party socialist system for yourselves? Answer: This is an issue for negotiation, none of which can happen while our leaders are imprisoned and the State of Emergency gives the apartheid state carte blanche in its campaign of terror against the forces of democracy. Question: I'm hearing mixed economy and the possibility of multi-party democracy? Answer: The present situation is untenable given the vast capital sums leaving the country instead of being redeployed to enhance people's lives. We need directed state intervention in the economy, education, housing and job creation to level the playing field. Question: Is the movement

130

concerned about perestroika and glasnost? What of Reaganomics and Thatcherism? Answer: When Afrikaners came to power their people had been impoverished by decades of government indifference. A program of state protectionism was developed to alleviate what they called the 'poor white problem'. This meant labor policies of capitalism for blacks and socialist protection for whites, in particular Afrikaners. Jobs were reserved for white Afrikaners; universities and teachers' training colleges opened their doors even to unqualified students; land was made available to white farmers through state subsidies and bank loans. If we look at Roosevelt's New Deal, we can see that in the USA, too, the problem of poverty and unemployment could not be solved without the state. No future government in South Africa — a country with a non-existent black middle class, no substantially educated elite, no sufficient infrastructure to provide housing, no police force to tend to the majority's needs, a healthcare system skewed against black well-being — will be able to transform society unless we take for ourselves the very policies that Americans and Afrikaners have used themselves. Question: How will the education system change? Answer: At present every white child has his education subsidized four times more than a black child. We will also have to look closely at the content of curricula, at how history is taught, at education's relevance to the needs of our times, at what values of community and accountability we wish our children to embrace. Question: How will you ensure women's rights? Answer, from the book woman: In other liberation struggles women were promised a voice, only to find themselves the day the struggle ended back, pregnant and barefoot, in the kitchen. Our movement has been mindful of issues around gender equity and we've taken lessons from other areas of the world. Our National Executive Committee comprises at least one-third women and it is a continuing debate whether some measure like this may be enshrined in all of our structures. Within South Africa, the United Democratic

Front and the trade union movement have excellent representation of women in leadership positions. The Freedom Charter clearly states *the rights of the people shall be the same, regardless of race, color or sex.* Women are the poorest of the poor and subject to triple oppression as blacks, as women and as workers. The migrant labor system on the mines places the brunt of child rearing, health, nutrition, education and discipline on black urban and rural women: it is an untenable situation and our entire future depends on how we will empower the mothers of the nation. Question: How does the movement view the question of gay and lesbian rights? Heads turn. He hears an Australian accent but cannot bring himself to look round. Answer, again, from the book woman: Gay men and lesbians are jumping on the back of the democratic movement and exploiting the struggle for their own ends. I don't see them homeless or hungry or suffering. Where does this business come from? It's very fashionable over here in the West. It will disappear along with colonialism and racism. We haven't heard of this problem in Africa until recently. In a liberated South Africa people will be normal. Tell me, are lesbians and gays normal? If everyone was like that the human race would die out.

Of what followed from the panel he heard little. Afterwards, the book woman was involved in heated discussion with white women and a young man with the blond look of a surfer. Michiel placed the book on the table and, catching the woman's eye, pointed and waved his thanks. Send a mule traveling the world, it still won't come back a horse. Let them stew in their hateful white and black fat, together. May that country burn with all of you in it. He never returned to anything hinting at South Africa; changed direction when the accent found him on the street, in bars and on Hampstead Heath.

He enrolled for a full load of classes. Requesting additional shifts, he remained mostly at reception, reading and writing papers. In class he rarely spoke. He lost count of the visitors to his room and the homes he fleetingly entered. With half a degree and an ESL teacher's qualification he lived with a steadfast headache certainly caused by the ungodly climate. With what little savings he had he took two weeks off and raced through France, Spain, Greece and Turkey. When one more summer departed before it had arrived he packed up and sold his books on Charing Cross Road. He booked a round-trip ticket to Australia and promised his employer he'd be back by the end of the month. On the plane he read Edmund White's *A Boy's Own Story* and believed his life changed for ever. Within weeks of arriving in Sydney he was in a relationship with a lawyer who offered *pro amico* legal aid to secure Australian citizenship. The application was based on what eventuality could befall him were he to return to South Africa. While Asians waited in backed-up lines for citizenship he was fast-tracked. He ate like a king for the first time since Salisbury Island, was wined and dined on the Gold Coast where, holidaying with the lawyer, he learned to dive. Even before he got his papers the lawyer found him in bed with a Samoan fisherman.

'You used me for the immigration thing.'

'I was — am — in love with you. I give you my word.'

'You haven't a clue what that means, mate. You don't own much but you'll need the big suitcase for all the crap in your head. Pack up and ship out.' Dropping *Giovanni's Room* on the coffee table in front of Michiel, he said, 'Lock the house key inside and call me once you discern your arse from your elbow.'

He found a crummy flatshare off Oxford Street. Could afford nothing he didn't need. He stuck to the phoney London accent. With new papers in hand he got a job as the maître d' at Luca's, an upmarket Italian restaurant with a view of the Opera House — as long as you keep that hair tied and trim an inch off the beard. He enrolled at the University of Sydney. The Berlin Wall came down. He saw pictures on the front page of the *Morning Herald* and other papers announcing *Mandela Walks Free*. At Luca's, growing

numbers of white South Africans were arriving for dinner. When on occasion his accent was questioned – even as he evaded intimacy with others like the plague – he offered the new South African traveler and émigré's stock phrase: *I left because I couldn't abide that terrible system.* No one, ever, black or white, had supported, been complicit in or privileged by apartheid or any other kind of exploitation. By its own magnificent volition, a system existed without human agency. South Africans he bumped into overseas seemed to believe that they had, one and all, slipped from their mothers' wombs with cries of *Amandla!* And their mothers had answered *Ngawethu!*

Sydney's students marched in their thousands against George Bush's pending invasion of Kuwait and Australian support of the war. On TV, a nurse from Kuwait City Hospital testified to Saddam Hussein's soldiers removing babies from incubators and leaving them to die. In class he kept his head down and completed his degree. As if out to prove the worthlessness and inherent futility of all education, reading and lived experience, no other student, ever, from anywhere in the world, had changed world views or shifted allegiances. No one had been wrong. Everyone had been born the way they are: if not progressive, then certainly liberal or open-minded. No one, ever, had been racist. No one, ever, sexist. Homophobic? Oh, for god's sake, my best friend is gay! Heterosexist? I don't know what you mean! But no, I've never been that either. A world chained and unchanging. As no one, ever, had been offside, it was best – easiest – to live as if he, too, hadn't. After graduation he took time off and returned to the Great Barrier Reef. By the time he got back to Sydney the war was over and Kuwait free of Hussein's forces. Another time, he backpacked through the outback. He camped in early winter beneath a grove of baobabs. From his sleeping bag he could look up into the trees' podded branches while he read *The Songlines* by Chatwin and *Voss* by Patrick White and *Waiting for the Barbarians* by Coetzee. From a campsite a short way from his, voices of men carried a mournful tune, over and over. He walked closer and stood at a distance from them, listening to the lyrics of 'And the Band Played Waltzing Matilda'. Nostalgia brought voices and faces to him from the land whence this one had drifted, taking roots and seeds and trees along as it inched off, becoming a continent apart.

Yet another fling begun with promise had gone sour, when he saw an ad for an experimental ESL job in a far-flung province of the Solomon Islands. The job was funded by do-good Australians and entailed teaching primary school children foundational English to counter the Pacific Islands' prevailing orthodoxy that Pidgin can get you anywhere in life. He applied even before consulting a map to find the scattered dots below Papua New Guinea. Hundreds of islands with white sand and coconut palms along turquoise lagoons. Pidgin the lingua franca with tourism actively discouraged. Timber the main export. A constitutional monarchy with Queen Elizabeth the ceremonial head of state. He would get lousy pay, but a house to live in as well as a return ticket. The diving was the best in the world, with an ocean littered by wreckage from the Second World War. He had the prerequisite citizenship, the degree and the diploma. In the interview he lied about two years of teaching English to youths in the townships of South Africa. 'The Solomons have the highest malaria death rate in the world,' they informed him. 'I know all about malaria,' he answered, shoveling back the invasion of Almeida's lips, a woman's face distorted and language lost over a tub.

He had a month left at Luca's and had already started taking chloroquin. One of his lecturers came in for dinner with colleagues. Michiel was introduced as a former student — 'one of the better ones, he could be writing a dissertation . . .' — and invited for drinks. The group returned a few more times, with among them a visiting lecturer from North America. Little about the short, curly-haired Canadian teaching post-colonial literature for a year in Sydney appealed to Michiel. Skinny, over-opinionated, pretentiously polishing his glasses as he held forth: dark-haired, olive-skinned and hairy. His assertive phrasing seemed to contain a theory of

everything. Over-confident, forbidding and camp. A member of
Act Up, sympathizer of Queer Nation and a recent PhD from
Stanford, Kamil made sure everyone knew he was on his way to a
postdoc at Berkeley. He had an answer to everything, from how
Luca's could ensure authentic al dente pasta to how the southern
tip of Africa would ultimately serve as a blueprint for Israel and
'Occupied Palestine'. *One Person One Vote in a Unified Israel–Palestine.*
If the blacks didn't murder the whites, why would the Arabs do
in the Jews? He was the son of a Palestinian father and a Jewish
mother, communists forced from their homeland. He loathed 'the
discourses' of Zionism (yesterday's victims, today's oppressors)
only marginally more than he distrusted Palestinian nationalism
(today's victims, tomorrow's oppressors) and disdained socialism
(zero ability to self-reflect or introspect) and despised capitalism
(a constantly adapting recipe to devour the world). Even among
professors nearing retirement, Kamil held court. He had a way
of anticipating or summarizing conversation and then moving
in with a premature knockout. When talk turned to Australia's
exploitation of aboriginal people, Michiel, in a rare contribution, referred to racial capitalism as 'false consciousness'. The
Canadian, in a mix of sarcasm and flirtation, responded: 'How
intriguing! You must educate me on the nature of *true* consciousness.' After a giggle and an arching of the bushy eyebrows, 'You
should write a book about this *true consciousness.* I doubt the text
exists in any of the world's great libraries. Could it have been
destroyed in the great fire at Alexandria?' Which delighted the
academics and provided impetus for Michiel to plead exhaustion
and say an early goodnight.

Kamil came back on consecutive nights and hovered till closing
time. They went home together: *All gay men do it with each other at least
once.* Kamil: What do lesbians bring on the second date? *A furniture
van.* And what do gay men bring on the second date? *What's a second
date?* And the following night, again, even though Michiel had

found the sex little more than tolerable. Years later, straining to squeeze the words like a confession from his throat, he would say: *too effeminate, too gay, not straight-acting enough, dick too small, not muscular enough; too obvious and oblivious of it.* Glassman: 'Like looking in a mirror?' Simultaneously attracted and repelled, Michiel allowed himself to be drawn in. In Kamil's presence it seemed no word was unheard and nothing made easy. Michiel recognized the feeling of threat, as he had often before: an instinct to flee while wishing the core of it to continue. Glassman: In cases where you weren't about to leave, you'd been a saboteur. Michiel: His eyes made me feel alive. I was like a sponge, listening to him. When I met his family I understood more. At their table, both the health benefits of salt and the hole in the ozone layer have led to family vacations being terminated midway. Two years of silence between Kamil and Nawal flowed from Kamil's refusal, once, to take Nawal's son along skiing when he'd wished to spend time alone with his sister 'outside the ambush of children'. 'Shande! You cannot force a parent to choose against her child,' Nawal snapped. 'But you're allowed to place me in the double bind of either taking him along or not seeing you?' Kamil shouted back. And then, 'I refuse to be cowed by a Darwinian supposition that procreators are entitled to *anything* that I'm not.' Whether Kissinger should be tried as a war criminal can have Malik pounding his fists on the table and Rachel smacking down pots in violent agreement. Glassman: He was the first well-integrated gay man you were with? Michiel: Kissinger? Glassman, smiling and peering over his glasses. Michiel: That I took time to get to know. Glassman: You invited him to the islands? Michiel: He wanted to learn to dive and the diving was part of why I was going. Glassman: How long after he arrived did things go awry? Michiel: Initially, things were fine. I knew no one so it was only him and me. I taught mornings, and afternoons we went diving. He stayed with me and then returned to Sydney. He came for one more visit. All of that was good, though he did start complaining about my smoking. The sex got better. Can one go from thinking someone is a stick insect to being unable to keep your hands off him? Glassman: Only in fairy tales and movies are love and desire reserved for the beautiful. Michiel: When the time came for his return to the US he raised the issue of 'us'. Once he left I was morose. I hated being stuck on the island and I was learning more Pidgin than the kids were learning English. I had little money. Letters took weeks – I faxed from the hotel. There were British volunteers and American Peace Corps types in town, who I got to know. Kamil suggested a scholarship for me here at Berkeley. The following year he flew out to stay for a month. Even before he arrived things felt wrong. Sodomy was a criminal offense under the old British laws: I feared deportation if anyone found out. I hadn't told anyone I was gay. I knew people by then. The Aussie and Kiwi expats were real bigots, but no more so than the British volunteers. When he got out of the island-hopper I resented his coming terribly. Glassman: You began acting out? Michiel: I guess. Glassman: What would you call it? Michiel: I slept with some of the local guys. Glassman: Local *black* guys, and you were instantly unafraid of deportation? Michiel, glaring at the shrink, wordless. Glassman: How did Kamil respond? Michiel: He spat out every platitude I now know he learnt from you: how my fucking around was aimed at chasing him off. That my grow- ing irritation and disinterest sexually was a disingenuous way of making a case against intimacy. Glassman: You *wanted* him to leave you? Michiel: I found him repulsive. Glassman: Your country of birth is finally shedding its racist government and you're in my office, staying away from compulsive casual sex with black men. Is this mere coincidence? Michiel: Why must you always explain who I sleep with in terms of where I come from? Why link it to shame and guilt or to defiance of the goddamn father? Can it not be some- thing as simple as I find black people rather beautiful? Glassman: Would you be here if you believed it were that simple? Michiel:

Therapy tries to do to people like me what the state has failed to: turn us into monogamous couples who pay taxes and raise two kids who salute the stars and stripes. Glassman, waiting, nodding. Michiel: It's less that I resent being pathologized than I fear being led into a new kind of psychologized racism. Glassman: That is a reasonable concern. I think I understand your fear. Michiel, with his eyes on the poem above Glassman's head . . . *give back your heart to itself, to the stranger who has loved you all your life, whom you ignored for another, who knows you by heart* . . . I distrust this psychobabble almost as much as I do your empathy sometimes. Glassman: Let's take a boat back to the islands.

Beside the stairs and at the base of walls, ice glitters like heaped silver. Scattered on top of piles of hail, something else sparkles: in the beams of flashlights they discover rivets that came off the roof. The children dart about on freezing feet, hunting for silver screws, bolts and rivets. Look, we're practicing for the Olympics, Kanu shouts, skating a path through the hailstones on the drenched lawn. Giselle and Karien herd the kids back inside: we'll have double pneumonia by morning and at least one case of lockjaw to boot. Thabiso and Thomas try to slink into the orchard's shadows but Dirk calls them back. The boys: Why must we be treated like the rest when we're older than everyone else? Dirk: Into the shower! Look, you're already sopping wet. Lerato: Wipe those hoofs before you come into the house.

They hear the rush from the spruit. Above the mountain lightning still splits the dark, illuminating remote squalls. Tonight no vehicle will leave the farm. Benjamin and Dirk will visit the bridge to check things there and in the harvest orchards. All but one of the shade-cloths above the cars have collapsed under the weight of the hailstones. Here, too, rivets and screws shimmer in the beams. The only vehicle left unscathed is Dirk and Karien's, under the one cover that held. The rental looks as if a hammer was taken to it. 'Gods,' Benjamin says, 'die fokken Japanese kak lyk soos 'n golf-bal.'

Michiel feels relief at having checked the box for additional insurance. Both the Volvo and Benjamin's Mercedes have only nominal damage. The electronic gate and its motor have been crushed by the branch coming down on the fence. They shine flashlights into what remains of the jacaranda. Where it has split in two, smoke smolders in the cold night air. But for a thick carpet of leaves and the scattering of lavender blooms beneath it, the other tree has been spared.

'Don't tell me,' Lerato says, looking up as Michiel enters the refurbished kitchen. From the house come the sounds of children being bathed, scolded and cajoled.

'A couple of small dents on the hood and a broken side-mirror.'

'The Swedes know what they're doing.'

'You should see the rental. Only the dominee's car is unscathed.'

'The gods take care of their own.'

'I wouldn't bargain on that bridge being open. Remember how Pietie had to drive us to school on the tractor?'

'At least you whiteys had wheels! Remember how I had to swim across, braving the waves . . .'

Alida cuts their laughter short. 'I've been saying to her, I think she must phone Gauteng and tell them what's going on. Before she gets fired. Jobs aren't easy to find and half of Zimbabwe and Nigeria has flocked to this country now.'

'O se ke wa nyeka marao makgowa jwalo ka ntja,' Kasigo mutters towards the back door.' To Michiel she says, 'I'll wait for Benjamin. If it's safe I must try to pass over.'

'She's not going over that bridge unless the water is completely down, Kleinbaas.' Alida glares at her daughter as she speaks.

Rolling her eyes, Lerato departs to fetch her children's pajamas from the rondavel.

'Has Kleinbaas looked at Ounooi's orchard?'

'I don't have the heart, Alida. Where's Ouba— my dad?' His eyes go to the door through which Lerato has just left.

'I've put him to bed, Kleinbaas. It's been a long day. I have my intercom if he needs me.' With the knife she is using to cut up meat for the dogs' dinner she points to the white gadget that resembles the child monitor in Nawal's home.

'I'll go and say goodnight.'

Little feet patter down the passage. It is Palesa, pretending to flee Karien, who comes by shaking her head, a jar of body lotion in hand. Giselle calls for the older boys to get out of the shower: The hot water is running out and you *might* consider leaving some for the adults.

'Pa?'

'Come in. I'll turn on the lamp.'

Michiel steps around the wheelchair and sits down on Ounooi's side of the bed. Mingled with his mother's familiar smell he finds something sweet that he cannot place. On his father's bedside table is the twin to Alida's intercom and attached by a rubber band around one etiolated wrist is the lamp's electrical cord and light switch. The cord, he sees, has been lengthened for this purpose. Does the old man remain all night long on his back, vigilant even in sleep so as not to tug the lamp off the nightstand?

'What did you see out there?'

Benjamin and Dirk will bring more news, he says.

'Wat van jou ma se boord?' What about your mother's orchard?

'We didn't look, Pa. We'll wait till morning.'

The old man stares at the ceiling, his head submerged in the top of three down pillows. His hands rest on his chest, one atop the other. From the eaves comes the steady drip of melting hail.

'Pa, will it not be best if Alida moves into the house?'

'Every half-arsed farmer and every Englishman in this town wanted her,' he says, eyes still on the ceiling.

'Ai, Pa.' Michiel has to look away. He settles his gaze on his mother's books. The red and black striped pencil is there with the metal sharpener. The small blue pottery jar into which she dropped pencil shavings. He looks back at the old man and undoes his tie, slides it from around his neck and smoothes the fabric down alongside him on the white duvet.

'I pretended I knew what I was doing,' Oubaas says. 'But it was all bark and no bite. She saw right through me. She chose me when she could have had any wealthy man in the Free State.'

But you were wealthy. *We* were wealthy. This Michiel doesn't say. In the hairline around the old man's ears are large liver spots, which he didn't see during this afternoon's bath. The eyes are squeezed shut. The gray hair has been slicked back, looking almost wet. Noticing that the pillow under the old man's head is wrapped in a white towel, Michiel at once identifies the sweet smell of coconut oil. A substance that altered the scent of villages as sure as wood fires, as much as the fumes of outboard motors stirring up phosphorescence behind canoes in quiet lagoons. He found it in his classroom when he bent to comment on a written exercise: 'No, not *him fella savi* . . . we say *this person knows* . . .' And on pillows after Kiko or another night visitor had left.

'I can't go on without your mother.' The voice is like a child's, with no trace of what it remains capable of. 'I can't see tomorrow without her.' Tears make glistening webs down the wrinkled cheeks. 'You and your brother must speak to Doctor Niewoudt. There must be a new law that makes such things possible.'

'Pa.' He stretches across the bed with his shoes suspended over the side and finds his father's hand. 'Let Alida move in and stay in my room. It will be more practical. Things will get better in time.'

'Time is what I don't want. With Beth I'd have lived another hundred years, even like this. It must have been difficult for her. Pushing me around in the chair. I'm no fool. Taking her before me is the bitterest punishment god—' He sniffs and produces from under the sheet a handkerchief, struggles to blow his nose between trembling fingers. 'Do you believe, Michiel?'

'I beg your pardon, Pa?'

'Do you believe in god?'

'I didn't know that you did, Pa. Ounooi had her quiet way with these things.'

'Your mother read to me from Psalms and Proverbs. We laughed about the proverbs, the new translations: *A nagging wife is like a tap that goes drip, drip, drip.* Song of Songs we liked too. Long after I was asleep she kept her lamp on and read from her books.' He clears his throat, coughs. 'You haven't answered my question.'

'I have some kind of belief, Pa. But I'm not sure it's in a god.'

'Your mother told me . . .' The eyes are still closed. 'Your mother said your friend is some kind of Buddhist.'

Your friend. This, then, is how Kamil is to be acknowledged. It is, in fact, more than good enough. He hears the house's silence. From the garden nothing, only from beyond the orchard, faintly, the river's rush.

'Kamil, Pa,' he says. 'His name is Kamil.' He sees in his mind's eye the White Tara above his side of the bed, the green one above Kamil's; himself grudgingly offering guidance as Kamil, standing on the mattress, positions the silk tapestries, *up on the left, more, no, down a bit.* 'He — we — try to live by some guidelines. Some are from Tibetan Buddhism. Compassion for self and others. Right action in the world. Mindfulness and staying present in the moment — the most difficult one. Some from Hinduism and before that who knows where. Some of it's quite Christian, I guess. Loving your neighbor as yourself is from the commandments. Seventy times seventy. Never do to others what you wouldn't have them do to you. There's a dose of Islam and Judaism from his parents, even though they're atheists. We're more interested in what we do than in what we believe.'

There is a knock and Giselle enters. Sleeping arrangements are being finalized. Bianca wants to know if she may have the extra bed in Michiel's room.

'As long as she doesn't mind that I snore like a bear.'

'Does everyone have a place?' Oubaas asks.

'We've put Karien and Dirk in Benjamin's room.' Giselle sits down at the foot end. 'Palesa will sleep with them. And we have the boys camping in the living room. They're playing video games now.'

'Enough blankets for everyone? Tomorrow's forecast says there's a cold front coming. The nights can still freeze.'

All have been seen to. Everyone is fed. The kids are bathed. Isabella and Grootman each have half a bone from the leg of lamb. No one is in need of anything.

'I'm off to have a bath.' Through the covers Giselle squeezes Oubaas's foot. 'I'm telling Bianca she can sleep in your room, Michiel.'

Once the door has closed Michiel and his father are quiet. The silence is about to become uncomfortable and Michiel is preparing to leave when Oubaas speaks. 'Ounooi was worried about Benjamin's marriage.' Then, turning his head to Michiel, 'Look on the bedside table in her book. She used something your friend gave her as her bookmark.'

Beside her Bible lies *Disgrace*, and under that Bessie Head's *The Collector of Treasures*. At the bottom of the pile, *The Collected Poems* of Audre Lorde. He opens the novel at the bookmark. It is the tarot card. *III: The Empress*. The priestess Serket, later subsumed by Isis, in gold, pregnant, with her open arms and the flower sprouting from her head. A bird has its wings extended over fields of poppies. His eyes go down the page to what has been marked in the text. He recognizes the moment. The disgraced father cannot grasp his daughter's resistance to offering him the story of her violation; he cannot make peace with her response to her rape. Earlier in the book whole paragraphs have been highlighted, notes made in the margins along with question and exclamation marks. On this page, only one sentence is underlined. Was this the last page she read? Sitting up against her pillows, she lifts the pencil, places the sharpened lead tip on the page and beneath these words draws the line: *what if* that *is the price one has to pay for staying on?*

He replaces the tarot card, closes the cover of the book that is a sensation wherever it is being read.

'And you, Pa, do you believe in some kind of god?'

'It's the only way I know I'll see her again.'

'You *will*, Pa. In the morning you'll wake with the piet-my-vrou. I heard it as soon as I arrived here at noon. It must be the tenth generation after the one that was here when I left. Or how many years does a little bird like that live?' He has remained sitting up and now turns to the mohair-draped windows and sliding doors. He hears the drip, drip. He thinks of making love to Kamil; swallows a lump in his throat. 'Once the river goes down you'll hear the turtledoves.' He thinks of the card on the coffin and the other in the book, the relentless fecundity of each image. 'There'll be the hum of bees, as if the world is vibrating. If even one of the blossoms is still on the trees you'll see Ounooi in that.' He says, 'Regeneration is composed mostly of a preceding process of decomposition, Pa. Nothing lives unless something dies.' He turns back to the face against the pillow, sees again the electrical cord attached to the wrist. 'That's what I believe god is,' he says. 'The energy that connects everything. It is in that sense only that god is omnipotent.' What he omits is that god is therefore also the dilapidation of the workers' houses and miserly wages, what is pent up from who owns what and who is owed how much more. That god is the fungus beneath the nail of Mamparra's thumb.

He finds his father's eyes on him; the child gone and the man back. It is clear that the moment has passed.

'You sound like your mother,' the old man says. 'Tell your brother to wake me when he's back.'

'Goodnight, Pa.'

'What time do you leave?'

'After lunch, Pa. My flight is late tomorrow night.'

'It's good you made time to come before you emigrate to China.'

'It's for work, Pa. Not to live.'

The lamp goes off as he reaches the door.

Other than the drip-drip from the hail melting in gutters, the house is quiet. Light and the electronic beep of simulated gunfire come from the living room. The armchairs have been moved to make space for mattresses on the kilim. From their sleeping bags the boys manipulate the controls of a video game: on the television screen lifelike figures run through a cityscape firing automatic machine guns, lobbing grenades, zapping lasers and blowing up buildings. They take no notice of Michiel, their concentration pinned to the spectacle of destruction. In the gurgle of explosions, in a tiny bundle beneath a blanket on the couch, Palesa has fallen asleep.

On the stoep, Karien and Lerato are sitting in wicker chairs, each woman covered in one of Ounooi's mohair wraps. The sky is clearing, with sporadic gyrations of lightning moving off. Above the orchard are the first stars. 'How is he?' Karien asks when Michiel sits down across the table from them. 'Wine or calvados?' Lerato offers. '*Meerlust, Rubicon,* 1994,' she says. 'Excellent if you like something with an old-fashioned floral scent.'

'A drink now would put me to sleep. Kids tucked in?'

'I need to go and check on mine,' Lerato says. 'I can see Kanu against the curtains. In and out of bed.' She points to the dull light of the rondavel window where Kanu's silhouette moves about. 'He's dikbek because I wouldn't let him stay up with the other boys.' She hasn't canceled her morning appointments. In an hour she has a telephone conference with New York. A section of the company is in the process of moving its primary market listings overseas. Her morning meeting is to report on tonight's discussions. Even here, Michiel says, in the middle of the old Orange Free State, no nook or cranny seems to be without connection to the outside world. Midway through the burial he saw a worker slip away from the cemetery, whispering into a cellphone. Remarkable.

'Wait. He's keeping Pulane up.' Michiel and Karien watch as Lerato walks along the garden path to Peet's rondavel.

'Your son sings beautifully,' he breaks the silence.

'Thabiso's voice will change soon,' she says. 'There is something sad about that. Remember when it happened to Benjamin, like a squeaky toy?' she chuckles. 'But yours deepened over time, almost unnoticed.'

'Where do I begin, Karien?'

'Surely with what it's like being back.' They study each other in the stoep's light, reading again, now without haste, the passage of years in each other's face. 'But I'm pretty sure the best place to start,' she says, 'isn't with my legs spread on the back seat of a VW Passat, bleeding.'

'Christ, Karien . . .'

'Come on, Michiel.' She laughs, making light of the enormity she has just handed him. 'Yesterday's another country.' She winks. 'Tell me, what's gone on since you arrived?'

He looks into the night garden before leaning across the table to pour a glass of wine. He meets her eyes over the rim of his glass, unable to grasp her mood or her intention. He speaks of the crawl of Johannesburg's morning traffic and the sprawl of new construction. Was that city always so big? His thoughts rebound to her, across from him. In his state of hyperconsciousness he wishes to stop his own tongue and to hear hers, listen to *her*, to let *her* speak *her* life, *that* moment that would lead to what must become an interrogation of himself, his own life.

'How are *you*?' he asks.

She smiles and says, 'Fok, Michiel! I can talk later.'

You do not sound like a minister's wife, he could say, but instead speaks of the season's shameless beauty: the redgrass that is still green, and sheep in the veld. Workers on the back of open pick-up trucks: illegal to transport people that way in the US. Red and orange sandstone buildings and wind pumps rotating above cement dams against the blue. Poplars. Willows. Migrant swallows nesting beneath highway overpasses. Seduction in the eye — in the heart and the mind — of the beholder: someone else may find it banal.

'What about the condition of our roads?' she interrupts, smiling.

The deeper he came into the platteland, the poorer the state of byways connecting the small towns. No longer the kept surfaces he remembers. Public money now has to go to more important things, he says. She snorts and asks: Is that what you call lining the pockets of fat cats? It can't be that bad, he says. As often as not it is, she says, though they're probably no worse than what we had before. With a free press it has merely become more difficult to hide the corruption.

When he speaks again he tells her that within an hour of starting the drive from Jo'burg — no, before, already at tens of thousands of feet — the tumble of memory had begun. The longer he talks the more possible it becomes to reach around the disturbing image she has for ever inserted into his mind: her white, skinny thighs on the back seat of a car, her young unlined face turned from him and whoever bends over her with some horrid instrument. He speaks about the stoep, barred like a prison. Grootman pissing against his luggage. The extraordinary presence of Lerato and her twins. His father ravaged beyond what Ounooi led him to believe, and seeing her painting in his parents' bedroom. Bathing Oubaas: how the old man had wanted him to come by Paradys not because the father had seen his son from a long way off and was moved by pity and tenderness, not to embrace and kiss him, but only because he imagined that's what the son's mother might have wanted. That he was called Peet.

'How was that, for you?'

'Is it Alzheimer's, not Parkinson's?'

'There's cognitive impairment of some sort. It's most likely progressive.'

'For a while he seemed to want a kind of reconciliation with me. Then he got angry. That life hasn't succeeded in toughening me up seems to piss him off.'

Her eyes on him leave no doubt of her fondness for him. She must know, too, that what he feels for her transcends the tyrannies of nostalgia, loss and guilt.

'A moment ago, in his room, it was quite touching. I held his hand for the first time since I was a boy.'

Karien smiles. 'He is unpredictable,' she says. 'But Ounooi wouldn't have told you that. Nothing about anyone unless it's good. No word out of place. Your life over there can't possibly be as Edenic as she reported.'

'I thought she had a good time with us.'

'She showed us pictures and went into lots of detail.'

'She liked Kamil, I'm sure,' he says.

'That's not to say it was easy for her.' They look at each other in silence and he tries to read her tone. 'We were close,' she says. 'You know we were . . . or maybe you don't: we became more so after you left. We missed you.'

In this moment his urge to touch her is almost overwhelming. 'Over there,' he says, 'it was as though nothing'd ever happened, as if things were just the way they'd always been. She didn't bat an eyelid.'

'To block it out may be the only way some can get out of bed in the morning. Here there's this obsession with remembering. I think it's because people can talk freely for the first time. Dirk says that it's because it was one small group, us whites, who did it to the blacks. But just across the border, in Mozambique, they don't pick at scabs. Millions died or were maimed or displaced there. Still, they've decided they can't afford to talk about it. I can't say they're wrong to do it that way.' She sips from her glass. 'Ounooi and I hardly spoke about how she dealt with you.' She looks out into the garden, where a single cricket has started to chirp. 'But she would have deferred to the Mozambicans, I'm sure. Both politically and personally.'

'And you? Personally?'

She thinks for a while. Frowns. Looks at him, then away. 'The others will be back any moment,' she says. 'We should have a few hours in the morning before you leave. Do you still ride?'

'Not since I left. But it's like riding a bike, isn't it?' He pauses. 'You *would* like to talk? About everything?'

'Well, *everything's* impossible. And I'm not sure that people can talk themselves better. How about you?'

'I've been in analysis on and off for years. It helps contain the neuroses before they trip me up. And I live with a man who talks even in his sleep: Michael — that's what he calls me — you either find language or take your ass out the door. By the time I got to him,' he says, 'you needed a can opener to get into my skull.'

'We've both been lucky with the men we chose.'

'I went around the world a few times first.'

'It must have been,' she pauses, 'quite a ride.' She leans across the table and seems intent on touching his forearm. Then, as she is about to, she draws back and instead runs her hand from her forehead backwards, across her hair.

'No more so for me than for you.' When she doesn't respond, he asks: 'Is it inappropriate,' he dislikes the word he hears from his lips, 'to ask whether you're happy?'

'With Dirk? It's a good marriage. You know what it's like.' She lifts the bottle of calvados. Without uncorking it, she continues as she now holds Michiel's gaze. 'Being *Mevrou Dominee* isn't what it was when we were growing up. Very little tea and sympathy these days, if that's how you've pictured my life. Dirk was tarred ever so lightly with the brush of Beyers Naudé and Tutu. He admires Óscar Romero of El Salvador. Now that there's this integration of sorts, dirty hands, in the most positive sense, come with the turf.'

'You're not sorry about giving up the other stuff? When you see where Lerato is? She must have been helped by the changes, but you could be an advocate or a judge or something—'

She laughs, throwing back her head, so that he hears her again as she was towards the end of high school. 'Only a few weeks ago, in a pep talk, Ounooi said that if I went to university next year I could still make it.' She shakes her head. 'Lerato isn't an affirmative-action case. She and her husband know what they want and they stick to it. She popped those twins out of that skinny body and was back in the office a month later. I could never have done what she has. Fifteen-hour work days. The laptop goes everywhere with her and tonight her phone rang ten times . . .' She studies her fingers, still clasped around the bottle. She holds it up, looking closely at the fluid refracted against the light. 'Was it Olive Schreiner,' she asks, pensively now, 'who said that genius is nothing more than concentrating on one thing to the exclusion of everything else? Schreiner or Einstein?' Again a chuckle before she puts down the bottle, still uncorked. 'I wanted color around me and in my hands. And to live here.'

He is unconvinced by her lack of regret or anger at him. 'Schreiner also wrote that all that's buried is not dead,' he says. If she has lived in him for so many years, has he not also been alive in her? Where is her rage, or at least her memory of it? In the absence of that, are there theological or spiritual metaphors that might explain why she dropped out of college and married the first handsome man that came her way? The way she tells it now undermines what he has presumed for so long: that in her life his place was taken by a wound. That is what he needed to *feel*, Glassman might say. Glassman: Why, week after week, are you late? Michiel: I don't think it's because I'm resistant to therapy. Glassman: How do you feel right now? Michiel: Like crap, for messing with your time. Glassman: Can it be that your being late, always succeeded by this abjection, feeds some base need to beat up on yourself? Michiel:

That's Christianity for you. Glassman: It may also be self-inflicted. What would be left of your feelings without the comforts of self-flagellation?

Karien has her elbows on the table. She rests her chin on her fists and is looking closely at him. As if she has an inkling of what he is thinking, she says: 'What happened between you and me . . . on the tail of Peet's death, forced me to make new choices. I was also lucky. With the abortion, I mean. Things turned out okay.' She leans back and again looks closely at her fingers. He blinks at the sting of tears. She has said the word he has wanted to hear and also dreaded hearing. In a session with Glassman during Ounooi's visit, he could say with a sense of greater certainty and relief what he'd suspected for years: There had been no child. *I took care of it* had indeed meant she'd had an abortion. And Glassman asked: How did you experience it, in your body (his hand goes to his chest, fingers open) before you asked and then after your mother's silence confirmed it? Michiel: I wanted to find out without giving anything away. I didn't know till then that my mother knew. My shoulders were tense, up, like this. If there was a child, a grandchild, even one given away, Ounooi couldn't keep it from me. Glassman: No sense of disappointment? Michiel: Why would there be? Glassman: Is there no part of you that wishes you'd fathered a child of your own? Michiel: Not under those circumstances. Glassman: Contemporary culture places a premium on man's worth as a procreator. If she had the baby . . . regardless of or even because of your being gay, would that not in a way have compensated . . .

Karien clears her throat. 'I do pretty decent paintings. I have a regional reputation and my stuff gets reviewed and exhibited. First National Bank bought a triptych of mine last year. After Thabiso goes to school the housekeeper comes in and takes over Palesa. Then I paint for four hours, five days of the week . . . I could have gone back to university. The law and the cloth under one roof could have been a *lekker* combination in this town. But I never again — I don't think I'm overstating when I say *never* — want to go and register for courses and get degrees. I still read, every day, but without the intensity. I read because it helps me to see the things I paint in new ways. And there's work to be done here, in town, good work that doesn't require my being a lawyer. I knew nothing about this place until I married Dirk. You know how we grew up.'

How much of what he has learned about this country while overseas did she end up getting, right here, on the job in the manse and from behind her easel?

The rondavel light has gone out. They hear the door close and see Lerato.

'If you're blaming yourself, please stop,' Karien says. 'I could have knocked your head in with a hockey stick. I was humiliated. I was beside myself with hurt. But I never blamed you for the choices I made. We were kids, for god's sake. I'm okay. It's not blame I want to talk about.'

'No?'

'I allowed you no say. I chased you as much as you took yourself away. What did we know about *anything* but that we were destined to be together? Gods . . .' Like Hansel and Gretel, with lives wasted on a stupid story. How does she know — till he abandons their legend — that his one and only love is the wicked witch?

'Your generosity astonishes me.'

'Without generosity as vast as the heavens we would by now all have had our brains blown out. Like the Oberholzers.'

Lerato has come up the stairs: 'Generosity my foot.' She guffaws and glides into her seat as if she has had a lifelong place at this table. 'It's the ten-foot wall around my house, with three strands of electric fence, that keeps the tsotsis out . . . The hyperactive brat is down and I must fortify myself for that lot in New York. Michiel, pour, please.' She shivers, flings Ounooi's wrap around her neck and rubs her hands together against the cold.

'Oberholzer had a fence higher than this one,' Karien says. 'Rottweilers trained to bark at any black man. You know how that old bliksem abused his workers.'

'No more than this old bliksem — no offense intended, Michiel.' Lerato nods at him, raises her glass.

'None taken.'

'And that is my point,' Karien says. 'Any one of the people on Diepfontein or on Paradys — without their forgiving spirits — could have knocked off Oubaas and Ounooi too, years ago.'

'There's no mystical spirit that keeps people up at the compound from sharpening pangas,' Lerato says. She frowns, shakes her head as if Karien's sentiments surprise her. 'It's the patience of being human. People believe their time *will* come. I doubt they sit there suppressing their hatred. Most just live their lives, like us. Try their best to raise their kids. How long the patience of some will last, *that's* a question.' Later, Michiel will think in near bafflement of the ease with which she spoke of herself and her children as apart, separate from *these people and their time, their* patience. 'We're in the honeymoon phase now,' she continues. 'Borrowed time. There's that Afrikaans saying, *spog met geleende vere* — boasting with borrowed feathers. Like you and I sitting here in Ounooi's wraps.' She hugs the fabric to her, slides her slender fingers down the soft mohair. The elegance of the gesture is at once studied and entirely natural. 'Her old clothes, remember!' Lerato hoots. 'Was I green when you got that turtleneck she always wore with the copper-colored skirt — remember that thing?' Plumage, time, stocks and bonds: part and parcel of the same thing. Ten, twenty, thirty years down the line this conversation will happen again, with the poor poorer and the rich richer, present company included. And not only in the good old New South Africa. No doubt they and others like them — their children too — will be called to account. 'Did those guys not take a phone to the bridge?' she asks. 'I have only a little time before New York calls.'

Karien takes Lerato's cellphone and enters Dirk's number. She repeats what she hears in the phone and shows thumbs down: water and debris a meter above the crossing. It looks like a mile of boundary fence has washed down with the flood, spun like a net over the logs clogging the bridge.

'That settles it,' Lerato says. 'I'll say goodnight. I have to make a few calls. We'll see each other in the morning.'

'Breakfast?'

'Oh sure, we'll come in. With all the kids, me and mine are lost in the fray.' Before turning to hurry off, her eyes find Michiel's. 'Ounooi was an inspiration,' she says. 'It's the fashion to scoff at those who didn't do enough to have a street named after them. But there was kindness in your mother, like a tiny ember of what was possible.'

'Thank you,' he says. Watching her again cross the yard, he asks Karien: 'Wat is die Afrikaanse woord vir *kindness*?' Something like 'goedhartig', she suggests. That, however, has a ring of charity that the English doesn't. Perhaps 'minsaam', but that word is rarely used in idiomatic speech. And 'vriendelik' means *friendly*, rather than *kind*.

In the US, Ounooi referred only in passing to the Oberholzer murders. For a while Michiel read online of the farm killings. On average, three a week in South Africa. By leaving the Oberholzers at a mention, it seemed his mother hadn't wanted to be seen as another white complaining in the face of otherwise abundant and miraculous hope. Out of concern for their fragile rapprochement he had not asked for details. From Karien's telling – based on word from laborers, township women, the police, newspapers and from the son Obie's mouth – the Oberholzers were assailed at their electronic gate. Armed men forced them from the bakkie. The dogs had already been poisoned by strychnine in meat thrown over the fence. The old people were taken into the house, stripped, their knees pulverized with Oom Oberholzer's golfing irons. Kneecapped. Hobbled like slaves from Virginia and Mississippi, Slovakia and Russia to Saudi Arabia and southern Sudan and the Congo: knees destroyed or Achilles' tendons snipped. No way out. How well the slave learns from the master. *Dismantling the Master's House with the Master's Tools.* In the film version of Steven King's *Misery*, someone who is slave only to her own insanity tells her captive, a writer, how hobbling was done to laborers on the Kimberley diamond mines. Then she breaks both his ankles with a sledgehammer. In the book, she cuts off his foot with an ax. Thus she coerces from him the book she desires — believing a story alone, rendered as she wishes it, will secure meaning in her life — only to have him smash in her skull with the typewriter. He will hobble through the rest of his writing life. The Oberholzers were forced to unlock the safe where they kept the rifles and the following week's wages. Michiel remembers Tannie Oberholzer from afternoons outside the high school's gate. Parked in her Peugeot station wagon, waiting for Obie and her daughter. And he sees her behind the tombola table at the church bazaar with her famously sour lemon meringue pies, the frosting three inches high. *More for the savage than the sophisticated palate*, Ounooi said, winking. And from the stands shouting encouragement to Obie, who was the school's star fifteen-hundred-meter athlete, her red rosette waving madly above her head: 'Dis Ma se kind! Dis Ma se kind!' That's this mother's child! While Ounooi herself sits in the stands grading Matric English essays. And he remembers Oom Oberholzer as the chief deacon in church, and with Obie in the bakkie, speeding with dust and gravel flying up the Paradys road, rifle barrels from both windows, out to get someone named Klaas who, they knew from interrogating *their other kaffirs*, had stolen a sheep. The Klaas in question was never laid eyes on again. That there was hell to pay in the Oberholzer compound they heard here at Paradys from Adam and Pietie. And from Peet, who'd heard at school from Obie. On their night of ill fate, with the homestead ransacked, both Oom and Tannie Oberholzer were shot, face down on the living-room carpet.

Hearing the shots, two workers from the compound came to the house armed with a spade and garden rake before the raiders could flee. Both were shot in cold blood. No arrests have ever been made. One of the dead workers' names, he now hears Karien say, was Klaas, his last name omitted in newspaper and TV reports. It goes without saying that the intruders had no jobs, no homes, no investment in not executing their deed. No motivation to adhere to morality or laws designed over three and a half centuries for the express purpose of keeping them out and in their place.

'Did you know about Mamparra's child?' Karien asks, frowning at him.

'Geel?'

After the murders, Obie went to the pastorie to see Dirk. In times like that, people still look to the dominee. Even if they think he and his wife are turncoats. Obie wanted to make a kind of confession, on behalf of his father. He told Dirk that Oubaas Oberholzer was the father of at least three of the kids in their compound. 'That's what people were already saying when we were at school,' Michiel remembers. Obie told Dirk that Mamparra – he called her *Mamparra van Paradys* – also had a child by his father. Obie had seen something as a boy of four or five. At Ounooi's farm stall. Mamparra was alone there. Oubaas Oberholzer told Obie to wait in the bakkie and to be on the lookout for traffic and to honk the horn if any cars looked like they were stopping at the stall. More times than he could remember, Obie saw his father drag Mamparra down behind the counter.

Giselle, with a blanket around her shoulders and bearing a tray of olives, sliced biltong and cheese, has come out to join them. 'Dispiriting talk for a night like this,' she says. The boys have been instructed to finish their game and get to sleep. 'No sign of the men?'

'No men in sight,' Michiel quips and it takes a moment before both women chuckle.

Giselle sits beside him with an envelope of photographs of Ounooi's visit: Ounooi in Times Square on her first day in New York. At the bow of the Staten Island Ferry. Here we are window shopping on Fifth Avenue and this is Broadway at night. A snow-ball the size of a boulder being rolled up a Central Park embankment by mittened and ear-muffed children. The snowball is larger than the smallest child. 'They pushed it up the hill,' he says, 'and then it rolled down. More children joined in and up they went again. Ounooi was transfixed.' Here, on the stairs before the columns of the Metropolitan. Was it an exhibition of Mayan art? A view of the bay from Coit Tower. The three of us on the Golden Gate Bridge. And now he thinks of the smiling family portraits on her desk. Why not this one, Ounooi, of him *and* me with you?

'And these statues?' Giselle asks.

'It's the Pool of Enchantment. A Native American boy piping to two mountain lions.'

'This?'

'Cervantes. Also in Golden Gate Park. She went there when I was at work. She found blue agapanthus and clivias — a few were still in bloom — and other plants from here.'

At the sound of an engine Michiel walks down the stoep. The bakkie is moving up the hill with searchlights, like beams fanning the crowd at a rock concert, grazing the branches of the harvest orchards. He is unable to remember Mamparra's child's face. All that he recalls is the name, Geel, the word for a color standing in for a whole being. *Yesterday is another country.* He pictures Mamparra disappearing behind the farm stall counter as the white man throws his weight on her; the money scatters as she drags the cash regis-ter down in her struggle. Does she call for help, to little Obie in the pick-up truck? What does she allow herself to feel, today, when the little boy from back then and his own offspring waddle on to Paradys to borrow the tractor or to offer condolence at Ounooi's passing? What happens on Sundays when their eyes meet in church, now that Mamparra is allowed in there? And Obie, what can he possibly feel? Standing here, looking at the sweep of the search beams, he is reminded of the stories of ghostly lights around the cemetery after rain. He becomes aware of his own deep fatigue. He still has on his church shirt. How did he and Kamil neglect to pack a sweater? When he says he's going in to take a shower Giselle asks that he check that Bianca is warm enough, and offer some disapprobation to the boys who have not yet turned off the TV.

'Your mothers are on to you,' he says to Thabiso and Thomas in the sleeping bags. 'If I were you I'd make an argument that with the flood there won't be school tomorrow. Why not be allowed another hour? Don't tell them it comes from me.'

'Yes! No school!' In Thabiso's company, Thomas has let down his guard and shoots a grin at Michiel. They pause their game and go to plead their case.

He turns on the hallway light. Bianca is asleep in his room. He takes the kaross from the end of his old bed and covers his niece. He tucks the jackal fur in on both sides of the pillow and, bending, stands for a moment, listening to her breathing.

Dressed in fresh clothes and an old jersey of his father's, he has joined the others on the stoep. He is aware of his weighted eyelids. Instead of invigorating him, the hot water has added to the lethargy.

Once, maybe twice every other rainy season this kind of storm hits. Judging by the volume of debris visible in the spray lights, Benjamin says, tonight's has been the worst in years. Mercifully only a small section of the harvest orchard seems scathed: the hail looks to have been concentrated on the ground around the manor. No one on the stoep has ventured into Ounooi's orchard. When Mamparra brought news from the compound — roofs leaking, Adam and Liesbet's window broken, a chimney knocked clean off — she said nothing of the trees along the path. They will wait for morning to confirm what they already suspect: with the fury centered about the house, it is likely that the preserve and jam crop blooms are decimated.

Children's schools have to be called in the morning. Meetings and appointments rescheduled in Johannesburg and in town for Karien and Dirk. Benjamin had been planning a week's stay on the farm, with Giselle returning to the business. Ounooi's passing has brought a thousand tasks that demand care posthaste.

There is agreement that Oubaas is not up to staying here without considerable help. Since his incapacitation, Ounooi has been the helmswoman. Pietie, knowledgeable and reliable as he is, cannot supervise the sprawling enterprise alone. Of fiscal intricacies and export contracts he knows nothing: the man has only a standard-three education. It's a long shot leaving him in charge of the harvest, though that might be what they have to do, with Karien keeping a close eye. Unless a temporary farm manager – no one says *a white man* – can be hired. Bookkeeping, accounts, ledgers, correspondence with exporters: no one but Ounooi has done that for years. Though Benjamin has a working knowledge of most of what goes on here, he and Giselle have their own lives and a business to run. He will fly to Bloemfontein on weekends to be here and keep his finger on the pulse. Karien will come during the week and see to the distribution of the Friday wages.

And in the long run? Paradys has to go the tourist route. A plan long advocated by Benjamin: sell or lease the outlying stock camps and retain only a hundred or so of the most picturesque acres: the koppies, the stream and the mountain as far as the boundary above the caves. Build chalets beside the stream, turn the manor into a top-notch guesthouse, keep a quarter of Ounooi's trees for their charm, but the views of the valley are too spectacular not to build on that land. Draw up a business plan for the next ten years: two or three new cottages per year, horse riding, trail hiking, rock climbing, the Bushman paintings, rafting on the Orange. The south-eastern Free State has become a tourist hotspot and, more important, farming on this scale is a dying concern.

'What about your son?' Karien asks.

'Thomas and Thabiso's idea of farming is a boy's fantasy.' Michiel is struck by the inclusion of Thabiso's name. 'By the time they're done with school and varsity, farming will have taken on an entirely different face.' Corporations, irrigation projects, special-ization, hybrid fruit for the voracious northern-hemisphere appetite: nothing like this antiquated sideshow. It's even debatable whether this is an ideal climate for cherries. Asparagus would prob-ably yield a greater income. As much as his heart is here, Benjamin says, these are the facts.

Giselle is all for selling up lock, stock and barrel. She is more than willing to have Oubaas in their Sandton garden cottage with a full-time nurse. The children dote on him. When the time comes, there's a hospice just down the road in Rosebank. Change is never easy for anyone, but is there really any other choice? This town's old people's home has a frail-care unit like a halfway station to the morgue. Oubaas would wither and die within a month. And he cannot be left on the farm: Alida, after all, is not today's child. 'Besides,' says Giselle, 'who knows when they'll decide to make a claim on this land?' Her eyes go from Benjamin to Karien and back to Benjamin. 'You'll turn it into a tourist haven, spend millions, only to see it taken away.' A click of rings on wood as she places both hands firmly on the table. 'We see the circus in Zimbabwe. I say sell before we're forced to give it away when some land com-missar decides that Paradys belonged to King Moshoeshoe's ancestors five hundred years ago.'

'Giselle,' Benjamin jerks his head. 'This land has been ours for generations. Even if a claim is staked here, the policy is one of compensation, not confiscation. That's what the Land Claims Court is for. You're being alarmist . . . at best.'

Speaking to Michiel, Karien says: 'They've set up a court with the same powers as the High Court to look at tenure reform. Land restitution and redistribution. Something that was never properly done in Zimbabwe.'

'I can't stand these comparisons with Zimbabwe,' Benjamin says. 'Blacks this and blacks that has just been modified to Zimbabwe this and Zimbabwe that, by whites, to hide their racism. This country isn't some banana republic. We're entrenched in a world economy and this government knows what it has to do.'

'That might very well be so, Benjamin,' Giselle makes no effort to hide her annoyance. 'But I object to the asinine claim that anyone who draws parallels with Zimbabwe is a racist.' She looks to the others. 'I'm sick of the race card being played to silence valid concerns. Where does one go once you've been called racist? How do I say anything about Sam Thabane standing in church lying about why the municipal pool was never reopened? The transition brought "other priorities" my foot!' Gesturing with her fingers to indicate the quotation marks. 'After I've been labeled racist, how do I ask Mayor Thabane what happened to all the money Ounooi collected for the project? I myself gave a thousand rand towards the restoration of that pool.'

'They are investigating what happened, Giselle,' Karien says.

'That's been your and Ounooi's excuse for the past two years. This is a small town, not a major metropolis, Karien.'

They sit for a while in silence. For a second time today, Michiel finds himself wishing for a cigarette. Then Dirk mentions land claims underway in Thaba'Nchu. The displaced have title deeds dating back a hundred and seventy years. And there is still the old talk in the township of restoring local areas to Lesotho, from which they were taken in the 1860s: everything this side of the Caledon.

'Lesotho didn't exist as an entity then,' Benjamin counters. 'If anything, it makes sense for that little kingdom to be incorporated into South Africa. The sooner the Highlands Water Project is entirely under our jurisdiction the better for Jo'burg's progress and peace of mind. Give the Basotho their hydropower, but take control of the water. The new government knows how to deal with the little landlocked territory. We saw that when the South African army was dispatched to Maseru to put down political unrest there recently. Unthinkable for the old white government to pull off that stunt without an international outcry. I can't stand the pessimism. None of us have had it this good. There's growth like never before and all I hear is naysaying. I agree with Mbeki: what a privilege to witness the dawn of the African Renaissance.'

'Renaissance *my hol!*' Karien snorts. 'And we're not witnesses, for god's sake. We're participants who are being further enriched.' Benjamin clicks his tongue, dismissive in a way that comes back to Michiel from their youth. 'If you do go the tourist route, which is the route of *dependency* as far as I'm concerned,' Karien goes on, looking across the table at Benjamin, 'there is the question of Paradys's workers. You won't be able to throw these people off. The new tenure laws make that a crime.'

'Karien, you know I won't make this decision alone, so stop saying *you* this and *you* that.'

The sad thing about the tenure laws is that they're not working, Dirk says. More people evicted from farms come to the township now than ever before. And if it's not evictions, it's the myth of a life of plenty in the towns and cities. The congregation grows exponentially. These people can stay on the farm, Benjamin defends. All of them. They have every right. The permanent workforce is relatively small. It's the part-time pickers who will be affected. The ones who've always been here can be retrained: anyone can mow the lawn, fold back sheets and prepare scrambled eggs and bacon for tourists. A few English lessons and you've got guides for the hikes and river walks. He speaks of starting a water-bottling plant. There is a growing craze for bottled water. *Water of Paradise* — there, a brand name ready to take the market by storm. 'All that water just spills into the dam,' he says. 'It's a dead loss in Ounooi's orchard. Those old trees should have been chopped down twenty years ago. Let's bring labor up to speed by putting that spring water to better use.'

At this, Karien and Dirk both laugh out loud. Benjamin looks at them askance.

'That *spring* water?' Karien smirks.

'You know the story?' Benjamin grins sheepishly.

'I've known for years.' She laughs, making a face at him.

The spring is on Paradys only in lore. The truth is that great-grandfather Steyn, in the few years of real drought that the farm ever experienced, had the workers dig a trench and put in pipes to an unmarked water source that bubbled up on to public land at least two kilometers away. In the sixties, under cover of darkness, sworn to secrecy, the workers laid new sections of piping to replace the old. Not even Giselle has known till now.

'Do you remember,' Michiel speaks for the first time, looking at Karien, 'the time we found the Mohlakwana graves? I thought of it today in church.'

'Mamparra Mohlakwana doesn't stand a chance,' Karien says. 'Women farm workers' tenure is always linked to a man's. If she'd married Pietie when she had the chance it would have helped her when the time comes. Someone like Liesbet has it better. She and Adam can decide to stop working tomorrow and that's it: you can't throw them off the farm.'

'Just *listen* to this, Benjamin!' Giselle's eyes are ablaze. 'You're inheriting a quagmire! Thomas and Bianca barely see us as it is. Now you want to invest more time and resources in this sinking ship!'

'We'd leave it to contractors, Giselle. We'd come for weekends and holidays.'

'No, I'm sorry!' Giselle gasps. She smacks her forehead and glares openly at her husband. 'Every weekend and every holiday on the platteland when there's a universe out there to discover.' She picks up Ounooi's photographs and drops them on the table in front of her husband. Their children need to see the world. They themselves haven't set foot in Eastern Europe. 'If we don't do Prague and Budapest in the next year they say those cities will be ruined entirely. I'm not raising my kids to become plaasjapies.' She has speared an olive with a cocktail stick. She chews, shaking her head. 'Forget it,' she says. 'It's not happening.'

'You've never had time for this place, have you, Giselle?'

'Oh Benjamin, please, let's not go there. Not on this of all nights.'

In the discomfiting silence there is the sound of drinks being poured. Michiel takes a handful of biltong. Over his own chewing he hears another cricket joining the earlier one. He thinks of Mehring in *The Conservationist*. The weekend farmer with his anglicized Dutch name and his maybe-queer son off to New York. Is that the first adumbration, ever, in letters, of something akin to his own story? Here they are then, almost thirty years after that, English-speaking Afrikaners all of them: boere, coming to the farms in their free time. Hobby farmers with the real business of making money and life elsewhere. And when the white man, disgraced, *leaves for one of those countries white people go to, the whole world being theirs*, it is the Africans (not the arrogantly misnamed Afrikaners now fluent in the language of transnational capital) who lay to rest the one who has no name. A name rarely sticks to a map for long. But bones remain under the debris of fences, streets and pavements. In lava rock and seabeds, in sweeping winds, bones lie across what was once or may be in future a brief boundary, a foundation or a border post, to be read, chewed on, mined, used as a tool or ignored for ever.

Giselle turns her head and asks: 'What would you say, Michiel, from an outsider's perspective?'

He is caught off guard by the invitation to enter the conversation, and its terms.

'I'm not sure I have a voice for this. And, in truth, I don't want to offend anyone tonight. But I'm not sure it's yours any longer to chop up or sell.'

Benjamin asks quietly, 'Are you really so well off as a teacher in America that your share doesn't matter to you?'

Michiel frowns.

'Contrary to what you seem to think, it's also yours.'

Michiel keeps his eyes on his brother's face.

'You haven't mentioned it to him, Karien?'

'We've had a lot to talk about. The estate hasn't been foremost in my mind.'

'One third is mine,' Benjamin says, his tone gentle as he continues to look at Michiel. 'One third is Karien's.' A smile plays at his lips. 'And one third is yours.' He awaits the prodigal's response.

'I had no idea,' Michiel says, looking from his brother to Karien. 'Ounooi said nothing.'

'Now that you know, is it still as easy to say let's give it to the likes of Mamparra? Under her ilk, how long do you think it will take before this place is bush again with just a few boerbokke running about in the kakibos? It's been tried all over the country. Within a year there was nothing. Bankrupt. Should we all go that route, like lemmings?'

'Benjamin,' Karien says, 'He's only just heard. Jirre. He no more has an answer than you or I.'

What I wonder is whether there is not a different way, Michiel thinks but cannot say. He cannot utter the childlike phrase: Can Paradys not be shared, somehow, by all the people who work on it? What he does manage: 'From what I can see, things for the workers here look as grim as when I left.'

It is Karien who presents something close to his own thinking: 'Unless you – okay, we – find a way to use it more fairly, *everything* will be lost anyway. There are models of profit sharing, of giving people stock in the land and an interest in the harvest. Empowering—'

'Bring me examples of those, Karien! They never work. But I'm open for convincing.' Looking to Dirk and Giselle, 'Have you two swallowed your tongues?'

'You've heard my penny's worth of racism.' Giselle glares at her husband. Then, looking from him to Michiel, 'I'm intrigued, Michiel. Is it a bag of gold or a hot potato that's been thrown into your lap?'

He thinks a moment, then says: 'I assumed I was cut from the will. That's what I got from Oubaas the day I left, unless I completed my time. In the army.' He cannot keep himself from glancing at Dirk. Their eyes meet briefly and the other man averts his eyes before Michiel goes on. 'I don't know what to say. I've assumed it was all going to you, Benjamin.'

'Ounooi wouldn't have allowed that. Not after she became the boss. Frankly, neither would I. And Karien . . . she stayed here with them when you left. How many harvests did you help with, Karien, after you were already in the pastorie?'

Karien shakes her head, dismissing the question.

'I was on pass from the border . . .' Benjamin speaks, looking away from the table. 'Up there I didn't hear anything. When I got back Karien was here and you were gone. I'd never taken much note of those kinds of stories, but I'd heard of an infantry captain in Oshivello whose troops lined up and stomped on his pips.' He pauses and casts a glance at his brother. 'What happened?' Michiel hears no demand, no entitlement or the usual confidence brimming in Benjamin's voice. His brother leans forward, his head now turned to Michiel, inclined, in a gesture of sympathy. 'I saw only the newspaper and heard a bit from Karien,' Benjamin says. 'Neither Oubaas nor Ounooi said anything and what good was there in the paper those days about, you know . . .'

Exhausted before this turn in the conversation, Michiel's mind has at once cleared. A story repeated in a thousand and one versions, snippets and asides to Glassman. To Kamil. To Rachel and Malik.

And to the Pauls. How and where to begin, in and for this little gathering? And what of Dirk, with his bit part? Does he skirt chapters that he would share with Karien? Time rushes about in the matrix of memory that comes to overlay the moment.

Just over ten weeks after we buried Peet. Karien knows the dates. No, don't say that. Go back, to before.

'You . . .' Michiel looks at his brother, 'had helped secure my transfer.' He finds Karien's eyes. Nothing there of the earlier avowal. I cannot help you, her eyes seem to say, this is your blank slate. He looks into his mother's dark orchard, settling his gaze where the stoep lights limn the tattered hedge of figs.

'My platoon had guard duties at a small radar station.' The place, if he is correct, existed to observe Soviet submarine activity. How much of the Middle East's oil traveled past there on tankers? We were sentries to things we never questioned. Two cement tracks went up into the bush above a seaside resort. Did the holiday-makers sprawled on towels and under beach umbrellas on white sand even know of the station's being there? Once a week Durban's naval base came to a standstill for sports parade. Over lunch he told the other platoon commanders and the padre (he was not designated chaplain) that he was headed for the radar station. 'Nice day for the beach,' the padre said. 'I won't be swimming alone,' Michiel answered with a half-smile. Instead of going all the way to the station, he'd pull on to the sandy track leading to the beach. He'd packed civvies for himself. The day was to be followed by a night out.

From the torn shadows of figs, he brings his eyes to look directly into Karien's.

'In the officers' mess I'd befriended a few people other than the platoon commanders, who were all my age. I liked the padre. He'd studied philosophy somewhere in Europe. There was also a female sub-lieutenant. Her name was Sonia. She'd done psychology at Tuks and worked in Com-Ops. She and the padre took black and

Indian kids out into the wilderness of the Umgeni Valley. "Hearts and minds" work. I had a misplaced admiration for people with degrees.'

'Lieutenant Sol Govender was on board the SAS *Tafelberg* when he wasn't in base. His ship was docked and he was on shore leave at Tongaat with his family.' Along with Govender's face and words, Michiel has erased the make of the little white car, already there, parked on the sandy track. They knew the risks of shirked duties and of skin color on a beach designated *Europeans Only*. Still, during other visits Michiel hadn't encountered another human being. Not a single fisherman. No father teaching his son how to control a rod.

Summer, and that constantly changing water presenting a different picture every moment. A scattering of black rocks clustered with mussels, and seagulls tumbling, and three freighters anchored on the horizon, waiting to enter the harbor. It might have been an ocean anywhere on earth.

'We walked a few miles north, went into the waves. On the dunes above us we saw a couple, white, of course, probably on honeymoon. In their bathing suits with a picnic cooler. They waved. We waved back. All quite friendly.

'We swam some more, then went back up to the vehicles.'

He breaks off. He has not taken his eyes off Karien. It is to her, he realizes, that he is telling the story. An edge of defensive spite has now risen in him. 'I'm not sure whether you'd like full details, in color, of what we did on the back seat.'

She purses her lips, otherwise shows no response.

Mosquitoes drifted from the bush into the car so they went back, naked, out into the dunes. They were baking in the sand, still up against each other, when a shadow fell over them. Even before he looked up — such minutiae he *would* always remember — he thought of the honeymooners. Instead it was two uniformed cops. One white, one black. He is picking through what to say and what

to leave out. It is only the detail that he ponders, but offering the
story comes easily.

'The police took us . . . they let us dress first.'

Underwear held as evidence.

There was no denying who they were or where they belonged:
there was the vehicle with military license plates. And in the car, in
his wallet, Govender's naval ID. The police drove ahead in the
yellow van to the police station while they followed in their separate vehicles. Ensign Steyn sat in the European charge office and
Lieutenant Govender was taken through the Non-European
entrance. A black constable fingerprinted Michiel, the job perhaps
too messy for the white sergeant who supervised the rolling of the
fingers in ink, the pressing of fingertips on to the little white
squares outlined in black.

'There must have been phone calls and some agreement with
naval HQ.' They would be escorted to the gates of the military base.
More than once, behind the wheel of the brown military vehicle
following Govender, Michiel thought of abandoning the bakkie,
disappearing into the crowds on the sidewalks along the esplanade.
It must have crossed his mind that the honeymooners had gone
to a phone and called the cops. That's what he accepted had
happened. Michiel looks at Dirk. For a moment he wants her
husband to see the accusation. In his mind there is the memory
of a young man, sempiternally powerful as the shepherd of the
town's flock. But then he lets go of the gloating. What might have
been going through Sol Govender's mind he thought of only years
later, often in Glassman's chair.

Benjamin has leaned forward and gestures with the bottle to his
brother's glass. Michiel nods.

'The commander informed us we were not to "consort" with
each other. No contact with shore, not even by phone.' Govender
had become a stranger, an enemy. Had there been an opportunity to
speak, could they, together, have come up with a denial, something

less damning? Had the navy decided on a court martial there would be a litany of charges: from sodomy to public indecency; the illegal use of a military vehicle; leaving a military vehicle in an undesignated zone; leaving naval property unattended; and bringing the rank of officer into disrepute.

He skips ahead now.

'I was demoted. I'd have to complete my national service as a seaman after a week's leave. "Go and sort yourself out, young man, and say your *mea culpas* to your family," the base commander said.'

Govender would be stripped of his rank and dishonorably discharged. 'You will have to find a way to live with this. I'm not sure what your family might say or where you will find employment with a stigma of this nature to your name. Needless to say, you have done the other non-white officers no service. Unless sedition was your intention from the outset.'

Faces wait for him as he casts about for where to pick up the story. Can he drag Karien into what he says, from here? Does she wish that part offered to this gathering? Is this time for the truth, the whole truth and nothing but the truth, including each comma and question mark? Is that for him and her to wade into alone, or is it the world's to know? And when he comes to the husband — *The Word tells us it is an abomination . . . with me were men who were cured* — how will he keep suppressed the anger already burning his tongue?

Abbreviate. Enough, already.

'I came back to the farm. I didn't know there had been some article in the papers with our names. I thought the navy would keep it under wraps. I told Oubaas and Ounooi that it had been a set-up, because of the race thing on the whites-only beach. That Govender was a friend and I had made a mistake by going where the law said we couldn't. Oubaas was as angry about my lack of contrition and the subterfuge as he was about what I'd done. What I'd become.'

Glassman: *By being found out.*

I was no longer the kid he'd known. I was the one he'd always feared. *Show me you can be at least some excuse for a man by doing the honorable thing and go and finish your two years. Humble yourself in the face of your disgrace. After that, we can talk.*

'What did Ounooi say—'

'Let him finish, Giselle.'

'She was astonishing.' He pauses, looks at Benjamin, unable to stop the burning behind his eyelids. 'She is so rehearsed at holding her pose. You know her.' He looks from face to face, skipping over Dirk's. It is on his brother's face that his eyes settle. 'I'm so sorry,' he says, knowing that he is apologizing for what all this did or may have done to them. Not in a single way for his life now.

'Kariena, I cannot say how I wish I could undo your hurt.' His flight and the pain she must have endured alone were but the grand conclusion to countless smaller treacheries. At the heart of human relationship is language and the notion of solidarity, two things melded together to constitute what we call trust. Their sitting here, at this table, is grounded in that before anything else. One need not overturn the table, send glasses and bottles shattering to destroy that. You need not plunge a blade into someone's heart to lose trust. One may do so simply by keeping quiet about what you can almost not imagine to be true.

Glassman: By omitting your other desires you deceived her?

Michiel: That too.

Glassman: In what language, with what moral imagination that you had access to in that context, could you have told her? Your survival depended on secrecy as much as that world depended on finding you out.

'You never let anyone know anything,' Benjamin says.

'He did come to me, in Bloemfontein,' Karien intervenes.

'You simply got on a plane and left?'

'I took my passport from the safe. Oubaas and Ounooi were in here. He was watching TV. She was busy with the ledgers. His bunch of keys were on the kitchen table. We all had passports for the Transkei and Lesotho.'

'I knew, of course, you were in England. From the letter,' Karien says.

'I didn't need a visa to get in there.'

'I gave Ounooi your address. And later Leon came back from Australia and told us that he'd seen you there. He phoned whenever he had news from you. That's how she kept track of you.'

'Why did you never reply to Ounooi's letters?' Benjamin asks.

Michiel hesitates. Because of cowardice. Because instead of standing up for me she took me to a preacher and abided by his verdict. Because I loved her it was easier not to have her near me. He can almost not bear to speak: 'I can't say anything about her. She was our mother, Christ—' His eyes are on his brother, who now drops his head into his hands, shoulders shaking. Giselle has placed her arms around Benjamin, her face, resting against his back, is turned away from the table.

'Look,' Karien says, glancing from one brother to the other. 'When Oubaas got sick Ounooi must have been doing a lot of soul-searching about the years to come and the choices she'd made. We were riding one day when out of the blue she wanted to know if I ever thought about what might have happened had I not married Dirk. As though, maybe, being with you, Michiel, would have been like being married to a man with Oubaas's illness. I was irritated so I asked outright, do you want to know what would have happened if it was me and Michiel? At hearing your name she started to cry. One of the few times I saw her weep. She unpacked what she was able to, in her way. She thought Oubaas had been insane with grief about Peet and with whatever your thing in the navy had triggered. She tried, in the years after you left, to reason with him. As far as he was concerned there was only Benjamin left. And, later, little Thomas. He also developed a soft spot for me. You'll remember that, before . . . he didn't have much time for the two of us lying around reading poetry or going off to roam the veld. To Ounooi, Peet was a wound that never healed. Neither did you, Michiel. It wasn't your leaving or your lifestyle that bothered her. She was ashamed of not standing up to Oubaas. What's the nature of love, when love is so intimately connected with fear? When your letter came he'd already been ill for years. As he weakened she seemed to grow stronger. Everyone in town was saying "poor Beth Steyn this" and "poor Beth Steyn that". In truth, she was soaring. She'd finished teaching and now it was going to be the farm and her project in the township. She did the house renovations. The day of your letter she came straight to me from the postbox in town. She was coming home to tell him she'd heard from you and she was going to visit. You sent her a ticket?'

He nods. I was not wrong, then, about Oubaas and me. With Glassman he has excavated the gritty trenches of memory. The father could somehow not deal with this son. The powerful gaze bore a hint of suspicion, enough to ensure that the child noticed it. The child's difference from others and the way the child carried himself: it was *that* more than a suspicion of the boy's sexuality — for were the eyes not judging long before evidence of the latter arrived? And what had Oubaas known, about Peet? Nothing in his bearing towards the eldest suggested any of the discomfort he felt towards Michiel. And these people, here, what do they know of the buried brother's secrets?

'What about you, Dirk?' Michiel asks. 'I don't think I ever knew your army history.'

'Before being called here I was chaplain at Valhalla.' There is a twitter and flutter of bats leaving the eaves, expertly slicing out between the white bars rather than through the gates that are unlocked tonight. 'Like with so much else . . .' Dirk has cleared his throat. There is awkwardness in his voice, an unexpected diffidence. 'We look back. We can't believe. There is incredulity at how things were. How we were. How we lived, among ourselves and in this country.' The contrast to the supreme eloquence from the height of the pulpit is startling. 'A few years ago,' he goes on, more confidently, 'a young man, sixteen or seventeen, from the township came to me. You can imagine he was not very welcome there. I went with him to his parents. I convinced them to sit down and listen. They took him back. And there have been others, in my confirmation classes. More frequently since the discussion here has opened up. And you know, Michiel, we now have laws that protect people's . . . preferences. I think and act differently from the way I did then.'

So do I, Michiel thinks, but doesn't say. And I am no longer much impressed by tolerance of sexual identity, Mister Johnny-come-lately: I have my eyes open and my tongue primed for gay men in movies and battle fatigues or re-enacting in vain before full-length mirrors in gyms, their own version of the boys still bullying them on the playground. Later, in bed, Michiel will think, I wish I'd had something magnanimous to offer you, as that moment called for, Dirk. But I cannot divorce you from the hateful institution you serve. You remain in your pulpit, after all these years, with the radical verse stitched into the blue draping. This all he will mull over afterwards. What he says in the moment is, 'Yes, we all change,' nodding at Dirk and managing a lopsided smile.

Sleep, he was certain, would take him when his head touched the pillow. Lying in bed he listens to his niece's breathing, his disconsolation tinged with a glow of release – elation even – from the talk and wine. Taking care not to wake the child, he'd opened the cupboard and taken down an extra blanket in the dark. In the bathroom he flossed and brushed his teeth. He stood over the toilet bowl for what seemed an eternity and when the face in the mirror appeared distant he realized he was a little drunk. From a bottle in the cabinet he shook two aspirin. In the kitchen, where the lights were on for the others to bring in empty bottles and glasses, he chewed and swallowed the pills with plenty of water. He wants Kamil in the single bed with him. A field day they'd have with all that has passed here. Jetlagged or drunk, Kamil would pick over every word and gesture, mine for clarity what he'd missed in the sprinklings of Afrikaans. When the call came they knew this had to be Michiel's journey alone; his flight to Canossa. Still, he longs for Kamil's reading of the day. His own tumult, grief and even the joy he can deal with, but comfort and affirmation, trusting his own understanding, would be secured by talking to Kamil. Now all that remains are tomorrow's hours, and till then to sleep alongside this child's breathing, in the growing chorus of crickets and a cow bellowing into the night. He thinks again of the white people and Alida's family on one side of the grave and the workers on the other. He placed the envelope with its card and dollar coin beside the sugarbush and honeysuckle on the coffin's lid. *Laat Heer U seën oor haar daal, U guns uit Sion haar bestraal* — Lord, let your blessings pour over her, let your favor shine on her from Zion — as the vessel was lowered into the earth. The dogs were alert, involved somehow in what was taking place. Tears stream from the corners of his eyes and dam up in the shells of his ears. He feels again his father's doddering head against his shoulder and, again, going down into the tub with Kamil in his arms. He is seized by the old terror of the touch-and-go days, when Kamil lost sixty pounds in four months of ceaseless diarrhea and Rachel and Malik came every fortnight to be with them. Though he has not said this to anyone, a part of Michiel is married to Glassman in anticipation of what may still be in store for Kamil. And through Kamil for him. Though there is nothing, other than perhaps the tight skin and grooves like pincers beside Kamil's mouth, to suggest anything but health, they live knowing that statistics for the treatment's long-term effects are new. Five years of chemicals, daily. For many, AZT had worked only for a year. About the new drugs rumors and speculation abound: the liver, the kidneys, the heart. What *does* it do to the body even as it inhibits degeneration? The preliminary findings look excellent, their physician says, time will prove us right. Michiel himself resists cholesterol medication for the sole reason that no one agrees on what it does over time. Instead, he relies on exercise and diet. No such choice for Kamil: swallow the pills or within a matter of months return to the brink. Under the care of holistic healers Ling, Michiel's deputy at International House, has tried more than once to go off the cocktail, replacing the daily dose with herbs and health foods, only to see her negative (which to their kind is positive) bloodwork reversed and forcing her hastily to retreat to the triple regime. Protease inhibitors. Proteus, Homer's old man of the sea, foretelling what is to come and changing shape to escape his fate. In Michiel's imagination – this, too, he shares with no one – the virus initially resembles bilharzia larvae. Curling and stretching, they drift and dart, multiplying through Kamil's narrow veins. When Kamil takes the pills the little creatures die and he pisses the corpses out. Only some of their eggs, or seeds, or polyps, find a place in which to lie dormant in the body: in the beds of fingernails, in lymph glands or in the testes, it is speculated. While Kamil stays loyal to the regime the larvae are asleep, suspended in the chemical haze. But the instant he misses his dose they stir into life, into new shapes, now like pygmy seahorses or baby nudibranchs released to spawn anew in the body's tides, insatiable lips sucking at the blood, ravenous like Pac-Man. In the Solomon Sea they went with flashlights to see the spawning of the corals. For seven nights they hovered in submarine fireworks, Kamil's eyes big, crinkling behind the mask, pointing his hairy arm that looked so white down here towards an ecstasy that lasts for hours. The planet reaching an orgasm in trillions of tiny capsules, no color spared, popping, shooting, drifting, gliding, squirting, maybe becoming planula, some drifting for days, weeks and months in the currents before they may settle and might grow. At dawn you see what happened at night, like red cream on the swell. In shared images of death and life he imagines the spawning of corals when he thinks of Kamil's blood. Across the kitchen table, before hope would return with renovations and the granite-topped island and them still together today, Michiel faces Malik. Rachel is in the bedroom with Kamil, who two weeks ago attended his forty-third funeral. (Twelve missed during his time in Australia and his visits to the Solomons. He goes only to funerals of friends and good acquaintances: *I am not a funeral junkie*, he insists). Michiel, with Malik in front of him, cannot begin to think of saying that on this night of wet sheets and two towels on Kamil's stained pillow, of shit (again) on the sheets and what (again) seems like delirium (Michiel thinks more than once of dementia and a head forced under water, a mouth producing something garbled; of themselves speaking in tongues as Mamparra stands, facing white boys on the stoep); he wishes only to find these words: *Malik, you and Rachel will have to make a plan. This I cannot go through. Take him to Vancouver, I beg you, just get him out of my sight*. Malik's face is lined. His bald head furrowed. His fingers with the same square fingernails as Kamil's are clasped on the table littered with half-eaten take-out boxes. Tonight Kamil has eaten only light broth. The fungus growing in his throat makes swallowing painful. A faint reek has lingered in the apartment for months: when he defecates, it is as if his intestines spill out. The past week Michiel has carried him into the bath three of the seven times. Will this be Malik and Rachel's final visit? Should Nawal be summoned? But this has happened once before, only for them to see Kamil recover and go back to teaching. But this time, after tonight's sheets, Michiel contemplates calling friends who have access to things that can end it. It has been done for half a dozen men they knew, in even earlier stages than Kamil's.

'When we left Jaffa,' Malik says, 'he wore a blue sailor suit for the airplane. We had a dog named Malaika who could not come with us because everything was done in great secrecy. Rachel and I could not bring ourselves to tell the kids that they would not see Malaika again, though Nawal was old enough to know. When we went to leave the dog, Kamil promised to bring a moose bone from Canada. He was only a tiny boy. Where in Palestine could he have heard of a moose?'

Rachel enters. Her son has fallen asleep without pills tonight. *A good sign.* Her face is serene, like wax glowing from the inside. It is as if her husband carries each layer of their shared concern, while she, with her brown pixie hair and eyes behind little round glasses, has within her some fountain from which she draws strength and light.

'He finished the whole cup of soup,' she says. 'He has good color tonight.' Tomorrow morning he might wake up singing. She asks whether Michiel will again stay in the guest room with Malik, or on the couch in here. She will remain with Kamil. 'You both need a full night's rest.' Malik protests, his eyes glistening. 'I will be with Habibti tonight, Rachel. You and Michael sleep.'

The old bald man is in his pajamas on the king-sized bed when Rachel and Michiel go in to say goodnight. The lamp is on. Above Kamil is the Green Tara, leg extended from the lotus leaf, the blue bloom across her left shoulder, her right hand granting the boon. Malik's face on the pillow is turned to his son's. His hand rests lightly where the pajamas stand away from the prominent collar-bone.

In the bedroom, where years later Ounooi would sleep, once Michiel hears Rachel's regular breathing from the other twin bed he sees Peet's footprints from the bundle of clothes to hollows in the wet sand. His brother's ankles and strong calves wade into the waves. He sees Leon leaving the beach, head held low. When they meet, in the days before he flees to London, the man's eyes exude something more disturbing than sorrow. Years later, in Sydney, the look is still there, a glint that binds smile and laughter to perplexity, as though an occurrence he knows will never be over is being repeated behind it. Michiel submerges his face in the pillow and weeps.

Within days he will be back with Glassman for what becomes

the second series of long-term visits. Glassman: Walking out on your dying lover. Now there's a colorful quilt for you to spend the rest of your days under. Michiel: What if it is guilt that keeps me with him? Glassman: We have our work cut out for us, I see.

Territory re-covered from the earlier 'prematurely terminated' therapy and each new day's trivia revisited. Professional interactions at International House: Ling's unremitting passive aggression. Her wedding – to a Mexican–American – Michiel resents being invited to. Paul and Paul on the ground floor, who have just returned from a holiday in Cape Town with the story that South Africa's new constitution prohibits the death penalty and, astonishingly, contains a clause protecting people from discrimination on the basis of sexual orientation. He relives the incidents at the Commonwealth Institute. Was that not only the other day? How could Africa's oldest liberation movement so rapidly have changed its mind? So much for democracy: let courageous elites change policies behind closed doors and drag the great unwashed kicking and screaming into the new millennium. Kamil's organic diet and the cost of everything at Whole Foods. Washing soiled sheets himself, instead of leaving them for America. The intolerable intimacy of nursing someone you love towards death. Reciting the Pledge of Allegiance in a hall with a thousand others from fifty-seven countries, fingers crossed behind his back. Nawal, thinking of naming her new baby in memory of Kamil, but if Kamil doesn't die would two Kamils in one family not be one too many? On Powell Street a black man holds a sign that says *God Hates Fags*. Within ten minutes a white woman arrives with another that says *And She Loves Niggers*. Concern about being infected by Kamil and Michiel's shame about that concern and when his latest test results come relief and guilt comingled. Kamil's will leaving to Michiel the house he himself was left by one of the epidemic's earliest casualties. Should they sell the bottom unit of the old Victorian that was once a single home to the Pauls, who rent there, to make paying for the drugs easier?

Kamil on a confidential trial of new drugs that may kill him even sooner. Fear. Terror of abandonment. How at moments he still sees himself as single, maybe back in Australia. He wants to dive again, in warm water, among pygmy rays and mantas and sharks. Instead, his life has become this disease. Then, months after he has decided, *knows* he cannot, will not and does not wish to leave, ever, the rapid return of Kamil's T-cell count: victory, joy unbridled, Beethoven's Ninth Symphony played loud with open windows: *Freude, schöner Götterfunken, Tochter aus Elysium, Wir betreten feuertrunken, Himmlische, dein Heiligtum . . . Alle Menschen werden Brüder, Wo dein sanfter Flügel weilt . . .* Schiller's poem ringing out over the balcony and backyard, 'let them hear it in the Castro', as if the Lower-Haight were Vienna almost two centuries ago. Friends arrive with champagne and a hundred and one red roses. They get happily drunk and stoned. All over Eureka Valley people will live! Ordinary complex lives will again be the order of the day, not lives reduced to ways of dying. At dinner something is said about rent control, about Harvey Milk, Princess Diana – now also rolling out a prayer rug – the wonderful weather they've been having, about American football's homoeroticism being akin to that which exists between soldiers. Michiel is irritated; already high, he initially demurs; smokes more pot. Through a muddle of paranoia violent memories flood back, of fire and movement, of the thing he sees again on the night before he leaves Namibia. 'I felt ridiculous,' he says, 'like an impostor in the army and in the scrum.' 'You're joking! Beside them every night, in the scrimmage, all sweat and testosterone!' from one of the Pauls. Bullshit, Michiel says. He was never able to suspend disbelief: someone was always being hurt. The stuffed bag for bayonet drill, the target with its human silhouette. Never succeeding at forgetting ('dissociating'), relentlessly ashamed of being part of it and at the same time so apart from it: a fraud, an interloper in the conspiracies of violence. Nothing sexy about that, he mutters, fed up with their company on the night of Kamil's celebration. Glassman: That may be where both football and war can be read as erotic: you can touch as long as you violate. Michiel: Instead of fucking? Glassman: Even fucking may be a defense against intimacy. You know that. Michiel: What if it is just part of healthy, normal masculinity to give and receive sexual pleasure widely, like animals? Glassman: I have known many more who need the comfort and intimacy of a deeper relationship – with all its shortcomings. Michiel: In some ways I still feel ashamed of that, in myself. Glassman: Of wanting to be loved, wanting to give love? Michiel: As though I am a lesser male. Glassman: Tell me more about this *normal masculine*. Michiel: Just being a regular guy. Glassman: Who is this regular guy? Michiel's eyes go from the shrink to the seascape painting on the wall, to the black-and-white photograph and poem. He drops his gaze to the carpet, waiting for the shrink to answer his own question. He looks back at Glassman and sees Oubaas at the dam wall, Miemie beside him, the tips of reeds drooping into the water. They stare into each other's eyes, unspeaking, for what feels like minutes—

He wakes, shouting. Oubaas has hanged himself. He is on the bed in the guest room with Rachel beside him. Rattled, he fumbles for the light.

'Uncle Michiel?'

Bianca.

His old bed.

'I'm so sorry, my girl. I need to turn on the lamp.'

'That's okay.'

He finds the switch. Bianca sits up, squinting. A bad dream, he says, a silly nightmare. He throws back the blanket and gets quickly from the bed. I'll be back, he says, I need to use the bathroom. You can turn off the light, Bianca, go back to sleep, my dear. He has to stop himself running down the passage and waking the house. Heart pounding, he turns his father's door handle, bracing himself. His hand runs along the inside wall, searching for the switch.

'Is dit jy, Alida?'

'It's me, Oubaas.' He breathes. Whispering, 'Can I turn on the light?'

The bedside lamp goes on. The old man doesn't open his eyes: 'What is it, Michiel?'

Michiel's eyes find the tie, purple on the white duvet where he left it.

'Nothing, Oubaas. I couldn't sleep. Sorry for waking you.' He passes soundlessly from the door into the room and takes hold of the tie's tip, drags it to him and crumples it in his fist.

'Goodnight, Oubaas.'

'Night, Michiel.'

While using the toilet he thinks of the dream: he is in Glassman's chair, but *here*, in the overgrown rose garden and he has long hair, tied in a ponytail. The garden is from a painting by Rousseau, bright colors, insects droning from flower to flower. Someone he cannot see grabs his hair from behind and forces him to look at the jacaranda in flames; a body hangs there from a burning branch. A dog? A tiger? A half-skinned carcass? Something about the tree bothers him. The shape is wrong. He tries to free himself: if he can prevent the body from falling before the flames burn through the tie it will not be dead. He calls *Habibti, Habibti* but the branch is engulfed and he hears the crack as it separates from the huge trunk and he dives, yelling, trying to catch the body before it can strike the ground.

He looks at his watch. Five pm on the West Coast. Kamil will be on BART, heading back into town. Did he find a tank and has he managed to coax Xanthippe back into it?

Bianca has arranged the kaross around her shoulders. She smiles shyly and yawns, running the jackal fur against her lips. He is about to turn off the light when she asks about the nightmare. 'I'll tell you in the morning,' he says, leaning on his elbow towards her and placing the tie on the nightstand. 'No need for *you* to be having bad dreams on my account.'

'I'm wide awake,' she says. 'Will you go straight back to sleep, Uncle Michiel?'

'In a while,' he replies, though of that he is unsure.

'Can I come and lie down with you? Just till you fall asleep?'

He throws back the covers as she leaves her bed. She slides her arm over him, rests her cheek on his chest. From the practiced gesture he guesses that she still sleeps, occasionally at least, with her parents. She asks for a story. He thinks of reading to Nawal's children.

'If I tell you one about rats do you promise not to have nightmares?'

'I'm not scared of rats.'

'A hundred rats?'

'I'm not scared of a hundred rats.'

'Well, this is about a hundred thousand million rats that can swim over oceans!'

She giggles and with her fingers pinches his belly. 'Tell the story and stop pestering me, Uncle Michiel.'

'There is a town that has a humongous problem with rats.'

'*The Pied Piper*,' she whispers. 'One of my favorites.'

'The rats are everywhere. In the streets, in cupboards, in food, in churches and on farms. There's been one big takeover.'

'In the schools, and in shops too. And in the circus tent,' she whispers.

'In people's shoes, in their beds, under the judge's robes, on their plates, in their peppermint tarts!'

'They didn't have peppermint tarts in the olden days! You can't have peppermint tart without Peppermint Crisp, can you?'

'They used goat's milk with ground-up honeycomb and peppermint leaves. And who said anything about the olden days, anyway?'

'I still think you're wrong.'

'Would you indulge me? May I be allowed narrative control?'

Again she pinches him, giggles, 'What's nattinive control?'

'Mmm . . . that's a different story. One day a man playing his recorder comes to town.'

'Flute. And he wears a suit like a court jester, with red pointy shoes.'

'Any further editorial?'

Again the pinch: just get on with it.

The piper offers to solve the problem by playing the flute and leading the vermin from town and the people undertake to pay him for his help. On a sunny afternoon the piper walks the streets piping his tune. Rats come crawling out of desks, from orchards, from plates, from every building, every sewer, every nook and every cranny.

'And every peppermint tart, I suppose,' she mutters, giggling.

He pretends to pinch her and she laughs softly.

In a wide ribbon the rats follow the piper to the river. As he stands on the bank playing his flute they all go in. In their hundreds and thousands. But now the townspeople refuse to give him his dues. He goes to the mayor, to the town council, to the legislature and to the queen. The grown-ups hurry about on their way to work in offices, in the army and factories and parks and beauty salons and high-rise buildings and hospitals and universities. The piper lifts his pipe and begins another little tune. From all over the town children come, in tens, then hundreds, then thousands, all singing and dancing along to the piper's new tune and following him as he walks out of town.

'Back to the river, where they all drown,' she murmurs, her voice now sleepy.

No, he says. No one drowns because of what grown-ups who always think they know better did or didn't do . . . He leads the children safely up the mountain to a cave. He asks them to wait there. Then he goes back to the town, where the adults — horror, horror, horror — have found their children gone. Again the piper asks for his dues. Now the people run to their safes, their mattresses, their checkbooks and bank accounts and stocks and bonds. They place everything they own at the piper's feet with his upturned red shoes. The piper lifts the flute and plays a new little tune. And slowly, all singing and dancing, the children come back into town with incredible stories of their journey and what they saw on the mountain.

In the morning, bringing coffee for Michiel and orange juice for her daughter, Giselle will find them like this, the old Basotho blanket askew, the bedside lamp glowing dull against the bright sunlight outside the blinds. Oh, this child of her and Benjamin, who takes every chance to crawl into bed with them, who cannot talk to a living thing without touching. Bianca, fair beloved. How long before the world does its dirty job on you? For a moment Giselle will forget that she cannot call Ounooi to share the moment.

This she will repeat to Benjamin in some detail, who in turn will tell it to Michiel in the hour before he leaves.

'Michiel . . . Bianca . . .' she says softly, blinking to clear her vision, 'time to start the day.'

A blanket of mist envelops the town so that the church steeple floats like the mast of a ship, adrift, cut from its moorings. The thermometer stands at eleven degrees. Fifty Fahrenheit, he guesses. There could be snow on the Malutis. He finds Oubaas in the living room, watching *Good Morning South Africa*. Familiar white faces presenting news bulletins have, in the time since he left, been replaced by younger black faces, the program now punctuated with words and expressions from African languages amid the predominantly English reportage. The lead segment of news is about the country's currency plunging to an all-time low against the dollar and pound; the reason, he realizes, that he received almost double the money he thought he was exchanging. What he doesn't need for gas he'll leave for Alida and the others. Another segment of the bulletin deals with opposition from local environmentalists to a US warship docking in South African waters. In international news, three people have been killed in a Turkish suicide bombing.

'Did you manage to get back to sleep?' Oubaas asks in the break between the news and weather report.

'I did, Pa, thank you. How about Pa?'

'I haven't slept since the night your mother died.'

At breakfast he receives a text from Kamil: *Off to bed. X still on the loose. Have food out to trap her. Got new tank. Love K.*

Karien is in Ounooi's jodhpurs, boots and black riding fleece. The Levis in which he flew make do for him, along with a pair of Oubaas's old riding boots: no socks as the boots are half a size too small. Against the cold he has put on last night's jersey, and Alida brought a faded brown army jacket of Benjamin's that has *Steyn* in faded letters above the heart-pocket.

By the time they ride out, the workers are in Ounooi's orchard raking up leaves and petals like a thin layer of molten wax. On stepladders, pruning shears are used to snip off the narrow ends of branches enfeebled by the hail's force. These are to be gathered from the wasteland into great heaps, then shoved into transparent garbage bags and trailered up to the compost dumps. Once the new layers are almost dry, and while there is no wind, they will be set to smolder, quietly, for days, like incinerators, the humidity incubating the mold acid for next season's fertilizing.

A spring in rags. Bark, chipped and torn, stands up and away from stems and branches like flesh wounds. The few blooms that remain hang flaccid and bruised. By lunchtime they too will be a dull brown, all hope of the trees bearing fruit wilted. Ounooi's orchard entering its own twelve months of mourning. No bottling, no sales; Paradys's lucrative home industry in remission. No weeks in the shady summer shed with music and talk radio for Mamparra and Liesbet. They will be sent out into the sun for their real job of scaring off birds and baboons from the harvest. Mamparra with her tin unused, singing the lines. And next spring? Summer? After a year without fruit a tree often returns with abandon. *Expect a record crop*, Benjamin and Oubaas will surely say. Who will steam the bottles, then, order the sugar, design new labels and enter the new harvest's dates, send the truck out to cafés, grocery stores, gift shops? For a moment he can see himself at the long tables, hear himself dishing out orders, the banter with whomever is shirking duties, and on the phone to expand their market. Each image and sound more appealing than peddling English in Beijing. A vision of himself which is no less a pipe dream than his nephew's and Thabiso's, of one day becoming some kind of Oubaas here; *one day when I'm grown up* has arrived. And where, he wonders, would Kamil be while he is in the shed? And how do I say – looking away while I wash the spinach – *a third of the farm in Africa is mine*? I had no idea, Kamil, but I would like to run my mother's orchard. Will you come with me? There is a university only a few hours away where you could teach; with your color you may even be seen as a special case . . . And how do you meet Malik and Rachel's eyes when one of them tilts a head and says: *Let me tell you about an orchard in Jaffa. Let me tell you about orange trees chopped down and salt rubbed into the earth's wound.* And Kamil as Meryl Streep as Karen Blixen: *I had a farm where Tel Yafo grows higher every decade beside the blue Mediterranean. Where orange trees*— And Malik interrupts with: *Irony will only take us so far, Habibti.* And Rachel, with arms wrapped around her husband's shoulders, whispers: *But which ways of knowing teach humility, my love?*

Side by side he and Karien ride down lanes of unscathed trees in the crop orchards. They will pass through here and then over to the Oberholzer land. From there, through gates and across the next farm all the way down to the Caledon. It is the route Karien rode often with Ounooi. Michiel is keenly aware of leaving Benjamin and Dirk to the business of overseeing the clean-up: while he and she malinger down memory lane into a wonderworld that once was theirs, the other brother and her husband get their hands dirty at the bridge.

'How's it feel?' Karien asks.

'Like I've been here every day of the last fifteen years.'

'You were.'

'My shrink would love you for saying that.'

She's on email now, she says. She'd be happy for them to correspond. She'd like to know what music he's listening to, the exhibitions they're attending and what he's reading. Maybe exchange reading lists? She belongs to the book group that Ounooi founded. With the library and Sam Thabane's help she's starting another with women in the township. She would like to become fluent in seSotho. And a world is opening up here through the pens of old writers like Mphahlele, Modisane and Kuzwayo, who wrote in English. And voices she has just now been discovering: Njabulo Ndebele, Zoe Wicomb, Damon Galgut, Zakes Mda, Marlene van Niekerk and Mandla Langa. Oh, and Yvonne Vera from Zim. She and Dirk — they read to each other in bed — are almost through a novel called *The Quiet Violence of Dreams* by a young writer called K. Sello Duiker. From among these, one will arise to take over from the great Gordimer and the even greater Coetzee. Oh no, Michiel says, now you're putting Ounooi's boot on holy ground, and besides, you're comparing apples and pears. Then there's Krog's *Country of My Skull*, a book Kamil has taught alongside Fanon, Todorov and Bakhtin in a course on postcolonial confession, memory and trauma.

'Remember how we—'

'Yes! Wasn't that how we fell in love with poetry!'

'When did Krog start writing prose?'

One of the things they missed out on by not being full-time students together is the bond forged between those who together discover the great books and poems of their lives. Instead, in Sydney and London, where he still held himself aloof, he sat in student unions overhearing what was passing at tables beside him: he'd hear an excitement — a belief in a sentence's force, a life changed for ever by a single line — announced in voices whose compulsion to share what has happened was volcanic.

From blooming orchards they ride out into the weak sun and green veld. She is the one to dismount and open the gate between Paradys and Diepfontein. Long gone is the split-pole stile beside the gate for the black schoolkids to climb over instead of risking them leaving the gate ajar. On plowed land, hazy green with new mielie plants, a secretary bird walks with stiff legs, its neck moving from side to side as it looks for prey, gray head-quills fluttering in the breeze. They pass through another gate that Karien again hops off to open. 'When we get to the river,' she says with a smile, 'you'll see that I've brought you here partly under false pretences.' He waits as she closes the gate and remounts. From the inside pocket of Ounooi's fleece she produces a pack of Camel Lights. 'I have one a day. Your mom and I smoked, secretly, whenever we were alone.'

'Ounooi?'

'Just a few. She'd never get hooked, with the running.' She looks at him. 'When did you stop?'

'Kamil refused to kiss me if I'd been smoking. And smoking in public in the US — like having your dick sucked in private — is a greater crime than backing coups in Latin America or bombing Serbia. So I started running. Replaced nicotine with endorphin.'

She doesn't smoke in front of Dirk and the kids, less because of Dirk's dislike of what she's doing to her lungs than not to set a bad example for Thabiso and Palesa. Then, almost without a pause, she says: 'I couldn't carry a pregnancy to full term, afterwards.'

He had guessed as much.

'Last night,' she says, and he feels her eyes on him, 'when you were speaking, I could hear your brain clicking with what to say and what to leave out. Also for my and Dirk's sake.'

It was not for his sake, Michiel thinks.

'There is a part of me that wants to tell you exactly how it was.' She is quiet for a while and then clears her throat, sniffs from the cold and wipes her nose on her sleeve. 'But then, that's impossible. I'm also concerned about the pornography of it.'

He adjusts the boots in the stirrups and turns his head to meet her eyes.

'When you spoke,' she says, and pauses. 'About going back to the car with him I filled in the pictures anyway. I wanted you to tell me who did what to whom. What his face looked like. His legs. His chest. His penis. It's the way I am. I want to know, even if I can't, really. Dirk and I have been to Europe twice. One of the first things I dragged him to see was a porn movie. It's legal here now, but I'm not all that interested. I mean, it's not as though I'd like to have it in the house, with the kids. But there was something about sneaking into a show in Munich and, later, in Paris. I wanted to see for myself. There was something liberating about it! Can you imagine this lot here — the poor dominee caught in a cinema watching porn with his wife?'

'She with the scarlet letter on her chest.'

'How much do you want to know?'

'Tell me the way you want to. I've had time enough with my imagination.' He looks from the horse's ears to her. Now you can tell me in your own words so I can own my part of what is ours.

'I still prefer big brush strokes. In bright colors.' She smiles. 'Interrupt,' she says, 'if you have questions.'

'I should have said the same, last night.'

Her friend the primaria was from Zastron. The family had a cottage at the dam where weekends they went to boat, water-ski, swim and braai. No one there during the week. Key under a stone at the front door.

They take towels and sheets from the Emily Hobhouse laundry.

They borrow another friend's car.

They don't go into Botshabelo, where SADF troops and the police are swarming. There is a national State of Emergency. They pick up the nurse from a street corner outside the township. If anyone stops them or comes to the dam the white girls will pretend they're on break from varsity, with the black woman their hired help. When they get to the cottage, the key is not there. They cannot go back: this is the one day the nurse has off and the pregnancy is at twelve weeks. They shatter a windowpane to get in and open the door from the inside. The window frame will not budge. She lies down on the back seat. A wire is inserted into a thin plastic tube that is then pushed into the uterus. The wire is forced through the tube and jabbed about, feeling for the fetus. The plastic tube is left in her to irritate and drive down whatever is clinging to the womb. She starts to bleed. There is not enough cotton wool and sheeting and towel to contain the flow. The friend goes to the cottage window and from outside rips down the curtains. With these they line the seat for the drive back. Before dropping the nurse off they make a detour so the friend can go into the bank to cash a check from her scholarship fund. It seems like the bleeding has stopped. They drop the woman off at a different location. In the middle of the night the bleeding resumes. The fetus will expel itself at any moment; then it will be over.

'It clung on as if for dear life,' she says.

Karien cannot stand the pain. If they go to the hospital in Bloemfontein the police will get involved. And her father is a cop.

Ahead, at seeing the horses, guinea fowl scatter with a tinny din, some flying a short distance before landing in the veld. The horses head into the hills above the river. The land here is dry; no rain has fallen for days.

'We came to Paradys.' Their eyes meet. 'It was the middle of the night.'

They have reached another gate and before she can get off, he does. He winces as he remounts, realizes he jumped off in apprehension of the memory of her physical pain.

'I couldn't go to Dad. And not to Mom, where every cake recipe becomes a melodrama. There was never any doubt that Ounooi—' She has tugged at her reins. His horse is a few strides ahead of hers. He turns his head. Her face is held up to the sun. 'I still can't believe she's gone. I don't trust the bullshit of too much gratitude,' she says, 'but I do owe her my life.'

The horses follow their well-trodden path to the river. Below them, the Caledon threads silver through the new green of trees. Down there on the riverbank, beneath the poplars, Christmas or New Year's Day was spent with the extended family of Steyns and Fords. Fold-out furniture, lamb splayed on the spit, potato and beet salads, oven-baked bread, and trifle, oozing Oude Meester brandy or Three Ships whisky, for dessert; the boys and their cousins running upstream, drifting down on inner tubes then running back up, drifting again, for hours, blissful in the knowledge that all their days were to be but a continuation of this moment's extravagant joy.

The stoep light went on even before the girls got out of the car. Oubaas came to the door; it was before the burglar bars. She had a towel pressed to her pelvis. He carried her into Michiel's bedroom. They wanted to take her to hospital. She begged them not to. Ounooi sent Oubaas to town. 'Remember the midwife, Tannie Salie Pienaar? She helped a few girls over the years. Her daughter Pamela — remember her? — lives in New Zealand now. Salie looked me over and said it was too dangerous because I was at least four months pregnant. I said that was impossible. Karien doesn't need to give you a date, Oubaas said, I know the day, the hour and the place this happened. Abortions can be done till three months, I said. Of course I know how far you are and you're too weak, Salie said. You can die. All I can do is help you survive what has been done to you. And save the baby.'

He looks down at his fingers plaited with the reins and swallows whatever is pushing up from his chest.

Ounooi sent Karien's friend to inform her lecturers that she was down with pneumonia. Salie came to the farm once a day. 'God knows what Oubaas paid her.' Ounooi convinced Karien that they needed to bring in Dirk: she and Oubaas alone couldn't deal with Karien pregnant with their grandchild while her parents in town thought she was at her desk in Emily Hobhouse. Salie saw Constable Opperman on his motorcycle or Gerda Niehaus in the butchery and had to pretend it was just another 'hello' passing between them. Once Dirk was brought into the inner circle he offered to speak to Karien's parents. 'I said that if anyone went near Mom or Dad I'd get out of bed and never stop walking. I had scholarship money and would go and have the baby in peace some-where else. I was in your bed for ten days.' Alida washed the sheets and towels but they wouldn't come clean so she burned them with the compost. Ounooi called the university and pretended she was Gerda Niehaus. There had been a misdiagnosis, she told the lec-turers and the house-mother: pneumonia was in fact mumps and Karien would soon be back. They hatched a plan for Ounooi and Alida to raise the child at Paradys without denying it was Michiel and Karien's, while Karien would rejoin the path of the capital G. 'Oubaas said nothing, but he smiled a lot. I think it was in those days that we became quite fond of each other. Any baboon could see how the thought of a grandchild excited him, though he wasn't ready to forgive you and no one knew where you were. Men in uni-form arrived at the front door. I was sure it was the Botshabelo police. Ounooi's first reaction was that something had happened to Benjamin in Angola. It was terrible. She stayed in the room with me and sent Alida out.' She pauses and looks at Michiel. 'They were looking for you.'

He sees the river is swollen, but not in flood. A wide sandbank reaches from the Lesotho side to mid-stream, where the reflection of the cold sky is broken. They stay mounted and allow the horses to graze; grasshoppers skitter up in rapid color; butterflies tumble over yellow and orange wild flowers.

Oubaas grew angrier with each call or visit from the military police. Karien kept in touch with her parents so they wouldn't know she wasn't in residence. Dirk was now there every day, clearly no longer only as the family's spiritual guide. 'There was nothing about him I didn't like. With looks like that, who needs to develop their brain, I asked. He said: If I can forgive your beauty, then surely you can forgive mine. I was exhausted. I had no energy. Dirk gave me balance. His confidence reminded me of Peet's. I felt replenished, though it was a stretch to get used to the idea of being pregnant with you while falling in love with someone else.'

He feels her eyes on him but looks away.

Eventually they could not keep from telling her parents. From Gerda Niehaus there was much wailing and tearing of hair. Karien had ruined not only her own young life but the entire family's. Gerda mailed a ten-page handwritten letter to Ounooi, begging forgiveness for ruining the Steyns' fleckless name right on the heels of the family's terrible loss. Constable Opperman called police stations across the Orange Free State to be on the lookout for Michiel. His fury at the *koelie-loving homosexual who did this to my daughter* gripped Gerda like a stranglehold once Ounooi refused to play the game of suffering or blame brought on by *this slut I raised*. The town too was in the know once word got out of Dirk's daily drive to Paradys. He was summoned before the church council. His refusal to desist from openly consorting with a *fallen woman*, and his insistence that she be allowed to attend services *in her condition*, led to his being disbarred from the white church until after the child's birth. He ministered in the township. Karien, already showing, was welcomed there.

When she miscarried she chose to have the hospital take care of what came out of her. What is not born alive, she says, doesn't require a funeral. 'I didn't ask for details. It seemed better to live without that picture in my head.' Dirk's censure was immediately lifted. Michiel tries to remember himself in London. Where could he have been at the instant the womb's lining finally let go?

'For days afterwards, when I sat in the hot bath on the farm, things came out of me. Pieces of red tissue. Fine, like torn lace or rose petals, drifting around me in the water. The first time it happened, I called for Ounooi. She kneeled at the tub to hold me.'

Recuperating at Paradys, she started drawing and painting again. In the weeks after the pregnancy terminated she decided she would not return to law. She had fresh paint stains on her fingers and beneath her nails. It was not Ounooi's style, but Karien she begged and flattered. To Ounooi, bound in a vision of intellectual achievement and its public display, life's real meaning lay in books, in formal qualifications and in Karien getting silk, then the red garments and the bench. The country had only ever had one female high court judge. That Karien was taking a different turn — as a woman — vexed Ounooi particularly. She herself could have been a more snazzy professional but had opted for teaching. Were his mother's dreams rooted in an unspoken regret at the paths she herself had not taken?

'She was fond of Dirk. And she loved the kids. But right to the end she was hoping I'd walk the walk, restore myself to glory and vindicate her and me in public. Even you. I should have written to you again,' she says. 'With time, I let it go. Life goes on. Accounts, committees, servicing the car, children's sport, arguments, the church choir, bake sales, snotty noses. When you did come into my thoughts I told myself it was up to you to pluck up the courage and find your way back. Or write again. Dirk likes the way Jews ask forgiveness three times and then stop. The times you tried were enough. In a way it was also easier, not having you here. Resolving conflict is such fucking hard work.'

'Last night, on the phone,' he says, 'the only person Kamil asked about was you.' Then, 'Do you think of that time . . . of us?'

'It's there . . . When Ounooi was going to you, while she was away, and since we heard you were coming it's been with me, on and off.' She looks at him, wavers, then says, 'We miscarried twice.' He notes her choice of pronoun. They could do in vitro, she continues. There is a chance they could have kids of their own. She has friends having first babies as late as forty. But neither she nor Dirk is keen on that. His and her discomfort with the culture of 'a child of one's own DNA', the whole idea 'that we need little penis and vagina sculptures of ourselves' may be a practical rationalization, but whatever it is, she wishes it were an issue people would think about. Different, she thinks, but related to the breeding of specialty pets while pounds overflow and the abandoned and discarded starve or are put down en masse. There is the Chinese state's policy of one child per family, he says. Imagine proposing such a law in Europe or the US. I'm probably in favor of it, she says, if the sex of the fetus doesn't determine who survives. 'But then, what is a family? Who'd be allowed to have the one kid, anyway, these days?'

They tie reins to stirrups, loose enough for the horses to graze. She points to the rock where she and Ounooi came for their cigarettes. He and she sit there, tightly against each other, with a chilly breeze blowing across the water from Lesotho. 'I want you to know,' she says, her hand finding his in the coat pocket, 'that in most ways it was a relief. Giving you up.' Their fingers intertwine and he squeezes her hand. In herself she'd known from early on that they were lovers through familiarity and fondness. Although it was subsumed by righteous anger the day she turned her back on him, she also had a sense of being set free, that he had made it possible for her to leave him, and thus also for her eventually to walk away from Ounooi's spell. It was wonderfully terrifying.

'We put an easel on the stoep. I drew only what I saw from there. In our sitting room is a sketch, from then, of Miemie on the steps between the strelitzias. Workers went by with sheep going to the abattoir. I painted the back of the herd passing by the ripe pomegranates. It seemed such an important thing. Then, just a single sheep, looking back. More than anything I wanted to make art.' She tried, over the years, to explain this to Ounooi. 'She couldn't get it. Maybe I was the daughter she'd never had. If I were hers, I may have despised her.' She laughs, wiping off tears. 'It's strange,' she goes on, 'a parent's obsession with a child's career and coupling. I'm already in knots about where and with whom my two will end up. Ounooi's great relief when she came back was that you have a good job and that you have someone.'

'Mine too,' he says. 'Though I'm still uncomfortable with how ordinary those two things seem. How over time we lower our expectations.'

'You happy with your job?'

'So-so. I'd have to do a PhD to become an academic proper. Or I have to teach high school or otherwise stick with ESL.' After Berkeley, he interviewed for a position as an English teacher at a Bay Area private academy. He was certain he'd nailed the job, until the last evening's dinner with the faculty and the principal. A question was asked about his accent. He had it down close to a generic US phonology, but when self-conscious he sounded Southern, and certain words were almost Canadian, from living with Kamil. One of the teachers was from the UK. He responded to Michiel's gloss of his time as a conscript by relating his own status as a former Royal Marine. He spoke vaingloriously of fighting the IRA in Northern Ireland: *We were fighting real terrorists.* Michiel, forgetting interview etiquette, replied: *If your terrorists were real, then so were ours.* It was as though a viper had been thrown on to the table. Kamil, after the debacle: In parts of this city, like in parts of New York and LA, you may not have to bite your tongue about being queer. But nowhere here do you utter a word about what England does to Ireland, and you simply pretend never even to have heard about Israel in Palestine. And you don't ever, *ever* use the phrase *Occupied Palestine* — even after you have tenure. To an ex-officer of the English Imperial Army, Michael!

'Clearly you didn't want to follow in your mother's footsteps.'

Karien chuckles. From above comes a dull whistle. A falcon swoops in the blue, swirls on the wind and wings back, higher into the sky.

'There are times I'd like to do something else. But then, perhaps I'm too timid to change direction this late in life.'

'Surely you have more imagination than that?'

'I can hear Kamil saying something to that effect.'

'You love him.'

'My shrink says he was Psyche to my Eros. Only instead of a candle, it was the can opener.' They laugh, she clapping an open hand on her thigh.

'And you, Dirk?'

'I do,' she snorts, but how different it shows itself from the poetry the two of them thought it would be. 'Love is like a berserk Psyche running after a fleeing Eros with role changes every few days.'

The horses' ears are forward, their necks strained as far as the reins allow, their eyes intently across the river. Down an eroded gully, a woman and a boy accompany a herd of goats. Once they reach the grassy plateau the sounds of bells reach Michiel's ears. The woman is at the back shooing on stragglers, the boy at the front carrying a short whip. The goats trot bleating down the embankment, their muzzles going down into the water.

'One of our deacons . . . a nice guy . . . He's gay and married to a woman in my reading group. It must make everything easier for him.'

'And for her?'

'What do you mean? He gets a free ride through life!'

'Surely *you* have more imagination than that? We have friends in a marriage of that kind. A good marriage.'

She is quiet for a while. When she eventually speaks she says: 'I'll have to think about that.'

'How are your parents?' He thinks of Gerda Niehaus in the line-up at church, yesterday. How hard time has etched itself on the exquisite face he could still see from before, at the butchery counter, rows of carcasses on metal hooks suspended three-deep from the ceiling behind her.

'Ma sold the house to the first black family who moved into town. She's divorced again and lives with Auntie Antoinette. Last month I had to fetch her when Antoinette threw everything Ma owns out on to the pavement. Ma was standing in the road shouting: *You're a whore, Antoinette! You've been a whore since we were kids.*' Karien shakes her head, looks at Michiel and shrugs. Nothing has changed on that front, the look suggests, I can't be bothered. Then, 'I'm quite fond of Dad. He's getting old. They forced him into early retirement.' She smiles and leaves the subject for another. 'Dirk wasn't much help, was he, back then? Mind if I have my cigarette now?'

'Stand over there, because of the smell.'

'*You* push off,' she says. 'This is Ounooi's and my smoking spot.' She lights up and walks off. From there, she asks again: 'How do you feel about Dirk?'

At least some of what he thinks of the man she married is colored by events that are far removed from the day in the vestry. In Gizo, Kiko brought news of South Africans in town for wreck-diving: 'There are two very sexy women from South Africa going diving with me this morning. This afternoon I'm taking them to Skull Island. Maybe today is my lucky day!' Michiel was less interested in meeting South Africans abroad than locals or other expats seemed to think he should be. He didn't recognize the woman at first, out of her uniform. When she spoke her voice touched a scar of memory only occasionally fingered: Sonia, from Salisbury Island. His face flushed as he took her in, in her red bathing suit, her lover at her side. At her insistence he joined the two women for lunch. Kiko was there again, now masquerading as a waiter ready to serve. Sonia wanted to talk of what had happened, back then. *That was long ago, I scarcely think of those days,* he said. She, though, had something she wanted to get off her chest. The partner already knew the story.

It hadn't been the honeymooners on the beach. The truth, as Sonia gave it to him, was a little more surprising. On one of the nights the four of them had gone drinking on the beachfront, something had tweaked the padre's attention and he mentioned to Sonia his suspicion of something afoot between the Indian lieutenant and the white ensign. While studying in Europe, the padre had witnessed first-hand *the dangers of men in dresses marching down the streets, kissing, eroding the cornerstone of our civilization.* Michiel's aside of 'not swimming alone' added up, in the padre's mind, to only one thing. Concerned that the military police themselves wouldn't act on this information, the padre tipped off the civilian police. When there was no civilian charge, it was again he who made calls to local papers. When the padre concluded his national service, he traveled the Front Line States as a preacher to the poor, in the pay of South Africa's National Intelligence Service. Were it not that Sonia had been living her own secret life in the officers' mess — already at the time of the padre taking her into his confidence — Michiel may never have heard this version of events.

Kiko returned with the dessert menu, his eyes sparkling. Michiel pulled a face at him and said, 'Today rabis day belong you ya. Hem nao iu no lucky.'

Kiko, in mock perplexity, 'No more ya. How now bae iu savi tofela hem no laaik hem local man?'

'Iu trastem me no more, Kiko. Bae me no try for lucky witem tofela ya, if me iu!'

'What was that about?' Sonia wanted to know once Kiko left.

'I was suggesting he take an altogether safer route than he'd been planning to Skull Island.'

'To think they were cannibals,' the partner said as Kiko left. 'This place seems so peaceful and civilized. *Lonely Planet* says that the headhunting went on well into the nineteen-twenties!'

And in forty-five we dropped the culminating glory of our civilization on Japan, Michiel would have responded under different circumstances, or had he known the two women better. Far more respectful, far more *Christian* – Kiko would pretend to meditate, pretend to search for proper English before tourists on his tours to Skull Island – to eat occasionally of another's body than spoil the human flesh of two entire cities with atomic radiation.

'Teaching a child to believe in heaven and hell is unforgivable,' he says, looking at Karien. 'Sunday after Sunday in that building. Taking communion: *this is the body of Christ who died for your sins.* Our own cannibalism. *I am the light and I am the truth.* That's how we gave our savagery moral foundation. I'm not sure what Ounooi expected of Dirk. Or I, for that matter. He didn't have the power to save me or to stop me from leaving. At a long shot, maybe compassion or empathy from him could have changed the old man's mind. Who knows? *Everything* about organised religion bothers me. I cannot get over it. How did you?'

'You don't go to church anymore?'

He shakes his head.

'In the end, our petty righteousness cannot stand up to imagination, Michiel. History doesn't have a snowball's hope in hell against it either . . . Jissis, here we are, after all.' Her eyes have gone across the river, to the goats, lined up in single file on the riverbank with their snouts down to the water. 'As they say, the difference between men and angels is that angels do not expect perfection of one another, but only of god.'

He has not set foot in a church for fifteen years: not in the Most Holy Redeemer from where a stream of friends were sent off till four years ago; not in Westminster, Canterbury, Notre Dame or Seville. He did enter the Hagia Sophia: a *mosque*, he told himself, no longer a church, though signs of an earlier epoch remained on its walls. He remembers the day he spouted off about the Buddha statue on their balcony: 'If we got rid of the clutter of religious crap, we might be able to fit an extra chair out here for someone to sit in.'

Kamil pounced: 'And what of our shelves of poetry, Michael?

Let's burn the books and stock that space with bread and cans of food for the poor. Do you think poetry has not been used to aggrandize dictators and genocidal presidents? And what of film? And what of love? Are people not murdered in the name of love? Have men and women not used love for centuries to ensnare one another? And parents to fuck up their kids? And what about philosophy? Let me tell you how Nietzsche and Marx and Fanon and Smith and Friedman have been used. Painting? Music! What of this English we speak and teach? Has the earth ever seen a more terrible, a more beautiful language? When you throw out the evil of our everyday lives and when you stop using the English language, *that's* the day I remove my Buddha from this balcony. It's not the thing itself, it's what we do with it; not what was done. It's what we do with it now. Perfection is stasis and that's fascism or the holocaust and finally the end of the fucking universe. I'm sleeping in the guest room tonight, you Afrikaner lunkhead.'

'Where are Hegel's dialectics in this little tantrum, Kamil? Where's the dialogue and the oral tradition of Silko! Dialogics my arse. I'm not one of your graduate students who needs you to lecture — to *preach* to me like some Dutch Reformed minister! Stay in the guest room for a month for all I care. And while we're at it, don't call me an Afrikaner again, you fucking mongrel.'

'Does cruelty not also stand or fall by empathy? Even the torturer relies on *empathy* for what he does to his victims, or what say you, Ensign Steyn?'

'Game, set and fucking match, Kamil Kassis! I'm going out.'

'Now *there's* something when you go sucking Glassman's cock on Monday.'

'Fuck you, Kamil. Who got me to go there in the first place?'

'You're worshiping at the phallus of psychoanalysis, Michael. Shall I tell you how shrinks have fucked over our lives?'

'Then why am I spending all this time and money getting more fucked?'

'Because shrinks have saved us.'

Being with Kamil is at times like being forced to take exams every day.

Karien digs a hole with the boot's heel. She drops the butt and covers it with river sand. When she sits down he tells her she reeks. 'Stop being so precious,' she says, 'you're sounding like an American.'

On the opposite riverbank the boy sits on his haunches, looking towards Karien and Michiel, then again down to the goats. He is dressed in a red jersey and torn jeans hoisted tight around his waist by a belt, the end of which is flapping loose. The woman has a tartan blanket about her hips and the sleeves of her thick gray sweater are pushed up to her elbows. On the sweater bold letters announce a slogan or advertise something that from here is illegible. On her arms are silver bangles and she wears old-fashioned white running shoes. Carrying a plastic can, she comes carefully down the riverbank. Upstream from the nearest goat, she goes down on her knees. When she bends to submerge the can she looks up, across the river and the stretch of sandbank.

Karien rises again from the rock. With hands cupped around her mouth, she calls: 'Dumelang!'

The woman, with her can now filled, calls back: 'Dumela, Mme!' She waves and with one motion stands and lifts the heavy can from the riverbank on to her head. With tiny steps she goes swiftly back up the bank, her back and neck straight, as if kept upright and taut by an invisible upward force.

'I often thought of the nurse,' Karien says, when she sits down, again slipping her hand into his pocket, finding his fingers. 'Had we been caught she would have paid the heaviest price. There are times I think I must find her. Though she may not even remember. Or she may not wish to be reminded. She may be quite indifferent.'

The woman and boy are moving off a way behind the herd of goats, disappearing into the fold of the gully.

'Would you go and look for her?' Michiel asks as they get up from the rock to untie the horses.

'Oh, I don't know,' Karien answers, turning her horse as they mount. 'They say you can't cross the same river twice.'

'Unless it's frozen.'

'Even ice moves constantly, baboon!' She laughs. 'We learned that in Standard Three!'

When she takes off — instantly, at a canter — he calls after her to take it easy. His heart pounds. She is being reckless. She looks back, laughing, calling to him that the horses can smell the stables and he'd best hold on for dear life. 'Stop being such a sissy,' she shouts as beneath him he feels the rhythm of the canter change to gallop. 'It's like riding a bike,' she calls and leans forward, her buttocks up off the saddle. Head down and eyeing him sideways, 'This is how Ounooi and I always went home.'

Thank god for the fences between here and Paradys; that we closed those gates behind us. His attention is riveted to the danger and vague recall of advice to always roll shoulder first. Today ligaments will certainly be torn; the collarbone could snap like a twig; not like when they came off as kids and after a good cry and a smear of spit on the graze were back up, going even faster. With the wind on his face his eyes water and his heart thuds in his contracted chest. He gets the feel of the animal beneath him. When he is one with the horse his body seems to swell and release. He feels tears coming off his cheeks and in the thrill of speed and fear he feels utterly alive, in his flesh an exhilaration that in a very long time — even without his feeling the absence — has not been there.

From Lerato and Giselle packing up their cars under already resecured shade-cloths, they hear that the kids have gone up the mountain with Mamparra and the dogs. They haven't been seen or heard for hours.

'What about Palesa?' Karien is irritated. 'That child can't walk so far. She's three years old, for god's sake. And she already has a runny nose.'

'It's been a madhouse here this morning,' Lerato answers. 'Mamparra took a doek to tie her to her back. It was the only way to get them out from under our feet.'

'While you two were gallivanting,' Giselle says, her tone not without edge, 'we made sandwiches and sent the lot off so we could clean the house. There's food on the kitchen table. Michiel, Alida is packing leftovers for you from last night. She's wondering whether you'll take biltong. There's a vacuum packer in the bottling shed.'

'Do the kids have jerseys?'

'We took care of everything, Karien,' Giselle answers.

'Where is our car?' Karien asks.

With the bridge clear Dirk took off for town for rivets and such, and he and Benjamin are back down at the bridge, aiding Pietie with the final clean-up. There is a ton of flood debris at the roadside.

On a counter top Alida folds aluminum foil around leftovers for all who are departing. Lerato comes in with her cellphone to her ear, while Karien and Giselle gather their children's belongings. Over lunch at the kitchen table Michiel skims the day's papers while trying to listen, intrigued by Lerato's language: *I say! Tsala, ke tla tloha ka nakonyana esa fedising pelo. Unfortunately, ke misitse phutheho ya bohlokwa . . . because o tlameha . . . hoseng self. Nee wat . . . Brother wa ka . . . lefuma . . . sebetsa Jo'burg next month.* Between his fingers the vibration of newsprint gives away his body's response to the speed of the ride home. He holds his hands above the page, unable to still the tremor. Tight shoulders and painful tendons in his forearms are a reminder of the force it took to rein in the horse. By the time he gets off the plane tomorrow morning he'll be strutting with the stiff limbs of the secretary bird. The smell of horse and leather on his hands is strong. A pity to lose this — like washing off a memory — when he showers for the journey.

The English and Afrikaans papers are similarly headlined: *Zimbabwe Land Crisis Plunges Rand to All-time Low*. Then there is an article expanding on the story of the US ship he partly heard on this morning's news: The USS *Enterprise* is due in South African waters. Listing nuclear safety concerns, local environmental groups have launched a campaign to bar the warship from docking. Tourism authorities, very much in favour (not spelled *favor*) of the ship's visit, eagerly await the outcome of an inquiry by the National Nuclear Regulator and the departments of Mineral and Energy Affairs, Foreign Affairs and Defence (not the s he now writes and teaches students). Both front pages carry stories on Thabo Mbeki's controversial position on HIV. Activists of the Treatment Action Campaign have expressed outrage at a letter written by the president, in which he once again questions the view that AIDS is one of the country's main killers. A picture, from the president's recent visit to the fledgling Scottish parliament, shows protesters holding signs saying 'You Have Blood on Your Hands'. Michiel's eyes run over the smaller headlines: *Single National Examination for All Matrics Planned; Maidens do Reed Dance for Zulu King*. A large color photograph shows 'Nelson Mandela's wife' addressing Women of the World, a Jewish organization formed to counter the country's pervasive sense of pessimism and to discourage people from emigrating: *Women Can Change the World, Says Graça Machel*.

'Do my ears deceive me?' Michiel looks up at the sound of Karien's voice and hurried tread.

'Hold on,' Lerato says into the phone. Through the orchard come children's squeals followed by splashing, laughter and the incessant barking of the dogs.

'Nee, Jissis,' says Karien, already heading for the back door. 'Today is the day I bliksem that Thabiso!'

'I'll ring you back,' Lerato says, shutting her phone. 'They'll die in this weather,' she calls after Karien and follows through the kitchen door.

'What's going on?' Giselle has also rushed into the kitchen.

'It seems that the kids are in the dam.'

'That's what you get for putting Mamparra in charge,' says Alida after Giselle goes out on to the stoep. 'I told Lerato.' She slips the roll of tinfoil into one of the drawers. 'But my child always thinks she's clever. What that Mamparra knows about raising children is just enough to be dangerous.'

Amused by the drama, Michiel leaves the papers to follow the women striding in single file up the orchard path. Behind stripped trees and bare branches there is already the sight of little bodies in various states of undress running along the dam wall and plunging in, shrieking. Mamparra, with Palesa tied to her back, and Adam are the only ones fully clothed. Pulane, tiptoeing like a fairy with Grootman balancing on the wall behind her, pretends not to see her mother and quickly dives in.

'No, Adam! Mamparra, I'm sorry!' Giselle hollers from a distance. 'How could you two allow this?'

'We tried, Mrs Giselle,' Mamparra protests, coming towards the mothers. 'But it's that Thomas and Thabiso. They don't have ears on their heads. I said to them Karien will strip the skin off you and I'll get the sack, but do you think they listen? And once the big boys went in Bianca and the twins couldn't be stopped.' Karien takes the sleeping Palesa from Mamparra's back. She lifts her daughter on to her hip and rests the little head against her collarbone, draping the doek over the child's shoulders.

Isabella, with hind legs quivering and front paws on the cement, stands yelping from the diving rock. Grootman runs along the wall, half-heartedly nipping at the water splashing over the sides. Adult faces appearing over the wall create a further melee in the dam's center, where the three boys sit with their legs interlocked on a huge red-brown inner tube. Bianca tumbles back, shoved off by Thomas and Thabiso's quick arms.

'Look at us, Michiel! We've won,' Kanu hoots.

'Mommy,' cries Pulane, treading water, 'they won't give me and Bianca a chance! Tell them, Mommy!' Giving up the fight, she swims towards her mother while Bianca valiantly continues to wrestle for a place on the tube. Pulane has reached the side and hangs from the cement wall, lips shivering.

'Enough!' Lerato shouts. 'Look at these blue lips. Get out! Kanu! All of you!' But Pulane has already shot herself off the wall and is swimming underwater back towards the inner tube.

'I want you all out of this dam in ten seconds,' Giselle commands as Karien holds her hand over her sleeping child's ear. 'I'm counting. Ten . . . nine . . .'

Lerato waves a finger at Kanu, who now stands on the tube, held in place by the other boys.

'Where did they get the inner tube, Adam?' Karien asks of the man who has now stepped off the eucalyptus stump to stand among the lilies with Mamparra.

'No, it was here, on the dam, Nooi Karien.'

Karien glances at Lerato and Giselle. They know all too well that the tire tubes and lilos are kept in the storeroom, deflated; pumped only in summer's full swelter.

'You're hurting us! Play fair!' the girls cry out.

A refrain Michiel remembers from childhood now comes from Kanu while the two older boys persist in pushing the girls off the tube: *I'm the king of the castle, and you're the dirty rascal.* This is followed by a conspiratorial huddle and whispers among the boys, leaning in over their bobbing float.

Lifting his head, Thabiso calls: 'Mom, what word rhymes with water?

'Daughter,' Karien answers, and then, 'Thabiso, get out. Now! I'm not speaking again!'

Instead of obeying, the three boys manage to hoist themselves upright on the tube together, arms locked, feet apart, stomping on the girls' hands still trying to get a grip on the slippery rubber.

Bianca gets hold of her brother's ankle but he manages to shake her off. The boys, balanced upright and firmly gripped to each other, sway furiously, make waves that force Pulane briefly to retreat to the wall. To Bianca, splashing them from below, they holler: 'We're the kings of the water, and you're the henchman's daughter.'

'Now *there's* a phrase to rankle the goddess,' says Lerato casting a glance at the boys chanting the phrase over and over, the old taunts transformed to a new refrain as Pulane returns and the two girls fight on bravely.

'No daughter of Africa worth her salt ignores such provocation.' Karien raises an eyebrow and tips her head towards the dam as she and Lerato share a grin. Lerato nods and looks to Giselle. 'Girl?'

'You are not serious!' Giselle exclaims.

'I can't either!' Lerato shivers and pulls a face. 'And this hair! I have a board meeting.'

'Ag, donner, Lerato, fuck Anglo American for once,' Karien whispers. 'Just put the doek around it. Here.' She gently hands Palesa off to Michiel and holds out the strip of fabric in which the child was bound.

'We're going to freeze our tits off,' Lerato mutters, nonetheless reaching for the doek.

Karien squats behind the dam wall, pulling her top over her head. 'Close your eyes, Adam,' she laughs up at the man, 'if you don't want to see the madams in their bras and broeks.' Adam, embarrassed, looks down into the callas. 'Adam!' Karien laughs, 'I've got nothing that Liesbet hasn't!'

'What the hell,' Lerato says, and she too unbuttons her blouse, bends so her head is hidden from the kids.

'I'm sorry,' Giselle says, 'I'm staying right here on dry land.' She comes to stand beside Michiel, who still holds the child against his chest. That Palesa has not woken from the ruckus is remarkable. She must be exhausted from the long walk.

On the wall and the diving rock the dogs have gone quiet. Mid-dam, the children too. The girls hang from the tube now, the boys' defense of terrain briefly suspended. When the women appear – disrobed to underwear, hands held, chins raised and stepping like queens on to the diving rock – all eyes are on them. But for their underwear they could be, there beside the overhanging reeds, Cleopatra and her lady-in-waiting above a pool on the banks of the Nile.

'We're not jumping from up here,' Lerato urges as she tucks the end of the doek tightly against her neck. 'Let's slide in, together, down the side.' With hands held, they step from the diving rock on to the wall.

'Hold the pose, Lerato,' Karien whispers, Isabella licking at her calf. 'Think of Ounooi.'

From a seated position, bracing (Lerato puts on a brave face at the feel of green tendrils floating from the side), they lower themselves into the water. The kids silently observe the spectacle being played out by the wall.

Once the women are in, heads still held high, they glide leisurely towards the tube. *Mommy's coming to help us!* Pulane shouts and when the boys register what may be happening the noise of battle resumes. Before the boys can steel themselves, the two women together lift the side of the tube and all three go tumbling off. The girls cheer, the dogs go wild and the adults clap while Michiel's hand covers Palesa's ear.

'Mooi so! Dis hulle verdiende loon!' Well done. They had that coming, Mamparra cries, doing a little jig on the diving rock, where she has joined Isabella.

As the boys flee to the wall, Karien hoists herself and helps Lerato up before the two girls are given a hand. Then it is the four of them, adrift, in the dam's center. Lerato laughs at the boys as she adjusts the doek and reties it in the nape of her neck.

'You cheated! You had grown-ups on your side. It's not fair.' The boys are lined up, hanging and sitting on the wall's far side.

Then, from Thomas, glaring at Michiel: 'What about you? You could have helped us, you fuckin'—' he stops, mid-sentence.

In the quiet Michiel, with Palesa against his chest, holds Thomas's gaze. Everyone's eyes go to the man whose eyes are still on the white boy, who has now dropped his head and is looking down, on to the water.

'You have no clue . . . You don't know what you wanted to say, do you, Thomas?'

Kanu, sitting hunched beside Thomas, has his one leg drawn up and is whimpering. He has grazed his knee while clambering up the side.

'Mommy, I'm bleeding,' he calls.

'Aren't there piranhas in this dam?' Lerato calls back. 'With the blood pouring in, your other leg could be chewed right off.'

Kanu quickly draws his other leg up. His face disfigured by anger, he splashes his mother from the side, calling to her, something in seSotho that Michiel doesn't get.

'No, Kanu,' Lerato answers, 'don't come crying now. And don't try emotional blackmail on me. I will not have you behaving like a skabenga to your sister. And if you get my hair wet — *any* of you!'

After a while: 'Come, you boys, let's see if we can all get on here together.'

The boys splash in from the wall. There's squealing and churning as they're aided on to the float, between the others. From among the reeds a red bishop darts, swerves from the float and disappears into the poplars. The women and children drift, all quiet now, in the cold spring sun, their arms, legs and fingers intertwined. Someone whispers and they lean outward with their backs touching the water, then closing up, unfolding again, their mirth now as if rising from a terrific drifting bloom. Then, with their hands in sync, they row, spinning slowly around. Again they lean out and fold themselves back in, sending laughter and waves across the dam. Michiel exhales, hugging the little girl to him. Elongated reflections of poplars wobble on the surface; in the distance the mountain is hazy green in crags and in the dark vein where the kloof leads up to the caves. A breeze stirs the leaves. A jet of silver cascades from the black plastic pipe protruding from the reeds. He turns his face to the light wind, getting the smells of the kraal, the dairy and the stables.

He lifts his wrist behind the child's back to check the time.

'I have to get ready,' he says to Giselle. 'I haven't packed.' He passes the sleeping Palesa to her. As she takes the child Giselle, with cheeks flushed, refuses to meet his gaze. 'I'll see you all at the house.'

'See you in a minute,' she answers, still looking on to the child's head.

'Goodbye, Mamparra. Ek moet padvat, Adam.' This time, at least, he is bidding people farewell.

'When is the Kleinbasie coming again?'

'Such a short visit! Ag, nee man, Michiel! I wanted to show you my new ballroom gown.'

'I'm not sure,' he says. 'Maybe soon. I'll leave something for you both, and for Liesbet, with Alida.'

'Wait,' Mamparra says. 'Mrs Giselle, you take over supervision here. Michiel, I know you're a man who can appreciate a creation like this. I'm coming to the manor.' She slips from the diving rock, trots down the path and turns up towards the compound, singing as she goes *Oh when the saints, oh when the saints go marching in* . . .

Walking from the dam he sees again the mountain, above the oversized lotus opening and closing and the lime-green tendrils afloat like seaweed from the dam's side. Through the tidied orchard the drift of the algae persists in his mind's eye . . . *you could have helped us, you fuckin'* . . . and over that himself and his two brothers naked in the dam and over that the spawning of the corals. The islanders of the Roviana lagoon, where women have not swum since the arrival of missionaries, say that the crawl – freestyle – originated there, from where it found its way in hybrid form to the rest of the world. *When is the Kleinbasie coming again . . . I know a man who can appreciate a creation like this . . .* What he would return to, if he does, he is not sure. To show the changed land to Kamil? Introduce old friends and family? The generous rhetoric of farewell, he knows, is but a feather on the titanic scales of life.

He makes his way to the cemetery. The dogs have remained at the dam and he feels their absence. The yapping has resumed and he wonders how long the truce, the new order, lasted up there.

The heaped red soil is outlined by a wide doily of pink. A spade today must have scooped up and tidied what ran off in last night's rain and hail. The mound again seems fresh, as though filled in only an hour ago. Adam's work, he's sure, directed by Oubaas or Benjamin. Michiel imagines Adam returning from the grave to the shed with the spade over his shoulder (no implement left unattended on the farm) and meeting the children coming from the mountain with Mamparra; the bigger boys, maybe running ahead of the little ones, begging, sweet-talking, offering a tip, *ag, please Adam*, and getting him to inflate the tire tube with the tractor pump and carry it up to the dam for them.

While his gaze moves between Peet's slab and the mound beneath which Ounooi lies, Michiel sees Oubaas in the future, brought once a week by Alida. He carries flowers in his lap and the wheelchair has cut ruts along its tussocked path, making it easier for Alida to push. In summer he has *Gloire de Dijon* in his lap. Or sugarbush. Or arum lilies. In winter, something else; maybe aloes from the ridge? Does Oubaas ask Alida to leave him alone for a while, here? Does she go off and sit in the shade of the oaks, perhaps still with an orange brought along in her housecoat's pocket?

'Giselle told me you might be here.' It is Benjamin. 'Adam must think he's in heaven, with all those half-naked women. You're leaving soon?'

'Just a shower, then I'm off.'

'My daughter's developed a crush within the last twenty-four hours. She's the one who sent me to search for you. She doesn't want you to go without saying goodbye.'

'There's something about Bianca,' he says. And your son, he doesn't say. 'Did Giselle go in?'

'She hates cold water. Our pool has to be solar-heated.'

Is the hint of derision evidence only of the idiosyncrasies of all relationships — the daily peeves pardoned and lived with — or is there something more?

'Karien and I will sort through stuff over the coming months. the attic and storerooms must have a century's worth of boxes, trunks of who knows what. Is there anything you want?' Michiel shakes his head.

'I don't envy you,' he says, 'everything that has to be decided here.'

'Now that we're in touch, I hope we'll decide the direction of things together.'

'Ai, Benjamin,' Michiel says, unsure how to respond. During the ride with Karien he admitted to himself that rarely, if ever, has he known fulfillment — happiness? — as he has here. Like something suspended that is ignited again. A tiny window or crack opened. Inside all he and she said to each other, her fingers finding his in the jacket pocket, was already a presupposition of knowledge and of lives shared, a language that cannot be had elsewhere. Oh, go on, allow yourself: the sense of belonging, almost; as close as there is any belonging in life. He looks at Peet's stone. Whatever that little crack is — even while you think you know its every problem, its nuanced and terrifying perversions — nowhere but here is it restored, does it remind you of what in your abundance of life, liberty and the pursuit of happiness you live constantly without. And you cannot say that it disappears at the first gate of Paradys or at the airport with its new name, or at thirty thousand feet above the coast with the seatbelt signs long off. It goes with you. And then it locates itself somewhere in the folds of your brain, in your thick Afrikaner skull, around the hairs of your forearms. It becomes part of your not quite forgetting, as you practice loving your man in your flat above the City of St Francis and you drink Napa wine and friends smile about your odd little pet from Pakistan and read symbols from the tarot and you go running all the way to Ocean Beach and wave at the American kids like the United Colors of Benetton at the bus stop and pay your bills and say the c in schedule as a *k* rather than as a *sch*. Through all this privilege *that thing* is dormant in you: until you hear an accent, notice a tree's shape on the hills around the South Bay or you catch the whiff of wood smoke from a basket sold at the trolley stop or you hear a word like terrorism or see a child that now could be fifteen years old. You drive along Big Sur and for a second recognize a familiar white rocky cove way down below you; you see Rooibos tea appearing on the shelves of Trader Joe's or you receive an online article from a friend about floods with a subject line that reads *Mozambique Woman Gives Birth In Tree* and while you run you wonder whether she spoke Portuguese or any language at all. Here, many hours later at your mother's grave, last night's dreamtree falls into place where it grows on a sidewalk in Monterey, above the ocean. You have seen it more than once when visiting the aquarium and have stopped to look into its blooms in April and May. What's up? Kamil asks. This tree, you say. Jacaranda, Kamil says, from South America. I know, you say, but they grow everywhere now. Then, if you risk it, you feel that thing has budged, reappearing from wherever it always waits.

'You have a different relationship to this land,' he says to Benjamin. 'You always wanted to manage it. You wanted to see the work done of making it produce. To me, being here is a little like being in a painting. Or a song. Or a novel. That you tell me a third belongs to me doesn't change the fact that I've never been a proper boer like you.'

'That's a cop out, Michiel. Between Karien and me we'll figure things out with Oubaas. But Paradys is your inheritance too. You can't just walk away. Give me some idea of what you want done or what you can do yourself. Or I could buy you out. What do you think of the resort proposal?'

'Remember way back, the day Ounooi dropped you off at the black school and forced you to walk?'

They both chuckle.

'I've also been remembering the weirdest shit,' Benjamin says. 'Too many memories.'

'When she stopped to pick up Little-Alida she said, *I can't live with myself if this child has to walk to school through the frost.* Something like that.' While Benjamin stays at the graveside Michiel turns and walks to the cemetery's ragged boundary. He looks up at the compound. He has not made time to go up there; instead, when he could have, he went riding.

'Look, Benjamin.' He speaks loudly so his brother can hear. 'Look how we make people live so we may live like royalty. To us, Paradys is an abstraction. It's a name with fence posts that can be moved, even overseas, in the blink of an eye. But for these people this is their lives, not just a word. I cannot live with myself even partly responsible for their living like this. I don't want that responsibility, cop out or not.'

'Does the proximity make it intolerable, Michiel?' Benjamin calls to him from the graveside. '*Seeing* their lives so close? Because I know enough about California's economy to know who does the work there. You can hold this pose only because you don't see the hands picking the strawberries and lettuce you eat. I have business partners there, Michiel, I know the shape of the eyes of the people who do the unskilled labor in San Francisco. Don't come and whine to me, to us in this country about exploitation, please.' He walks over to Michiel at the fence. He lifts his arm, pointing north, to the compound. 'From what Ounooi told us, you and your boyfriend live quite well with yourselves. Go and take a look at the land around Salinas and tell me what distance between so-called fucking abstraction and sweat makes your life in America possible. I thank god that you landed on your feet. It must have been quite a tumble. But I'm not going to bullshit you: I've been livid with you for fifteen years. I'm nowhere near forgetting what you did. You want me to buy you out and use that money to build better homes for these people, I'll do it. Even if you want me to sell pieces of land or give it to them, I will. But don't give me this sentimental crap, this crap of *I can't live with myself*. Why don't you and your clever boyfriend lobby to give back the place you live in to whomever it was taken from?'

'Benjamin . . .' He does not wish to respond to his brother's anger. 'As much as I love this, I don't *need* it. Nor does Kamil. It could feed many mouths if you share it.' They need a longer time, not the minutes remaining, for this discussion.

'It will feed more, I assure you, while we own and manage it. And I think you know that, Michiel. Secretly, but you cannot say it. You wish to evade even the responsibility of saying it, just as you always sidestepped the shit you caused.'

Then again, another hour or two and things could really come loose at the seams. He looks at his watch.

Now, once more in a tranquil tone, Benjamin says, 'You don't want to be late. Let's walk back.'

They return to the grave of their mother. Michiel looks a last time at Peet's stone. In Afrikaans: *Petrus Dawid Steyn, Dearly Beloved Son and Brother, 29 January 1963 – 16 December 1986, Returned here to Paradys*. That plot, Benjamin says, pointing next to Peet, is for Karien's family. Ounooi wanted it like that. She and Oubaas are the children's godparents.

'Oubaas Thabiso's godfather? God, this country. Just yesterday I heard him refer to Lerato's twins as piccanins.'

'You can always give your share to Karien. That way it goes to Thabiso and Palesa.'

Could it be less a question of who owns it than what is done with it? Or is it, in fact, for this moment in this place, still only about the race on the deed? How does it play if the darker heir turns out as

218

bad or only slighter better than the trembling godfather? And what of Mamparra's Geel, could he legitimately make the cut? 'Whatever I decide,' he says, only partly joking, 'I may hold on to one acre. Maybe the one with the dam and the spring.' That way I could still come, at times, to be in a picture of my own painting, in the tale of my own telling.

'The dam is one thing, but the *spring*, now that's an altogether different ballgame!' Benjamin guffaws. No need to resolve everything today. Now that they're in touch, they have time.

'When you go through her things,' Michiel says, 'if you find the letters. From back then. Maybe she kept them. I wouldn't mind having those.'

'If they're here, they'll be in her files. Anything else? What about her books? Any of the furniture? We'll have things crated and shipped to you.'

Michiel shakes his head as they leave the orchard pathway and walk out on to the green lawn.

He has sent a text saying he leaves within the quarter hour. Kamil can call before going off to Berkeley.

At Ounooi's desk he slips bills into envelopes: the money that would have paid for a hotel and meals. Only what he estimates for gas at Winburg and for the toll at Kroonstad remains in his wallet. He is writing the names on the envelopes when he hears singing. Envelope in hand, he goes through the sliding doors. The sun is netted behind a haze of cirrus, the afternoon cold overlaid by tones of gray. She is on the footpath, passing beneath the bare fruit trees. Like decorations, single white blossoms cling to branches along her way. The disappeared sun makes the red of the dress seem even brighter between the stark black stems and the matt green of the ragged fig hedge. One arm is covered in a red mesh sleeve from shoulder to wrist and she carries red pumps in her hands. The blood-red bodice is held up by one thin strap across her left shoulder and whatever suspension is hidden in the fabric. A wide skirt swishes in folds around her calves, above her bare feet, her stride confident and unhurried.

'What do you think?' she says, stopping at the base of the stairs to slip on the shoes. Before he can respond she has come on to the stoep and spins on the shining cement floor, making the skirt flare like a magnificent bell. She has on light-cerise lipstick; a suggestion of rouge on her cheeks. Her hair is pulled back tightly by a silver comb with a red ostrich feather.

'Beautiful,' he says. 'Is it chiffon?'

'Charmeuse,' she answers, lifting the skirts and swaying on the balls of her shoes, 'from the koelie in town. Two weeks to glue on all the rhinestones. The koelie had to make a special order from Jo'burg. The shoes, too, Paulus had to send me from Cape Town. This whole package,' she steps away from him and again swirls, once, twice, three times, like a dervish, 'is two years of my savings.'

She has brought along a small framed picture, a studio photograph of her and Pietie with arms interlocked beside Roman columns draped with fabric and palm fronds. She is in the dress; Pietie, smart in a tuxedo, his bow tie the same red as her bodice.

'You've managed to get Pietie smiling!'

'The Free State regionals for ballroom and Latin American. We came third in the tango. This year the trophy comes to Paradys.'

'Still no ring on your finger, I see . . .' His gaze is briefly on her left hand.

'And what's the story with that one on yours?' she asks, her neck inclined and her eyebrows raised.

'It's not quite a wedding ring,' he says. 'It's more a symbol of belonging. Of loyalty.' Then, 'And your son? He's in Cape Town?'

'He's a conductor on Spoornet. He gets a free pass every year. I take the train to see him for Easter, after the harvest.'

'He comes back to visit?'

'Paulus hasn't lost anything here.'

Alida has come out, holding a Pick n Pay bag. 'I have your padkos, Kleinbaas. Everyone is waiting.'

'I'm coming, Alida.' Then, to Mamparra, 'So you've seen the ocean, then?'

'It's too big, Michiel. There's no way I'll stick my toe into it. Before you know it a shark has you by the leg and your dancing days are over.'

'I love the dress,' he says, handing her the envelope. 'I would have liked to see you and Pietie dance.' She glides down the steps, the skirt sweeping behind her. Before crossing the lawn she removes the pumps. He is about to add something when Alida says, 'You're holding everyone up.'

He briefly meets her eyes. Then, before Mamparra disappears, he calls: 'Maybe Alida can get Lerato to let me know how it goes with the competition?' Half looking back, she has re-entered the orchard, again singing, the ostrich feather pertly bobbing as she nods: 'We will be the champions.'

'What is her real name, Alida?'

'Her name? *Mamparra*, till her deathbed. No red dress or holiday at the sea will change that. Give a monkey a golden ring, it's still an ugly thing. You're too behep with names.' He follows her back into the house, his eyes on the stooped shoulders, forceful, almost defiant beneath the blue cotton housecoat.

On the front stoep he stands now with the bag of padkos in hand.

The old man's hands are folded in his lap, his head nodding askance. Voices carry from the cars, where the others await his leave-taking.

'Die Kleinbaas se kamer wag.' The Kleinbaas's room waits, Alida says from behind the wheelchair; his designation, he notes, back in place. 'Kleinbaas will see there are lamb sandwiches and I vacuum-packed two pockets of biltong. And some raisins and dried peaches from last year's harvest. Two apples. Lerato says they don't feed you properly on the airplanes.' When they hug, her back and shoulders feel to him frail, like the bones of a bird. Of the arms that must have carried him as an infant, no physical trace remains.

He goes on to his haunches in front of his father. 'Give yourself time, Oubaas.'

The old man blinks, looks across the stoep, through the bars towards the orchard. At its sideways angle the head, on the pleated neck, turns back to Michiel. 'You have only that bit of luggage,' he says. 'Ounooi says it gets cold where you live. Take your kaross.'

Michiel is not sure how the blanket of skins will be transported, and is concerned that it may be confiscated by customs.

'The jackals weren't shot yesterday. The skins can't have rabies,' Oubaas says, his eyes suddenly wide. 'Tell them it comes from your grandfather. Put up a *fight* – in god's name, Michiel – if they try to confiscate it.'

Alida is to roll the kaross into one of the bleached calico bags she keeps to use for dried fruit in the pantry. He will take it as hand luggage and hope for the best in Atlanta.

A car's horn blares. Kanu, surely. Then there is indeed the sound of the boy calling: 'Michieeeeel, America is waiting for youuuuu.' Michiel could be overwhelmed by knowing this may be the last time he looks into his father's face. He sees again the body hanging from the branch in his dream; looking into the exhausted, almost powerless blue gaze he longs to know what may be going through the old man's mind. He leans forward. He goes on to his knees. When he embraces his father he feels the tremor of forearms against his back. He finds the smell of Palmolive in his father's neck and thinks for an instant of Ounooi, nine months ago, at the departure gate. *Through everything. A thousand ways and more.* He cannot, for the life of him, find the words to say to Oubaas.

Alida returns with the kaross rolled tautly inside a Bokomo meelsak. Bianca has come to report that everyone's wondering whether Michiel has decided to stay. He rises, his father's soft hand slipping from his. He receives the bag from Alida and, without looking back, descends the seven steps, Isabella skipping alongside and Bianca's hand in his.

'So, you *are* going after all!'

'Better late than never.'

'Don't forget us again.'

Padkos on to the passenger seat, kaross in the trunk.

Handshakes for Thabiso and Thomas, joined at the hip now, both in baseball caps. 'Don't stop singing once your voice breaks,' he says to Thabiso. The boy with the wide open face and big black eyes smiles, coy at being reminded of this gift when so many others should rather be mentioned.

'Look out for potholes after the Hobhouse turnoff,' come Thabiso's first words to Michiel. 'Mom blew out two tires and buckled a rim there last week.'

'Thanks for the warning.'

Thomas manages an embarrassed half-smile from beneath the cap as he shakes his uncle's hand. 'Good luck with everything,' Michiel offers. You will remember me, you little shit, the day you have to admit it runs in the family.

A kiss for the beautiful Pulane. Next year, maybe? The little girl smiles, shyly.

A kiss and a hug for Bianca, who quietly weeps as she clings to Michiel's hand. 'Ask your mom and dad to send you over with Lerato,' he says. Then, whispering in her ear, 'American chocolate is lousy, so bring Peppermint Crisp for us to make you know what.'

'Where is Kanu? Kanu!' Lerato calls for the boy, who has disappeared. 'We'll see what transpires,' she says to Michiel, running her hand down Bianca's cheek. 'We may very well meet over there. I'm off in a few minutes so we may catch each other up on the road. You can leave the gates unlocked.' They exchange business cards and undertake to stay in touch. When they kiss, his free arm goes around her back.

'Drive safely,' Giselle says. They hug and she loosens Bianca's grip from his hand by drawing her daughter to her side. 'Thank you for coming.'

A firm handshake from Dirk, along with a smile and a nod that tries to do whatever has not been, cannot (yet?) be said. The can opener, Michiel thinks; maybe the touch of a bayonet.

'Kanu, *get out* of that car and come and say your goodbyes!' Lerato has spotted Kanu's head where he pretends to hide on the rental's back seat.

'Who wants to drive in this old thing, full of dents, anyway?' the boy asks, pouting as he jumps out and slams the door. With Lerato's hand resting on his head, he shakes Michiel's hand. The boy's eyes are defiant, self-protective. 'We'll shoot past you on the highway,' he says. 'And I won't wave at you.'

'As long as you're wearing your seatbelt,' Michiel replies, catching Lerato's wink. 'Come, you two,' she says to her children, 'let's get our things.'

'Yes, come you all,' Giselle says. 'Time for packing and saying goodbye to Oubaas. Tomorrow's school and I want to be on the road before dark.'

Michiel is left with Benjamin and Karien.

'Let's get it over,' she says. 'I can't stand this.'

'Well,' Benjamin says. 'Send Bianca a pic of you on the Great Wall of China, won't you? We'll take things further on the phone and on email.'

'I wouldn't know where to start if I were you,' Michiel says. 'With Oubaas, I mean.'

'He'll hear me, eventually.' They hug. Before walking off, he says, 'And I won't let you go scot-free with the other stuff. Neither of you bleeding hearts.'

'Email,' Karien says, once they're alone. In the sun emerging from the layer of cloud he sees again the lines around her eyes. Her hair is still wet from the swim, pulled back into a knot. She runs a finger down his cheek. 'An eyelash,' she says. 'You know they've all gone off to give us a moment. You must go, now.'

'Have you not made it too easy for me?'

'We're thirty-five,' she smiles. 'With luck we have at least as many years left for me to ride your guilt bareback. And if that takes too much energy, we can always make it easier on ourselves, you know, by resorting to the mutual forgiveness of each vice that opens the doors of paradise.' We have scarcely begun hearing the story, he thinks to himself, on this day, here, rubbing the fine fabric of a burial shroud. Tomorrow has its own colors and different garments, where rice is served without turmeric and tongues are untied.

'You saw the kaross? He insisted I bring it back with me.'

'*Take* it back with me,' she says. 'In Afrikaans, when you're leaving we say *take* it back, not *bring* it back. Would Americans really say *bring*?'

'I think they do,' he says. 'I'm not sure where else I would have picked it up. Unless it's just one of Kamil's idiosyncrasies.'

From a carrier bag she produces a CD and two slender books. The CD is of Afrikaans folk music, rearranged by a new wave of young musicians. She wants him to hear how the fetters of language and music are being undone. Listen on the drive, she says. The new rendition of the old 'Sugarbush' is quite moving. She looks at the books she holds in her hand. 'Ounooi gave these to me. That time. We thought we were dissident for reading them, those days. Remember, the Red Menace?' She squints and raises a hand to shield her eyes from the sun. 'Let's skip the hugging and kissing. I must wake Palesa. She's been asleep for hours.' She hands over the CD and books. 'Watch for those potholes. I almost wrote myself off.'

'Already I'm remembering you.'

'I know.' She turns even as she speaks.

He squats to pet the dogs, his eyes following her as she goes, his head full of her and the afternoon's murmur of turtledoves.

When he's in the car he finds her again in the rearview mirror, barefoot, going up the stoep steps. Making sure he sees the dogs, he reverses from under the shade-cloth. At the gate, the jacaranda stands split like the prongs of a charred tuning fork. Branches have been sawed into sections, leaves and blooms raked into heaps with a purple glow. The twin stands majestic, intact. In the cracked side mirror he sees the dogs scamper after the car, then stop. He thinks he sees Kanu and Bianca dashing across the lawn towards Peet's rondavel. The valley shines in white bloom. There is the tip of the church steeple and the mountains, with the river between. He rounds the koppie to start down to the bridge and the road to the gate. He slows to look back, but what he wants to see is already gone, behind overhangs and outcrops.

He can make good distance before dark and get to Jo'burg at the tail end of the rush-hour traffic. He has only the one case to check, and that is small enough to go as hand luggage along with the kaross if need be. Near the bridge, two men are going at a log with a chainsaw. They look up, lift their hands in greeting. He recognizes Pietie crossing the bridge, water splashing his gumboots. He has little memory of Pietie other than of his aloofness and omnipresence, everywhere and always on the farm. There are children, he knows, from an earlier marriage or pairing. Michiel has not anticipated seeing him again and has neglected to leave money with Alida. To suggest now that Pietie ask for a share from the others' envelopes would be awkward. And he can't offer the gas money: from yesterday he knows stations here don't take credit cards.

He turns off the ignition.

'Michiel alweer oppad, landuit?' Leaving the country, again?

'I need to get back to work, Pietie.'

'That's how life is,' the older man says, sniffing. He looks from Michiel in the car to the others. They are now taking axes to segments of log lying like the stripped backbone of a Tyrannosaurus Rex on the riverbank. Pietie clears his throat, spits.

A smile a year on your chops during the samba will not win Mamparra's heart, Michiel thinks. Whatever her other reasons, no wonder she will not deign to marry you. But then, what can he guess of Pietie's bearing when out from under a white man's eyes? What does he know of the rituals of courtship and lovemaking in the Paradys compound, their profanity and poetry?

'There's big work here now, Pietie. With Ounooi gone and my father like he is.'

'No more than always.' He doesn't look at Michiel as he speaks. 'Benjamin and I talked. We'll sort this place out.'

'Paradys cannot survive without you, I know.'

'How is it, overseas?'

'I have a good life. Everywhere has its issues.'

'Mamparra tells me you're childless. You better make a plan before you get too long in the tooth.'

'I didn't see your children at the funeral.'

'Sem got a job in forestry, with Mondi. Through Little-Alida. He's there in Mpumalanga at God's Window. The girl is in Botshabelo. She has a baby.'

Michiel glances at his watch. He is cutting it fine. They shake hands.

Michiel crosses the bridge slowly, water sloshing at the wheels. He has already driven up out of the dip when he again looks at his watch. He brakes and puts the vehicle in reverse. Foot on the brake and eyes in the rearview mirror, he allows the car to run back down to just before the bridge. He stops and this time gets out. Pietie has again crossed the bridge to him. Michiel unclips the watch.

'Pietie, this is not new. But it's a very good make. It's a Rolex. I'd like to give it to you, if you'll have it.'

Pietie takes the watch and pushes up his overall sleeve. He slips the strap over his hand, clips it to his wrist. Still no smile. Astonishing.

'It can last a lifetime. I got it when I was living on the other side of the world. To go diving, under the ocean. It was given to me by a dear friend. The man I live with.' He wants to say: I'm not giving it to you because it's old. I thought I'd wear that watch for ever. I love that watch.

'You can put it in the water?'

'Look, on its face it says *water resistant to a hundred meters.*'

'It's a strong watch.'

'If you don't want it, you could sell it or trade it,' Michiel says. 'But don't let them do you in. You must get what it is really worth.'

When Pietie shakes his hand, Michiel feels him do the thing he saw pass between the men at church: palm, to thumb (not wrist) and back to palm. By the time Michiel is in the vehicle, Pietie has crossed the bridge and is taking a rope to attach to the back of the tractor.

On the straight stretch between the bridge and the gate, Michiel imagines Ounooi in sweatpants and a gray sweater. Puffs of dust explode behind her shoes as she runs. For a moment they are again side by side, inhaling the smell of the Pacific, then back here, somewhere in late adolescence with his long skinny legs and acne at his temples as Miemie darts after francolins ahead of them. If he could fetch back his mother's words now from when they ran here together – *any* word from her . . . His one hand comes from the steering wheel to his mouth and his vision blurs. He stops for the gate. In the dust on either side of the cattle grid tracks, footprints and the marks of hoofs tell him that last night's storm did not reach as far as here. He opens the gate and stares back, towards the koppie. He crosses the grid and stops to close the gate, leaving the car idling. As he turns to step back into the vehicle he sees again the score of footprints and his eyes go to the dilapidated remains of the farm stall. For a moment he is suspended in the open door, one foot inside the car, the other on the ground. He sees the structure as it would have been, back then. A bakkie is parked there with a boy looking back through the glass. Hello, he says, without thinking. No matter who passes here or what goes on in there, on photographs and bookshelves, in letters returned unopened to sender, on the linens and kindness of a thousand and one strangers. No matter where earth or water receive you into the great embrace, there you are: my boy, my man, my heart, my beloved. And lowering himself into the car, pulling the door shut, he knows he will tell Kamil and Glassman of this moment. *We have our work cut out for us.*

On the open road he lets the speedometer climb to a hundred and twenty kilometers per hour and then clicks on the cruise control. He lifts one of Karien's books from the passenger seat and looks ahead, scouting for potholes. At a page marked by a dogear, he reads Ounooi's handwriting: *Kariena, I suspect he's impossible to translate, but you can still hear what he's saying:* September Sea . . . *Too much travel leaves the heart dumb and waterlogged, like a sea turtle depositing her geometrically perfect eggs on distant shores, before again swimming off wobbling into the vast blind expanse — and whoever reads the words while their shells are still soft? . . .* He shakes his head. He cannot read Breytenbach at this speed and this is not the time for tears. He replaces the book on the passenger seat and lifts the Pasternak, then swerves when the circular shadow of a hole suddenly looms in front of him. Ahead the road again looks clear. His thumbs rest on the steering wheel as the book sits against his fingers. Here too, Karien or Ounooi has folded in the corner of a page: The Grown Marksman . . . *A tall, strapping shot, you, considerate hunter . . . Phantom with gun at the flood of my soul . . . Start me, I pray, from the reeds in the morning, Finish me off with one shot in my flight . . . And for this lofty and resonant parting Thank you. Forgive me, I kiss you, oh hands of my neglected, my disregarded Homeland, my diffidence, family, friends.* Master at arms, rifle extended with bayonet, square colossus in browns and boots, a stone rhinoceros, shoulder to shoulder with the unit commander beside the padre. In his whites, dwarfed by the master, the padre has his Bible open. Not the entire base on parade. Only one platoon, with two killicks, in browns. The ensign alone, of the conscripts, is in whites. No other officers or ratings. It is not to be any of the spectacles conjured during the night of waiting. Behind the armory's walls serial numbers are called out in an Indian accent as a section checks in automatic rifles. Camel-colored trucks and brown pick-ups rattle by. A ship's horn sounds. Voices and vehicle engines slow down, then accelerate and slow again for the speed bumps. Base life continues, unknowing the ceremony underway. His platoon's weapons — thankfully without bayonets — are at their sides. Behind the browns, across docked ships and swaying masts of yachts are the tops of tall coconut palms and the city's harbor-front skyscrapers. Life on the city streets, stunningly normal. A plane's rush and vibration, passing low over the base in descent towards Louis Botha, interrupts the padre's reading midway through Psalm 23.

He does not know, till today, how it happened for Govender. After being taken back separately to their overnight cabins they did not see each other again. For Govender it may have taken place — no, *may have been done*, he must use a transitive verb — on the main parade ground above the docks, right there, with the SAS *Tafelberg* tied by heavy ropes to the quay. Instead of a bayonet, the commodore or captain may have used a sword. Stories had come to Michiel during the despondent hours of night: base commander or ship's captain marches from the dais to where the disgraced officer waits under the gaze of his entire crew. Ceremonial sword extracted from sheath, the captain uses rapid motions to dislodge the rank from the disgraced shoulders. Members of the crew do an about-turn so their backs greet the dishonored. Accompanied by drummers the former officer is drummed off parade. Whether that had already happened for Govender earlier in the morning, Michiel would never know: the wind was blowing from the south and all sound would have been carried away from the mess.

He stood at attention throughout, facing the commander and the parade at ease. The heaviness — he would never forget — pushed from the navel down, dilating his anus and flooding his legs, his face radiating heat. As one, master at arms and commander stepped forward. From his rifle, the master unclicked the bayonet. The commander, the former Selous Scout, came to stand in front of him. With his eyes on the ensign's shoulder, he slipped the dull blade in under the fastening laces and sliced off the left epaulette. When he stuck the bayonet in under the other the blade seemed to slip, and the insignia, instead of falling, remained in place. The commander lifted his free hand and placed it on the space between Michiel's shoulder and the remaining epaulette, the skin of his hand touching the skin of Michiel's neck. With his hand resting there, Michiel felt the motion repeated. At the command of the master at arms, the former ensign, together with the chief petty officer, made a right turn. No roll of drums. No trumpets. A convoy passed on its way to slops or the repair shop. Outside the gate, where civilian police would have picked them up had civil charges been pressed, his sports bag was waiting at the guard post. 'You have a week's pass,' the petty officer said, knowing full well he needed no reminding. 'No more eating off menus for you, seaman. Your bunk will be waiting for you alongside the troops.' And, with a smirk, 'As will the base. We're going to have fun.'

For the sham game in which terrified boys fail constantly to pass as men you *need* him. He acquiesces. Leaves. Fights. Resists. Unbecoming a man. Somewhere in this small world. Always.

Soon, towering behind green mielie fields and clusters of euca-lyptus, he'll see the concrete grain silos of Tweespruit. He glances from his bare arm to the digital clock on the dash. He could fill the tank on this quiet back road rather than waste time at the Winburg station on the highway. He is slowing down at the cross-roads to Thaba'Nchu when the cellphone beeps.

Can't get thru. I'm safe. Have u heard what's happening here? K.

There should be fair cellphone reception in the little village, he thinks. With the thumb of one hand he types: *On the road. Stopping for gas. Earthquake? Will call U in a few min. M.*

In the shade of the towering silos he finds the forlorn station with two pumps on the town's rutted main street. The only other vehicle is a beat-up white pick-up. The farmer smiles in sympathy, shakes his head at what he recognizes as hail damage on the car pulling in. While the attendant (a woman, Michiel has noticed) fills the tank and prepares to wipe the car's cracked windshield, he walks out on to the quiet road. The phone's signal bars remain weak. He taps in the international code followed by their home number. He gets no indication that the call even registers. He types, to Kamil's cell: *No luck. Will try later.* The pump's clicking black digits from a different era have stopped with the second number turned halfway between nine and zero. The attendant brings back enough change for him to leave a reasonable tip: two silver five-rand coins. A note it still was, he thinks, not a coin when I left, and men at the pumps, not women. To receive whatever he is holding out to her the woman drops her chin, cups both hands together and curtsies with a soft *dankie baas.* Christ, he thinks, nodding at her, how do we undo this?

Back on the narrow road he speeds up, sets the cruise control. He is well underway and negotiating a strip of scars in the tarmac near the Westminster turn-off, when at last a stronger signal appears on the phone. He's about to push redial when the phone rings.

'Is your radio on?' It's Benjamin.

'I'm listening to a CD. I filled up at—'

'You won't believe this. We're all in front of the TV.'

'What's up?'

'They've flown into the World Trade Center. Passenger planes. It's all over CNN. They've crashed into the Pentagon too. Both these skyscrapers are on fire. Jesus, I know someone who works there.'

He looks in the rearview mirror and gears down with the phone clutched between his shoulder and ear. He hears Karien and Giselle; one of the boys, shouting, *Ma, look, Pa!*

'It's coming down, gods, Michiel, *hier donder daai bliksemse toring ineen.*' God, that bloody tower is collapsing.

'What are you talking—' He slows enough to steer the car on to the narrow roadside.

'You should see these people running through the streets. The banners say *America Under Attack.*'

'Is this some kind of prank?'

'God, Michiel! We're watching live as it happens! Unless the whole world is in on the joke. Have you seen Lerato? She left shortly after you.'

'Is it only New York?'

'Washington too!'

'What about San Francisco? I got a text from Kamil.'

'This is all we know. I'll call you back.'

The road behind him is clear. He re-enters the single lane to the sound of gravel under the wheels. Within seconds he is back at speed. He pushes redial on the cell, hears the call go directly to Kamil's voicemail. 'I'm on the road,' he says. 'I'm in and out of signal. I've heard what's going on. Call me. I trust you're okay. The news here says nothing about the Bay Area. I'll try the home number again. I love you.' From his call log he redials the home number; hears his own voice in the awkward American accent: *You've reached Kamil and Michael, leave a message and we'll call you back.* 'It's me,' he says. 'Call as soon as you can.'

He ejects the CD. From the radio he is unable to find anything consistently audible in English or Afrikaans. When he thinks he hears seSotho he retains the station for a moment before accepting that he understands barely a thing. He switches a few times between FM and AM, taps the search arrow. Here and there are brief snatches of song, what resembles words, distant and broken, only sporadically something he either grasps or thinks he does: Aaaailalla . . . mmmmmpashhhhhhAaaa . . . tir, tir, sjip,sjip, wrrrrrrrr . . . X!XiiiXt . . . mmginnntritrimmm..sssssssshhhhhhhhh-hhhhhhhhh . . . H//MTsjjjjjrrrrrrrr . . . //X!!!QTA . . . Xha . . . !!XC . . . Six, five, three . . . Mi ta twa ku nandziha ngopfu, swi famba a moyeni . . . uMadagascar . . . mich sehr, es is ein d . . . Ditaba ke tsena le di ballwa ke . . . the minister said . . . kwatsha! . . . everyone over ten . . . zonke . . . New Amste . . . matla ha a na setlhare . . . bhash..!!.. grr,kr,kr,hr, laaaaa . . . setlhare se pelong . . . And I think

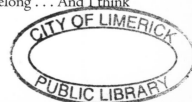

to myself ... Ncino wa maguva lawa ... Mp ... Mpppp ...
aaaaichaanXmmm ... Aaaaaiiiiiiiiiii eyyyyyyeeeee ...

He is twenty kilometers above the speed limit when Benjamin
calls. Banners running along the bottom of the screen on CNN
now announce that all flights within the US have been ordered to
land as soon as possible. US-bound flights have been redirected to
Canada. Karien is trying to get through to Jan Smuts for information on Michiel's flight; he hears her voice in the background.
Then, while she is still speaking, Benjamin says, 'They're telling her
all flights to the United States are canceled. The news says there
may be other hijacked planes in the air right now. You might as well
turn back.'

'I'm already hours away.'

'You're wasting your time going to the airport.' His brother's
voice is fading. If he's set on continuing to Jo'burg — Michiel can
barely make out Benjamin's words — he should spend the night
with Giselle and the kids, who are leaving Paradys shortly.
'Otherwise, come home.'

In the rearview mirror he sees a truck a way off. He gears down
and pulls on to the gravel. When he gets out, the eighteen-wheeler
swishes narrowly by, forcing him up against the side of the car. 'Jou
fokken poes,' he curses, glaring at the vehicle already hurtling into
the distance.

The road is now clear. The asphalt stretches to the orange sky in
the west and over a hill-top in the east. Power lines scallop one side
of the road between towering pylons; on the other side, telephone
poles lead their drooping wires uphill to disappear over the horizon. He stands at the car's hood, holding up the phone to find the
clearest reception. He climbs on to the rutted hood, then the roof.
Turning uphill, there is a nominal signal, though not enough for a
successful call. Across a narrow belt of grass and wild sunflowers
is a fence. Beyond that, on a rise behind the pylons, he makes out
the ruins of a shed or farmhouse.

He clambers down. He slips through the fence and strides into the veld, passing beneath the twittering power lines. From a grove of eucalyptus a horse has appeared, throwing its head up and down before starting down the hill. The ruined structure's walls are at least a foot wide. Michiel climbs to the top of the one section that still stands. Up here, evidence of wooden rafters remains in what is mud or grout. A rondavel; a chief's hut? He lifts his arm high, the phone against the sky. Nothing. He wonders when Lerato and the kids will be here. He is cold; the breeze whistles softly through gaps and cracks in the wall beneath him. When he gets down, the horse — white, he notes — is still adamantly coming closer. Pushing down the middle of the three barbed-wire strands, he slips back through the fence. He'll wait here at the roadside and see what Lerato suggests. Again he feels the cold in his neck, the chill cutting through his shirt. How did they forget a sweater? Away from here, this place is doused in perpetual summer. He imagines Kamil, gaping at the television. He has slid off the sofa and sits dressed in jeans on the magenta living-room rug, cross-legged, elbows resting on his knees. Perhaps the Pauls are there with him, not going to the office this morning, drinking coffee, or is America heading for work, as if it's an ordinary day? He hears Kamil, on the phone to Malik or Rachel or Nawal. Still unbelieving what Benjamin said was playing out on TV, he tries to picture the building collapse, but cannot conjure the image. Can it really be true? His eyes go to the road, searching again for Lerato's car. In only a short while these fields will be expanses of gold as the open faces of sunflowers follow the sun each day, east to west. When he turns he sees that he has been followed. The horse tosses its head from side to side at the fence. You are an ancient thing, aren't you? Is there a tooth left in those jaws? Undernourished your whole life. Not white either, rather a mottled, moth-eaten shaggy gray with patches of tan and coal summer coat. Kin to a paint horse, Michiel thinks as he leans into the passenger side and reaches for the Pick n Pay bag. He steps back on to the strip of grass between road and fence. The horse's gaze is on him, ears now perfectly cupped. Michiel holds an apple out, farther for the animal to see and smell. The horse steps sideways, backs from the fence, throws its head and shies away. Michiel clicks his tongue against his teeth. Mare, gelding or stallion, he cannot make out from here. In the elbow and stifle ticks cluster like grapes. Clearly it spends its life in the veld. He extends his hand across the fence, clucking his tongue with a rounder sound formed against his palate. The horse comes closer. He hears the breathing through the moving nostrils, receives the scent into his own. He feels the velvety muzzle on the skin of his open palm, the vibration of crunch and chew. He touches with his free thumb the pus and drip from one scarred socket, sees the reflection of himself tiny in the pupil of each eye. The horse turns from the fence, seems to waver, then heads back into the veld. Against the cold of the falling sun Michiel rubs his shoulders and arms. In the wide silence he cups his hands and blows into them for warmth, finding the smell on his fingers.

Glossary

Ag, donner Oh, please; Oh, dammit

Amandla! Ngawethu! Power! To the People! A call frequently used during the struggle against apartheid

bakkie pick-up truck

behep caught up with, obsessed with

boerbok goat

bliksem *noun:* a dislikable person, a bastard; *verb:* to beat

broeks panties

dikbek sulking

doek a length of cloth, usually worn around the head

dominee minister of the Dutch Reformed Church

FAK Federasie van Afrikaanse Kultuurvereniginge (Federation of Afrikaans Cultural Unions)

Habibti my love (Arabic)

hol arse

Jirre, Jissis Lord/Jesus (slang)

kaross blanket made of animal skins

kaya native dwelling

kakibos khaki-weed, Mexican marigold, *Tagetes minuta*

klaar out clear out (from military conscription)

killick marine platoon section leader

kloof ravine, gorge

koelie derogatory term for an Indian person

koppie small hill (Afrikaans; *kopje* in Dutch)

mamparra country bumpkin, idiot

Matie informal term for a student at Stellenbosch University

meelsak cornflour bag

Ou Hoofgebou Old Main Building, the Department of Law at Stellenbosch University

padkos food packed for the road

padvat hit the road

plaasjapie country bumpkin, yokel

platteland countryside

poes cunt

Porra person of Portuguese ancestry (derogatory)

rondavel round hut, traditionally with a thatched roof

shande shame, disgrace (Yiddish)

shegitz non-Jewish male (Hebrew)

skabenga no-good, layabout

skedonk jalopy

staaldak-webbing-en-geweer steel helmet, webbing and rifle

stoep veranda

surmay arrasak! you deserve a shoe against the head (Arabic)

tsotsis black hooligans

Tuks University of Pretoria

vlaktes plains

Wits University of the Witwatersrand

Acknowledgements

I am indebted to many South African works as well as other world literature. In addition to writers and texts alluded to within the story, the novel quotes and/or paraphrases from the following:

James Baldwin, *Nothing Personal*, with Richard Avedon, Atheneum, 1964. Dambudzo Marechera, 'The Waterman Cometh', from *Cemetery of Mind*, Baobab Books, 1992. Leonard Cohen, 'Anthem', from *The Future*, Columbia Records, 1992 (p. 1). André Brink, *An Instant In the Wind*, Penguin, 1985 (p. 2). Zbiegnew Herbert, 'Lament', from *The Collected Poems 1956–1998*, Ecco Press, 2007 (p. 10). Sol Plaatje, *Native Life in South Africa*, Ravan Press, 1996 (pp. 13, 71, 94, 95). Pablo Neruda, 'Every Day You Play', from *The Essential Neruda* (ed. Eisner), 2004 (p. 16). Nadine Gordimer, *July's People*, Penguin, 1982 (p. 54); *The Conservationist*, Penguin, 1983 (p. 165). Antjie Krog, 'Omdat', from *Eerste Gedigte*, Human & Rousseau, 2004 (p. 68). Margaret Atwood, *The Handmaid's Tale*, Anchor/Random House, 1998 (p. 79). Derek Walcott, 'Love After Love', from *Sea Grapes*, Jonathan Cape, 1976 (pp. 82, 139). Eugene Marais, 'Die Dans van die Reën', from *Groot Verseboek* (ed. Brink), Tafelberg, 2000 (p. 84). Alice Walker, *Possessing the Secret of*

Joy, Harcourt Brace, 1992 (p. 99). J. M. Coetzee, *Disgrace*, Penguin, 2000 (p. 144). Olive Schreiner, *The Story of an African Farm*, Penguin Classics, 1983 (p. 151). Laurie Anderson, 'The Dream Before', from *Strange Angels*, Warner Brothers Records, 1989 (p. 153). Michael Cunningham, *The Hours*, Picador, 2000 (p. 175). William Blake, 'A Vision of the Last Judgment' (p. 202) and 'The Everlasting Gospel' (p. 225), from *Complete Writings with Variant Readings* (ed. Keynes), Oxford University Press, 1966. Breyten Breytenbach, 'Septembersee', from *Kouevuur*, Buren Uitgewers, 1969 (pp. 229). Boris Pasternak, 'The Grown Marksman', from *The Poems of Boris Pasternak*, Unwin Paperbacks, 1984 (p. 229). The free translations of sections of poems by Breyten Breytenbach and Antjie Krog, as well as the paraphrase of Eugene Marais, are my own.

While preparing this novel for publication I have incurred debts of gratitude to Mic Cheetham, Mariana Cooke, Lauri Dietz, Percival Everett, Sandra Kiersky, Dana Levin, Oksana Luybarski, Elisa Majaoetsa, Kathryn Newton, Paul Theron, Ian Wolfley, Kolisa Xinindlu and N. S. Zulu. Particular thanks are due to Edwin Cameron, Leslee Durr, Annie Gagiano, Paul Morrell, Gerrit Olivier, Margaret Randall and Kfir Yefet for their time and insightful observations. Elizabeth Dietz and Zoe Gullen read and commented on the manuscript numerous times. Thank you, for your kindness and support. Where I have not heeded advice, I alone am responsible.

Mark Behr's previous novels are *The Smell of Apples* and *Embrace*. *The Smell of Apples*, which won awards in South Africa, the United Kingdom and the United States, is now considered a South African classic. He divides his time between South Africa and the United States, where he is Associate Professor of World Literature and Fiction Writing at the College of Santa Fe, New Mexico.